Reader Reviews

The Dreamer- the Beginning is a captivating tale, giving a convincing and passionate voice to a young man from humankind's early history. It is well researched and based on scientific study, lending additional credence to a very creative story involving a time in our history that is very much shrouded in mystery and conjecture.~ N. I. Bourdeau

As an avid reader I am always excited to step out of the box and read something different, The Dreamer Series delivers! A delightful journey set during the last Ice Age brings to life a Neanderthal family; their lifestyle, daily struggles to survive, love and loss. The author delivers a story set in prehistoric times described so well, so vividly it leaves the reader wanting more! Write faster, we want more! Donna R. Fox

Fascinating saga of the times and life amid a Neanderthal family as seen from the perspective of a man with a special gift and a love of his family. It's just like being there; you become involved with their trials and joys. The dreams give you a glimpse of future dangers and events, leading you through an engrossing journey. ~ C. H. Beusee

This is not the usual type of book that I read but I was fascinated and could not put it down. The author did so much research that it felt like I was reading a true story of a family and how they lived during that time! I wish the author could write faster so I could get my hands on those next ones...keep them coming!~ L. B. Collins

This is a unique and interesting read. I couldn't put it down–almost missed my flight! ~ J. Simmons

Just like The Dreamer – The Beginning, once I started reading Dreamer II – The Gathering I could not put it down. It is so interesting with a great personal story line. And I love all the historical information. After reading the first two books of this series I cannot wait to get the third one! Keep it up! – Patti Stribling Lauer

I read this book and thoroughly enjoyed it...so exciting that you can't put it down. Kept me on the edge of my seat. Great writing. ~ J. Stuller

I've read the whole Clan of the Cave Bear series by Jean Auel, and I was bummed when it ended; you got the ancients going again in totally different happenings and people's! I will probably read all three again. Can't wait for book four! ~ John G. Smith

Books in this series:

The Dreamer ~ The Beginning (2016)

The Dreamer II ~ The Gathering (2017)

The Dreamer III ~ The People of the Wolves (2018)

The Dreamer IV ~ The Cave of Bones (2019)

The Dreamer V ~ The Blood-Red Skies (2020)

The Dreamer VI ~ The Outsiders (2021)

Coming in 2022!

The Dreamer VII ~ The Challenge Circle

Much more to come!

The Dreamer VI

THE OUTSIDERS

The Dreamer Book Series

By E. A. Meigs

Dreamer Literary Productions, LLC

2021

Copyright ©2021 E. A. Meigs

All rights reserved

For information regarding this novel or permissions to reproduction selections from this work, please visit

Dreamer Literary Productions at:
www.dreamerliteraryproductions.com

ISBN: 978-1-7350558-3-1

 First Edition 

Cover photo by my friend Paula Krugerud
www.PaulaKrugerudPhotography.com

I dedicate this book to J. S.

Thank you for your friendship.

 Fonts used in this novel 

Papyrus was created by Chris Costello in 1982.

Garamond was designed by Claude Garamond in the early 1530's.

The Dreamer VI

❧

THE OUTSIDERS

The Dreamer VI ~ The Outsiders continues an ongoing saga that follows the life of a young Neanderthal man. The story takes place at a time in history when much of the world was experiencing brutal climatic changes and man's position within Nature's food chain was indeed perilous. The Dreamer VI is written as a stand-alone novel, meaning it is not necessary to have read the preceding volumes to understand the plot. An updated version of the original Introduction is included for those who are new to this time period.

Introduction

This tale takes place approximately 40,000 BCE (Before Common Era), when the last Ice Age was well underway.   At the peak of the Great Glacial Maximum, nearly one-third of the earth's surface was hidden beneath a thick layer of ice.   A substantial percentage of the planet's moisture was frozen solid, causing the oceans to recede and coastlines to become greatly expanded.

At that time the Eurasian landscape consisted of vast, wind-scoured tundra and small pockets of woodland populated by at least three groups of people: the Neanderthal, Homo sapiens (in this case, the Cro-Magnon), and the Denisovan.   These populations probably coexisted in parts of Eurasia for only a relatively short period of time, geologically speaking.   It was likely that they lived a seasonally nomadic lifestyle. We can only guess at what their lives would have been like: their languages, their social behaviors, their spirituality. Due to the passage of time and the impermanent nature of most materials they would have used in their day-to-day lives, there is little to tell us about their existence besides the tantalizing clues left by their remains, their tools, their art, their burials, and . . . their refuse.

Analyses of fossilized Neanderthal skeletons show that the males averaged five feet, five inches to five feet, six inches in height. The tallest Neanderthal men found to date were five feet, nine inches. The females were five feet to five feet, one inch. Their bones were about one-third stouter than ours. They were heavily muscled and had tremendous upper-body strength. The Neanderthal had the largest brain size of any known humans. Initial DNA testing showed that they likely had fair coloring: red to auburn hair, green or hazel eyes, and pale, probably freckled skin. Later genetic research on Neanderthal individuals found in different parts of Eurasia revealed that some had brown hair, brown eyes, and dusky skin. It is now considered likely that the Neanderthal had the same variety of skin tones, hair and eye coloring as do modern Eurasian people.

The Neanderthal roamed the earth for roughly 200,000 years (longer, if you include the proto-Neanderthal) before their trail went cold around

37,000 to 42,000 BCE. That said, the Neanderthal may have persisted to eke out a living for some time afterward. However, since most modern humans outside of sub-Saharan Africa share between one and four percent Neanderthal DNA, it would appear that the Neanderthal are still with us even now, albeit in diluted form.

Homo sapiens may have first appeared in the European fossil record as early as (approximately) 200,000 BCE, but more conservative estimates range from 40,000 to 65,000BCE. The previously mentioned Cro-Magnon have been dated to 42,000 to 47,000 BCE. They were named for the rock shelter in which they were discovered in the Dordogne Valley in France, in 1868. At one time, early anatomically modern humans in Europe were often referred to as Cro-Magnons, but that term has since fallen out of favor. However, since these novels take place almost entirely on the ancient lands we now know as France, my Homo sapiens characters actually are Cro-Magnons.

Over a period of tens of thousands of years the predecessors of the Cro-Magnon migrated out of Africa, gradually making their way into Eurasia. The men averaged about five feet, nine inches in height, but it is thought that some taller individuals may have been upwards of six feet, five inches. Like the Neanderthal, their brains were also bigger than those of today's people. They are believed to have had dark coloring: dark brown to black hair, brown eyes, and tan or olive-toned skin. (Blond hair and blue eyes are a relatively new development in modern humans, having first appeared about 6,000 to 12,000 years ago, long after the pinnacle of the Ice Age, but possibly coinciding with the end of that last glacial period.)

This novel reintroduces the Denisovans to the series. Not much is known of these people at this time. What little information we have comes from a few teeth, a handful of bone fragments, a number of artifacts, and what can be gleaned from the study of their DNA. The physical characteristics of the bones suggest that the Denisovans were a sturdy people, perhaps with a build resembling that of the Neanderthals. Their teeth, on the other hand, were quite large, about one-third bigger than that of either the average modern human or Neanderthal. We might then surmise that they probably had a heavy jaw to accommodate those teeth. DNA from a finger bone disclosed that it was taken from someone with dark hair, brown eyes, and brown skin.

When we consider the artifacts that have been attributed to the Denisovans, it must be acknowledged that they were an intelligent, skilled folk. Their needles (dated to approximately 50,000 to 60,000 BCE) look much like our needles of today. A bracelet of green stone shows that they had sufficient technology to drill holes and to shape and polish stone. We can only hope that further discoveries bring us more data on these intriguing people.

* * *

It is my humble opinion that after so many years of existence in a world that often presented extreme challenges, these intelligent beings would have been at the top of their game in leveraging the available resources to ensure their own comfort and the continuation of their species. Some indications suggest that early man was potentially much more advanced than is generally credited, and it is my guess that we will continue to be surprised by what is revealed when ongoing and future anthropological studies peel back layers of time as we search for ourselves within the lives of our ancestors.

* * *

An animal index is presented at the end of this novel for the convenience of those unfamiliar with the animals of Ice Age Europe. It gives basic information about most of the creatures mentioned in this book. It might be useful to know, for example, that a wisent is a species of European bison, and that the animal North Americans refer as a moose is called an elk in Europe.

* * *

This is a work of fiction and it is not intended to hold up to scientific scrutiny. I merely seek to tell a story that is set amid this ancient backdrop. I have peopled it with those whose lives — when broken down to their most basic elements — would not have been so different from ours: sharing care and concern for loved ones, enduring all life's hardships, and reveling in serendipitous moments of love, beauty, and joy when they grace us with their presence.

 **Chapter One** 

The sun sinks low under slowly darkening skies. A crackling blaze provides welcome comfort at the center of our camp. Emerging from the gloom, a group of men steps into the circle of light surrounding our fire. As we rise to greet them, one of them speaks. "We have been looking for you." There is malice in that voice.

"Puh-Puh!"

A finger poked my chest.

"*Wha* . . .?" I mumbled.

It required some effort to extricate myself from the Dream. I opened my eyes to quite a different fireside scene.

"Puh-Puh," my son Fox repeated. "You were sleeping! The food is ready!"

I had not intended to doze off as I sat amongst my family and friends, awaiting our evening meal. Several of us had spent the day on a long and nearly fruitless hunt. Just before we were bound for home, we were delighted to flush a large boar from the brush.

It had been a splendid late-summer day. We were going through a long dry spell, and the earthen trail beneath our feet was parched and dusty, and littered with fallen leaves. Barely a breeze stirred the sun-dappled forest. We had traveled some distance in search of prey and, having found none, turned for home.

The animal must have been napping, as these creatures are wont to do after a night of foraging. But his sharp ears soon detected our presence, and he charged forth from his nest within the thicket. This boar was enormous, possibly the largest I had ever seen. I had only a moment to wonder how this animal had survived to attain his great age. He must be a cagey creature, indeed. As he drew nearer I could see that his well-honed bottom tusks were longer than my forefingers.

The boar was feisty; he wheeled this way and that, tossing his head to slash at us with those impressive canines as he tried to make his escape. We blocked him at each turn, thrusting our spears to good effect. A boar of this maturity was not our usual prey.   At other times, we might have just parried with the surprised animal until he felt he had made his point and withdrew to find more peaceful surroundings; however, we needed to feed our families. His flesh would be tough and gamey, but it had been a long time since our last big kill, and we could not afford to be choosy.

After a prolonged and somewhat breathless battle, the beast at last expired. Even after he was gutted, he was so heavy that it took the four of us to carry him on a hastily produced pair of rails. The saplings that were harvested and stripped of limbs and leaves before they were to bear our prize still had plenty of spring left in them. We found we had to shoulder the burden as close to animal's body as possible to keep it from bouncing with each step, and further taxing our physiques. It was a long and arduous trek.

After waking from the brief nap, I was still somewhat weary. I flexed my tired back from left to right and then looked down at the two children who sat by me, my son Fox at my side, and my eldest daughter Pony on my lap.

"Food is ready? That is good," I responded to Fox. "My stomach is empty and it is quite ready to be filled."

"I am hungry, too," Pony piped up. "Puh-Puh, we will eat the big boar tomorrow?"

"We just might," I replied, pulling her closer for a cuddle.

Pony grinned as she put her soft cheek against my bearded face. There was a time when Fox would snuggle with me, too. But now at five winters old, he deemed himself too grown up to be as openly affectionate with me as he had been in years past. Fox was a large boy for his age and, in addition to a lively mischievous streak, he also had a great curiosity. He would ask me penetrating questions such as the one he had posed to me recently, "Do the trees become sad, Puh-Puh?"

"*Sad?*" I repeated, "What do you mean?"

"Trees are not able to run and play," Fox pointed out. "I would be very sad if I had to stand in one place every day. And winters would be so cold."

"A tree knows only a tree's life," I told him, wondering if I had asked such questions when I was a boy. "They are made to endure their existence in the same way we all must."

Fox still looked puzzled.

"I hear them creak and groan during storms as though they are crying out in pain," Fox said. "I am glad I am not a tree."

"The squirrels would tickle you as they ran up and down your trunk," I teased Fox, tickling him a little to lighten his mood.

"The good thing about being a tree is that animals would not try to hide from me," Fox stated as he squirmed under my tickling fingers.

"Nor would most of them care to eat you," I added.

Fox just shrugged. He had already heard many stories of what happened to children who did not mind their elders: they usually met with some dire fate, such as falling victim to a hungry bear. Fox had witnessed several confrontations with aggressive creatures; nevertheless, he seemed to feel an almost unnatural affinity with them.   From the time he began to form words, he was querying about all manner of animals, insects, and birds.   Fox was enthralled with the name we had picked for his sister Raven. They were not as common as crows in this area, but whenever he saw one, he would point it out to his toddler sibling and make a raven's squawk at her.   Poor Raven would just gaze at him in bewilderment with her wide dark eyes.

My daughters were quite different from their older brother.   Pony, at four winters old, two-winters-old Raven and our infant, Lily, were still willing to be kissed and hugged by their Puh-Puh. They resembled their petite, dark-haired mother, although Lily was losing the soft black down that had covered her head since birth, now gradually being replaced by hair of an indeterminate shade. I wondered if she might be another fair-haired child. So far, Fox was the only one who resembled me. He alone had my bushy, curly red hair, robust build, freckled skin, and green eyes.

My mate, Morning Star, approached with six-moons-old Lily perched on one hip and a birch-bark platter braced to the other, as Raven tagged along, clinging to the hem of her mother's garment. Morning Star smiled as she passed the platter to me and settled down by my side. Raven immediately crawled onto her mother's lap, looking up at her Muh-Muh expectantly as she anticipated her evening sup.

"Tris, you are awake," Morning Star said, with a hint of jest in her voice. "You fell asleep just moments after you sat down. Was it a difficult day?"

"It was a good day. We were lucky to find a large boar. We will eat well now," I told her.

A wry expression appeared on Morning Star's face and she wrinkled her nose. She too had noted the strong smell that emanated from our prize. But then she said brightly, "Yes, it was most fortunate. I am so glad you were able to harvest such a magnificent animal. We have not seen so much meat since that last seal was killed at the shore."

I nodded. This was true. We had returned from the coast just last moon. We usually spent a good part of the summer at the beach where we could forage for various foods, and catch a considerable amount of fish and, often, a few seals as well. Most of this was dried or smoked and added to our winter stores.

"We may get to sample the boar later on," Morning Star's father, Black Wolf chimed in. He was a giant of a man, whose thick black hair was worn in a multitude of braids that appeared to sprout out of the top of his head. "While we rested, some of the others made themselves busy. They have carved up most of the boar's carcass, and some of the meat is cooking over the coals, while some of it is being smoked.   The rest has gone into the cold-storage cache."

I nodded with understanding, impressed at how much work had been accomplished. How long I had been asleep?

"The cache was empty, but that beast's meat has half-filled it," my cousin Bror announced. "We filled the rest with as much dried grass and old hides as we could find before covering it with rocks and dirt. With luck, it will stay safe."

Our cold-storage cache was located a short distance from our small collection of homes. The smell of the meat, even hidden and buried, was enough to attract large predators.   The cache consisted of a hole in the ground that had been laboriously excavated and then enlarged by lighting fires within the permafrost to thaw the earth. Such excavations must be made during summer, since even on the hottest summer days, holes of any depth soon struck a layer of frozen dirt. To try to dig during winter when the ground was rock-hard would be futile.

As it was, it had taken many days and many fires before it was finally deep enough to serve the purpose of storing the flesh from our kills until we were ready to cure or consume it. The trouble was, not only was it subject to being raided by animals, but additionally, our precious stores could be damaged if rainwater penetrated the protective layers. We made every effort to seal it as well as possible, but the safety of our stored meat was far from a sure thing.

"I have not had fresh boar since Ria shot that little shoat last spring," my Puh remarked, speaking of his mate.

After my Muh passed, Puh became paired with a woman who bought a new weapon to our arsenal. It was a small bow that launched tiny spears into the air. It was not powerful enough to bring down large animals, but it served well to harvest fowl, young deer, and the like. Puh was extraordinarily proud of her ability to help feed our families. Everyone did their part to contribute in some way, but Ria was not only adept at foraging, she was also a skilled huntress.

"That was a succulent feast," Black Wolf said. "Today's boar will pale in comparison, but what it lacks in quality, it will make up for in quantity. I dare say we will probably be glad to see the last of it."

"Would you rather have more seal instead?" Ria asked Black Wolf.

"We have eaten so much seal meat since our return from the coast that I think I will soon be sprouting flippers," Black Wolf quipped.

"Just so long as you do not start barking like one," Puh teased.

Puh and Black Wolf had been close friends since childhood, despite our clans being of two different peoples. Black Wolf and his family, including my mate, Morning Star, belonged to one of the tribes of The People from the East, while our clans were called Old Ones. The People often tended to be a little taller than most Old Ones, and they were more gracile in build. Some Old Ones had the same dense curling red hair, pale freckled skin, and green eyes as my kin, but others had darker coloring. The People, however, owned dark brown to black hair, brown eyes, and skin that varied from tan to brown.

The People sometimes did not care to associate with Old Ones and, conversely, some Old Ones were also not inclined to mix. But our families had been raised together for generations and I was ever grateful that Black Wolf had allowed Morning Star and me to be paired. She was the only woman I had ever loved. Now, four children later, we were still very much attached to each other. If possible, I thought I might be more in love with her now than ever before, even including the fervent days when we were first joined.

"Tris, would you break up some of the food into small bits for our little ones, please?" Morning Star requested.

I balanced the birch-bark tray on my knees and did as asked. The meal consisted of a combination of roasted foods: parts of a rabbit, served still on the bone, some boar meat, tubers, and also fresh foods like berries and greens. Fox was already picking out a few choice morsels. He began to gnaw on a chunk of meat. Pony was crowding in, so I gave her a few pieces in hopes she would settle down and give me room to complete my task. Similarly, Morning Star was reaching for bits to give Raven before finally taking something for herself.

Our morning meal was usually eaten at home, and midday repasts were generally consumed wherever we were at that time, but each evening all of us gathered at the center of our compound for the evening sup. Only fierce weather kept us bound to our own hearths to eat the last meal of the day. I was glad to have this time to be together, to talk of what we had seen and done, of the weather, and always, talk about hunting.

Not so many years ago only my family resided here, as they had done since long before anyone could remember. My Great Gran, who was by far the oldest person in my family, and in fact, the oldest person I had ever heard of, had told me that even her grandmother did not know how many generations of our clan had been inhabiting this site.

Now, many households had collected here. During my childhood, Great Gran requested a home of her own, so Puh and I dug out another earth-bermed domicile from the hillside, a short walk from our home. Later, when Morning Star and I were to be paired, Gran gave up her modest abode to us.

Soon after, Morning Star's parents, Black Wolf and Little Fawn, and all her younger siblings relocated to our compound. When my sister Ru became old enough to be paired, she and her mate Bror added yet another home, and the same for my brother Ty, and his mate, Aessa. Lastly, Morning Star's sister Petal was joined with Fish Hawk, and a final house was created for their use.

This once serene glen was now bustling with activity, and many noisy children and dogs. Sometimes I missed the old tranquility of the place, but it did not take long for me to recall that I could not imagine my life without all of these people.

As I ate, my mind wandered back to the Dream. It was not usual for me to Dream during the day, but then, my visions came at unexpected intervals. I sometimes attempted to fathom what brought them on and what they might portend, but mostly they just presented an enigma. Often, it was only much later that I discovered what was actually being shown to me.

I was somewhat surprised I had not dreamt about today's hunt. The gleam of the boar's piercing eyes and his large tusks were still vivid in my mind. We had been desperate to bring him down, and yet he had come very close to getting the best of us. Instead, I had Dreamt of those strangers. And one claimed they were looking for us. Who could they be? I must speak with Great Gran about this. If anyone would know, it would be she.

I looked across the assemblage of people and saw Gran gazing back at me. She smiled. I was ever conscious of her keen insight. Had she somehow perceived my thoughts?

Gran nodded to me, almost imperceptibly. I knew then that we would discuss my Dream sometime in the coming days. Gran was a Dreamer, too. She was the only other person of whom I had knowledge who shared this trait. My first Dream had frightened me; the clarity, even the smells of the scene as it played in my head, were striking. In the intervening years since then, Gran had patiently guided me through these experiences. Even though she had taught me much, Gran nevertheless had to admit there was a great deal about Dreams even she did not know. Sometimes they showed us something from the far distant past, sometimes they portrayed an event happening elsewhere, and other times, they were visions of a future yet to be realized.

I then felt a drop of liquid land on my bare leg. Summer days meant that we men were dressed only in loincloths, and I could feel the warm liquid run down my thigh. I suspended my enthusiastic consumption of food to glance at my dog, Raena, who was drooling, and becoming impatient for her share. She woofed softly to me.

"Poor girl," I said to her. "Is everyone eating but you?"

I held out a chunk of the boar meat to her. Normally, Raena would swallow such an offering, hardly pausing to chew. She sniffed at it quizzically, and then looked at me as if to say, *Do you really expect me to eat that?* But then she gingerly took the meat from my hand and walked away with it, head hung low as though she were disgraced to be seen with such a poor dinner.

"She did not seem impressed," Morning Star noted.

"I do not believe she was," I agreed. "I have seen her roll around in a long-dead elk carcass, but yet it appears she does have some standards."

"It smells funny, Puh-Puh," Pony said.

"Tastes musky," Fox added.

"Until recent years, we have been fortunate to have a large number of animals in this area, and we were able to take only the choicest prey," my Puh said. "Until we find a new place in which to move our homes, we will be forced to eat whatever we are lucky enough to bring down. Now that we have brought in a large kill, perhaps it is time to go on another foray."

"Yes," Black Wolf concurred as he helped himself to more meat. "Are you thinking of going up to the Lake Region?"

Morning Star gave me a sidelong glance. She knew this meant I would be gone for an extended period, probably for the remainder of the summer and into early fall. She hated the long separation and the accompanying nagging worry regarding the dangers we might face. I tried to give her an encouraging smile, and she smiled wanly in return.

"Who will go?" my sister Ru queried.

She had good reason to ask. A group of this size required the labors of all its inhabitants to keep us supplied with food, water, and the firewood needed to feed our fires. In addition to those chores, processing hides and making clothing, weaving baskets, making twine and rope, creating tools, and raising the next generation also left little idle time during the day. Plus, it was important to have those on hand who were capable of defending our homes from marauding invaders, of either the two- or four-legged variety. But I already knew the answer.

"Tris, Tor, and I will go," Black Wolf proposed.

We all nodded in agreement. It had been the same during past years when we set out to look for fresh lands. We three were the main hunters in our conclave, and after landing a big windfall, we could then leave our families, knowing they were well supplied.

I thought Ru seemed relieved that her Bror would not be one of those tapped for this quest. They had a toddler and a new daughter just half a moon old. Many of the other men in our combined clans were also new parents this summer, but somehow, Morning Star, the eldest sibling in her family, was expected to cope with four small children while I was away. Morning Star did not complain, but her introspective look spoke of her true feelings. I knew she was cognizant of the inequity.

Black Wolf's visage also betrayed a man lost in thought. He shifted position, now stretching out his long legs before him. Black Wolf was the tallest man any of us had ever seen. I was considered to be quite tall for an Old One, but the top of my head just reached Black Wolf's shoulder. He was a formidable man, in both temperament and stature. His booming bass still startled our infant whenever he spoke. He and his mate Little Fawn had coexisted in a state of perpetual discord for many years, but he continued to share a home with her so as to provide for Little Fawn and the four remaining children who still resided there.

"When will you leave?" Morning Star inquired, her voice somewhat tremulous.

Puh glanced from me to Black Wolf as he weighed his reply.

"A day or two would give us time to bring in some extra firewood and prepare to leave."

"Yes," Black Wolf said happily. He was always eager to depart from his humdrum existence with a mate who barely tolerated him. "I can be ready to go by then."

I merely nodded without enthusiasm, mentally tabulating all the tasks I would need to accomplish before we left and calculating the readiness of my gear.

After the food was eaten and the cool darkness of evening had descended, a little more wood was added to the coals over which our meal had been cooked. Morning Star then herded our children over to the water bag that hung from a branch, so she could wash their face and hands.

I remained by the fire, continuing to mull over the coming journey as everyone else dispersed to tend to chores before the last of the day's light had vanished. Gran helped clear away the various platters, shell bowls, and wooden utensils used to produce and consume our meals, but then she approached me. It always pained me to see how unsure her step had become. She smiled as she sat down beside me and patted my hand.

"You have the look of a man who has a lot on his mind," Gran stated.

"It is just that I know we will have to be on the trail for a long time. Perhaps almost a moon," I said shaking my head. "I will miss my family and being home, but I especially dislike that it causes hardship for Morning Star, even though I know the others will try to help her as much as they can."

"Morning Star will be fine," Gran assured me, patting my hand once more. "She may not like it, but fortunately for her, she inherited her father's disposition rather than her mother's."

I was startled at this thought.

"What do you mean?" I asked.

"While Morning Star is very small, unlike her very tall parents, I find that she mostly takes after her father," Gran told me. "She has his good looks, his sharp mind, and most important, she has his happy nature. They both may be volatile and at times stubbornly opinionated, but Black Wolf and Morning Star share a sense of optimism and a pleasant outlook on life. Nothing against Little Fawn; she is a devoted mother and housekeeper, and a loyal friend, but she is not a happy person. She sees the worst in everything. And to be frank, she has a face like an elk . . . however, Little Fawn's appearance would not be much noted were it not for her disposition. Morning Star's sister Petal may physically resemble her mother, but she is prone to be merry. If I had to choose between inheriting good looks or a happy nature, I would choose the happy nature."

"I suppose you are right," I said, speaking slowly. "But then, you are always right."

"It is one of the benefits of living a long life," Gran said with a shrug, "After many long years, you eventually see it all. And I have known Black Wolf and Little Fawn since they were children. Some days it does not seem that long ago. Black Wolf was a youngest son; he was doted on and he was always noted for his great size – almost from the time he left the womb – and for being handsome. Little Fawn was also noted for her size and looks, but it was not in a way that would please most women. She was very self-conscious about these things. But then when their parents arranged for them to be paired, Little Fawn was immensely relieved to be joined with a man who was actually taller than was she. Black Wolf, on the other hand, was less than overjoyed. But, as you know, back then, children did not attempt defying their parents without great consequences."

I nodded. I knew only too well. My mother's parents had refused to associate with her and Puh after they had become paired; they had wanted her to be joined with a cousin. After all, most pairings were not bonded with love. It was simply hoped that the couple would go on to beget the next generation and raise a successful family. Anything more than that was considered to be extreme good fortune. I could well imagine that Black Wolf was also not terribly concerned over his parents' choice, since monogamy was also not strictly adhered to in many such relationships. He had felt free to indulge in occasional dalliances with women who owned more obvious charms. And what with his striking features, he had no lack of willing partners.

"It was a sad pairing for Little Fawn," Great Gran went on. "It is very sad to be bound with a mate who does not love you as well as you hoped. But it is sadder yet for Little Fawn, because her own proclivity for unhappiness has worked against her."

"Her outlook probably would not have altered her circumstances," I speculated.

"No," Gran started, "but even if you should fall and land on a porcupine, you do not have to stay there and sit on it. Take Ria, for example. She also does not have beauty. Her former mate treated her atrociously. Have you ever noticed that she is missing a few teeth on one side of her mouth? It is not because she is old like me and has lost them; it is because he knocked them out of her head. But you almost never see a frown or displeased look cross her face. Ria has immense strength of character and a determination to be happy."

I was shocked to hear this revelation about Ria's former mate.

"I did not know that about Bakkae," I admitted.

"I only know because while we were collecting kindling together one early morning, she happened to yawn and I noticed the missing teeth," Gran started. "I remarked that she was young to have lost several teeth already. Ria then told me that Bakkae had not been an easy man to live with."

"I had heard that he was not a sociable person, but I did not know Bakkae to be violent," I said. Then I added, "I do remember that she once said that she loved him but she did not always like him."

"Yes," Gran began. "When he disappeared she did not know whether to be heartbroken or relieved."

"No wonder she adores Puh," I observed.

"Yes. Your Puh is a good man," Gran agreed. "He has not said so, but I know he is hesitant to relocate our families because of me. He does not want to put me through a long trek. And I am sorry for it. I see you all working harder to procure the things we need to survive and I see you all becoming thinner, and I know it is my fault."

"No, Gran," I said quickly. "It is not your fault. We just have not found a new place yet. We will, and then we will make a comfortable seat for you on a sled and bring you to that new home."

Gran shook her head.

"You are so like your Puh," Gran told me, as she had many times throughout my life. "I am not afraid of making the journey. But your Puh fears for me, for taking me from the only home I have ever known."

"It is the only home that many of us have ever known," I began. "We all dread leaving it. But while I am sure that Puh is concerned for you and wants to make the trek as comfortable and safe for you as possible, I would not worry that he lingers here because of you."

But as the words left my mouth, I wondered if they were in fact true. Puh had never discussed this with me, so I could not say with surety whether he was or was not delaying our departure. However, just then Morning Star returned with the children.

"Hello, Gran," Morning Star said cheerfully. "Our little ones are now clean and ready for bed."

"So they are," Gran responded, reaching up to caress Lily's cheek as she dangled from her mother's arms. Lily grinned a toothless smile. "I will bid you all a pleasant evening, then."

"Pleasant evening, Gran," Morning Star answered. "Say good night to Gran," she instructed the children.

Fox and Pony obediently complied, and Raven simply waved while saying something that sounded vaguely like *pleasant evening.*

I rose and helped Gran to her feet. She grasped my arm affectionately before tottering off to her own lodgings.

* * *

We stayed just long enough to take leave of our neighbors, who were also preparing to take their families home for their nightly rest. Some would return to the fireside to talk over the day's events after the children were settled. In years past, Morning Star and I would stay to socialize with sleeping children on our laps. But now, what with four youngsters, it was easier to simply bring them all home and end our day within our own household.

The sun had long set and the moon was ascending a nighttime sky as we made our way up the hill to our little abode. Our dog Raena was alert as she accompanied us, and I watched her closely for signs of alarm. But she remained calm as she escorted us home. Raena and I were the last ones through the door, stopping to empty our bladders before I paused to fasten the door-flap behind us.

The three eldest children knew to wait at one side of the main room while their mother carefully stirred the red coals within the fireplace and coaxed a few shy flames to life. Morning Star added bits of kindling, and once they ignited, removed a small stick to light a lamp.

"Fox, Pony, Raven, it is time to get into your beds," Morning Star told them.

Morning Star still carried Lily on her hip as she helped to tug the children out of their clothing and put them to bed. I gradually added more fuel to the fire but stopped long enough to give the children a kiss and brief snuggle before they fell asleep. They were already drowsy, and it was not long before the sounds of their relaxed breathing reached our ears. I was feeling refreshed since my nap, and I was glad to have a little quiet time with Morning Star after such a strenuous day.

Little Lily still needed to be nursed one last time before she was laid down to sleep, so Morning Star sat in her customary spot on what had once been our sleeping platform and opened her garment to expose a breast.

"You and Gran seemed to be having a nice chat," Morning Star said, speaking softly so as not to disturb the children.

"We were," I said with a nod.

"You two looked rather serious. What were you speaking about?"

"Oh, many things." I hesitated as I tried to think of something in our conversation that Morning Star would find of interest. "Gran commented that you are much like your father."

Morning Star seemed taken aback.

"You are not displeased, I hope," I said. "I believe she meant that you had his intelligence and good looks, and his happy nature."

"Oh, I guess that is not too terrible," Morning Star replied. "When I think of my father, I most often picture a big dark man with enough body hair to make a bear proud, a loud voice, and an odd hairstyle." Morning Star giggled a little. "I am thankful that Gran was speaking of his other attributes."

Morning Star gazed down at our infant, as the baby suckled halfheartedly. Lily returned her mother's gaze as she grasped at the shell necklace that Morning Star wore around her neck. The decoration had been my pairing gift to her, and it was now rather shabby in appearance in comparison to the original present. My mate, my one love from boyhood, had inspired me to begin collecting the shells during our summers at the beach. The dainty shells were from mollusks of various species, but matched for color and size. I had bored holes into each one, sometimes simply enlarging a pre-existing hole, and then I had twisted the twine, rubbing beeswax into the finished length to help keep the fibers from unraveling, and painstakingly strung each shell. By now many of the shells were lost, and the twine had been broken several times and reknotted in places. I had offered to make a new necklace for Morning Star but she refused, saying she wanted to keep this one.

Morning Star gently untangled Lily's fingers from the strand of shells, and then stroked the baby's cheek.

"I do not think she will have dark eyes," Morning Star noted. But then she looked at me and said, "My dear Tris, you are staring."

"I am," I said with a smile. "I am staring at you. As you know, it is one of my favorite pastimes. No matter where we are, my eyes will always seek you out."

Lily was too tired to nurse for long. In fact, she fell asleep and even slept through the attempts to elicit a burp or two out of her before she was swaddled and laid down for the night.

While Morning Star finished her own evening ablutions, I set a few larger pieces of wood on the fire to help light and warm the room. Our home was dug out of the hillside, and while it was easy to heat during the winter, it was cool even during the hottest days of summer. I then brought a lamp into our bedchamber. It was a tiny enclosure, just big enough for us to sleep in.

Until recent years, our bed had been in the main room, but what with the accoutrements that came with a family of six and a dog, we found we needed to enlarge our home. Our children's chamber had been expanded in size to allow them to sleep undisturbed from the goings-on in the largest room, and we finally were able to retreat to our own little nest at night. I actually preferred this, not only for the privacy it accorded, but also because it was cooler.   I have always slept better in colder temperatures. And, it meant that I could count on Morning Star staying snuggled up to me all night long.

Chapter Two

I had made it through my twenty-second winter this past season, but the twenty-third anniversary of my birth had taken place several moons ago. I was no longer the naïve young man I had been at my pairing ceremony. I was feeling my age and the weight of my responsibilities. Morning Star bemoaned my increasing lack of fat, but like the rest of us, we were working harder to gather the necessities of life, with fewer than usual rewards. She had observed that with each passing year, I was coming to resemble my father more and more. I did not believe this to be a bad thing. After all, I strove to be like him in all ways. He did appear to be rather old, but I assumed she did not mean I was developing creases in my face such as those he wore, or that my hair and beard were showing strands of silver. However, my Puh – to the best of my memory – had ever been very lean. And he was scarred about his face and body. Puh had the look of a man who had been sorely tested by time and trial. This, I assumed, was where she was drawing her comparison.

But now there was little time to dwell on such things. I had only this day to prepare my family for my lengthy absence and make ready for the long trek. Fox dogged my every step.

"Puh-Puh, will you see hyenas while you are away?" Fox asked as he watched me stow items in my pack.

"We have not seen many of late, but it is possible," I replied.

"What about lions?" Fox persisted.

"Not if we can help it." I looked up and smiled at him.

"Will you see any turtles?" Pony asked, coming over to peer into my pack. "Oh, Puh-Puh, such a lot of things! Is this your fire rock?"

"It is likely that we will see a lot of animals, my sweet little Pony," I told her. "Yes, that is one of my fire rocks. It is a chunk of iron pyrite."

"And this is the other. It is flint," Fox said with pride, as the knowledgeable older brother.

"Fire rocks," Pony repeated stubbornly.

"Let your Puh-Puh alone," Morning Star said, trying to spare me from these constant interruptions.

"I do not mind," I said. "I will be missing you all soon enough."

Morning Star suddenly became somber.

"Yes, you are right," she admitted. "And we will be missing you as well." Morning Star paused before going on, "I have hung up your cloak to let it air out. I will look over your best tunic and leggings to be sure they are sturdy enough to survive the journey."

"Many thanks," I responded, reaching for her hand to give it a squeeze. "As soon as I finish packing, I will start to bring up firewood. Bror has promised to help me."

Morning Star nodded and turned to enter the storage area, where our extra clothing was kept. Like the other rooms in our home, this one had also been enlarged over the years. What had once been a small chamber to hold dry firewood, food stores, and various odds and ends, was now a series of rooms. The first now held a variety of clothing, snowshoes, tools and weapons, some as yet unfinished, and a large upturned animal skull for use as a place to relief ourselves in the middle of the night or during extreme weather. The next rooms stored foods. The deeper they progressed into the hillside, the colder the temperatures of the chamber. Normally we would be flush with stores at this time of year, after the spring hunts on the plains and our summertime coastal harvests of fish, seal, and fruit. Additionally, during late-summer we typically foraged vegetation and mushrooms.

We had done well on the faraway plains during the spring, but that meat had long since been consumed by our families. Our stay at the shore had been briefer than that of years past. After a hard-learned lesson, we had found out what might happen if we lingered there too long. Toward the end of the season the mild weather such as we were accustomed could suddenly turn wild and angry. The friendly blue skies became sullen and gray. The wind shrieked and screamed like a living thing, and the sparkling blue ocean was replaced by raging, roiling, frothing waves that attacked the shore with thunderous roars. It had nearly been the end of us. We would never again chance exposing our families to such danger, despite that the shorter harvest period obviously meant that we would bring home less food.

Nevertheless, we still had the fall rut to look forward to. After Puh, Black Wolf, and I returned from our foray, we would soon embark on the autumn hunts. Even if the other hunts were not fruitful, these expeditions almost always resulted in ample amounts of meat. The distracted deer were focused only on one thing – and while the bucks were certainly more aggressive, this was still by far the easiest time of year to stalk them. With luck, we would be plentifully provisioned at the start of winter, after which hunts would be few and far between until spring.

"Hallo, Tris," Bror said in greeting as he strode up the hillside, carrying two hefty logs on each of his shoulders. Other men might stagger under the load, but Bror was built like an aurochs and he had no trouble managing his burdens.

"Pleasant day to you, Bror," I answered. "Many thanks for bringing the first logs. I was just about to start lugging wood up the hill."

"I thought as much," Bror replied with a grin, setting the logs down near my pile of unsplit wood. "It is a nice day for such a chore, and besides, ever since I saw the size of that boar you helped bring in, I have been feeling guilty about my lack of contribution to our families. The least I can do is lend a hand to one of our mighty hunters."

Bror was teasing.

"You are very kind," I responded with mock solemnity. Then, in a lighter tone, I went on. "But you have done much to feed and provide for the comforts of our clan over the years. No one could begrudge you sitting out a hunt now and then."

At that moment, Morning Star's younger brothers, fifteen-winters-old Swift River and thirteen-winters-old Hawk came running up the path.

"Tris! Bror!" Swift River exclaimed. "My Da sent us up here to fetch you. Some men have arrived. They said that there is a bull mammoth not far from the Village."

"Yes," Hawk added, "but they need help to go after it. They do not have enough men."

The boys panted, but I guessed it was likely due to their excitement than the exertion of running up the hill.

Morning Star exited our home, holding Lily, and with Raven and our dog Raena at her side.

"A mammoth?" she exclaimed, seeming unsettled.

"Yes," Hawk said. "We are going after it!"

I was unsure about Hawk's usage of the word *we*, but I was also quite sure that Hawk and Swift River would do their best to persuade their father to bring them along.

I paused only to grab a spear before we ventured down to the main compound. The two brothers ran all the way, galloping ahead of us. We adults followed at a more leisurely pace. As we passed Bror's domicile, he stopped just long enough to take up one of his spears, as well. Then we proceeded on, with Bror at the lead, while I brought up the rear behind Morning Star and our youngest children.

Fox and Pony were already at the compound, where they had been invited to play with the other children. Fox ran up to greet me.

"Puh-Puh," he cried, "some men are here! They found a mammoth!"

"So I have heard," I said, placing a hand on his shoulder, and for once, he did not shrug it off.

The newly arrived men were strangers to me, but they were known to Black Wolf. When they caught sight of me, they immediately stopped speaking and gaped.

Black Wolf followed their line of sight and smiled as he walked toward me.

"This is my daughter Morning Star, and her mate, Tris. And this is Bror," Black Wolf said by way of introduction. "These are Quiet Foot, Horse Tooth, and Red Bear."

Red Bear was first to recover from his gaping and he came forward to meet us.

"Well," he said, addressing me, "I remember you from that bout in the Challenge Circle when you fought Snow Leopard for your mate. You were impressive in size then, and I think you may have become even bigger now; you are certainly big enough to tackle a mammoth. And Bror, you are a strong-looking man as well. I believe we have come to the right place for help."

"The Village is now all but deserted," Quiet Foot added. "We are the only able-bodied hunters left."

"And we can use as many as we can muster," Horse Tooth went on.

"Da, let Hawk and me go too," Swift River implored. "We will do anything you ask of us, we promise."

Hawk nodded vigorously at this statement. They must have already discussed this amongst themselves.

Black Wolf was silent as he pondered this request. The boys were well on their way to becoming men. Swift River already sported a light beard. While he was tall and lanky, I did not think he would reach the great height of his father – or his mother, for that matter. Hawk was still boyish; he was considerably shorter than his older brother and slight in build, much like his eldest sister, Morning Star.

"I will talk with your mama about this before I make a decision," Black Wolf finally told them. "Go find your mother and tell her I will speak with her."

The boys exchanged hopeful glances and left us at a trot.

"I go, too, Puh-Puh?" Fox whispered up to me.

"No," Morning Star said firmly before I could say a word. At his downcast expression, she softened her voice. "There will be plenty of time for hunting when you are bigger."

"Besides," I said to console him, "I will need you to protect our home while I am away."

Fox gave me a brief smile.

"I will take care of Muh-Muh and the girls," he vowed. "And when I am older, you will take me to hunt a mammoth? And bears? And lions?"

"Never fear, we will do plenty of hunting," I told him.

The men were discussing where the mammoth was apt to be by now.

"I do not recall ever seeing a mammoth anywhere near the Village," Fish Hawk, the mate of Black Wolf's second daughter, Petal, joined in. Fish Hawk would know. He had lived at the Village most of his life, until coming here to be paired with Petal a few years ago. "I wonder what has brought this one into the area now."

"He may be searching for water," Puh spoke up. "We have had a long, dry summer. If he is a newly matured young bull that has been driven from the herd, he may be seeking territory that is not yet inhabited by established bulls, and he will need to find a place with sufficient food and a water supply."

"Yes," Black Wolf agreed. "There is a large river and several creeks near the Village. And a pond and a lake not far from my old home."

"I would not be surprised if that was so. It has been a thirsty summer for many animals," Horse Tooth said with a nod. "The creeks are low, and even the river has receded far from its banks."

"We passed the pond near your former dwelling on our way here," Red Bear told Black Wolf. "It is little more than a mud hole, now."

"Not much to tempt a mammoth," Quiet Foot agreed.

"But perhaps a place to trap one," Bror spoke up. "Do you suppose we might entice him to the pond where he might be mired in the muck, in the same sort of way we trapped that other mammoth on weak ice?"

"If we do, I am not going to stand anywhere near its tail," Black Wolf stated determinedly.

During that particular mammoth hunt, the victim's final act in life was to bestow upon Black Wolf a mighty blast of excrement. This had happened quite a few years ago now, but the event remained sharp in his memory. The corners of Puh's mouth twitched with mirth, but he resisted the urge to smile. In fact, we all did. Poor Black Wolf had suffered enough indignity from that happenstance, and we strove to spare his feelings as much as possible.

"Well, that is one option, Bror," Puh said. "If we can devise a way to drive him into the pond. It will not be as easy as it was before. Then, the dense brush meant the mammoth had to travel down one of two paths, and Ria's arrows in his rump helped to urge him down the trail we chose. The land leading up to the pond is largely open. But first, we will have to locate the animal before we know what we can use to our advantage."

"Ria's arrows offer a definite advantage," Black Wolf noted. Speaking to Ria he went on, "Could you be persuaded to leave your little boy for a few days?"

Ria looked to Puh, who only smiled at her in response. I knew that Gran, and my sisters who still remained at home, thirteen-winters-old Twie, eight-winters-old Saree, and six-winters-old Mi, would be glad to care for their half-brother, little Mror, while his parents were away.

"If those caring for Mror would not feel put upon, I would go," Ria replied.

Black Wolf's mate, Little Fawn, now came into sight, walking toward us with her plodding gait.

Swift River had taken her arm as though to escort her, but he seemed a bit impatient to bring her to the group of people gathered at the center of the compound. I wondered if his assistance was merely a guise to hurry her along.

She was an enormously tall woman, tall enough to make most people stare. Now that she was nearing forty winters in age, her step had slowed and her back was bent from years of toil. I knew she was in constant pain, although she seldom spoke of it.

Little Fawn came to stand next to Ria, who was small even in comparison to my petite Morning Star, and side by side the two looked rather incongruous. But they were good friends, and they smiled to each other in greeting.

"The men are in need of your services once again?" Little Fawn said to Ria, having overheard just enough of our conversation to realize that Ria had been asked to partake in a hunt.

"No one can shoot the little spears like Ria," Bror proclaimed. "Although several of us have tried."

This was true. Ria had taught most of us how to shoot with a bow, but none of us was as proficient as she at hitting a target, especially a moving target. I could hit reasonably well if my target was stationary, but I struggled to strike anything that was either on the wing or on the run. While I hoped to eventually improve, a spear was still my weapon of choice.

"I see we have guests," Little Fawn said, nodding to the men, "I am Black Wolf's mate, Little Fawn. I hope you will sit by our fire and take some rest and food and drink while you are here."

The men had been openly staring at her, but now remembered their manners. They smiled at her and returned her greeting. Introductions soon followed.

"Thank you, Little Fawn," Horse Tooth said. "We were kindly given water and some dried fruit and roasted nuts when we arrived, but we would be very pleased to accept your invitation this evening."

Little Fawn smiled at them graciously, but then turned to Black Wolf and her tone became decidedly chilly.

"Have I been summoned here solely to cook, or do you have further need of me?" she asked him with feigned sweetness.

Black Wolf and Little Fawn could frequently be heard when they engaged in yet another verbal altercation, their raised voices carrying over our little settlement like the raucous calls of crows. Black Wolf did not typically suffer her gibes gracefully, and I could see that he was stifling a biting retort.

"I requested your presence because these men have brought news of a young mammoth. It was last seen near the Village, and we have decided to go after it. Swift River and Hawk have asked to accompany us," Black Wolf replied. He always became very formal when he was trying to hold back his temper. "I am considering whether or not to allow them to come, and I would like to hear your thoughts on this."

Little Fawn's mouth fell open in surprise. Her visage became that of a frightened and worried mother.

"This is sudden," Little Fawn said in a muted voice.

Their sons had been on a few brief hunts, but going after a mammoth, even a young one, was quite another matter. She stared at Black Wolf long and hard, as if to gauge his ability to keep their sons safe from harm. He returned her gaze expectantly.

"All right," Little Fawn finally said. "I know the boys will be in good hands. And sooner or later, they must learn all they will need to know when they are men. So, will you temporarily delay your trip to find new lands, or will you wait until next year to embark on the long trek?"

I did not envy her decision, and I admired her calm assessment of the situation. But Hawk and Swift River's jubilant reactions to her assent almost drowned Black Wolf's answer.

"We have not yet discussed that," he said, his voice rising to be heard over his sons' whoops of joy. "Perhaps we will speak of it over the evening meal."

Little Fawn nodded her reply, and then she hobbled over to Morning Star and me, holding out her hands to take Lily from Morning Star's arms. Lily, in return, reached for her doting grandmother.

"There is my little darling," Little Fawn cooed to Lily, rubbing her cheek against the baby's downy head while Lily tried to catch one of Little Fawn's long braids in her hands. Then Little Fawn looked to me. "Tris, you will help Black Wolf watch out for my sons, will you not?" she asked earnestly. Her eyes betrayed her desperation to have her boys brought safely home.

"Of course, Little Fawn," I answered. "We will all be sure to take good care of them. And we will not be that far away."

"Yes, Mama," Morning Star added. "All the men will be watching out for them, and Da will not let them do anything too dangerous."

Little Fawn just smiled faintly and snuggled the baby tighter.

"I know." Then she went on, "There are not many things that frighten me, but I am terrified that one of my boys will ... will ..." she seemed incapable of completing her sentence. After a momentary hesitation, during which Little Fawn seemed to compose her thoughts. "It is time to begin preparations for our nightly sup." Little Fawn placed Lily back in Morning Star's arms, kissing the baby one last time and patting Morning Star's shoulder.

"I understand, because I will feel the same way about Fox when his time comes," I said to Little

Fawn with sympathy. "But try not to worry yourself too much."

Little Fawn grasped my hand and squeezed it affectionately.

"Thank you, Tris. I know I can rely on you." She said quietly. Then she went on, "Would you bring up some wood for me? And a little tinder."

"Yes, Little Fawn," I replied. "I will fetch them directly."

Morning Star gave me a grateful glance for attempting to cheer her mother.

"F'well, Puh-Puh," Raven piped up from her Muh-Muh's side as I walked away, waving at me, even though I would scarcely be out of sight while I was gone.

"Farewell, my little Raven," I said to her, waving too. "I will be right back."

Tinder was easy to find now that it was late summer. The trees were just beginning to show the first colors of fall, and almost all the other plant life was crackling-dry. I had only to visit our firewood cache to choose a selection of various-sized pieces of split wood and gather up a handful of bark, twigs, and yellowed grasses from around the chunks of wood to complete my task.

* * *

The evening meal was a festive occasion for those who would be embarking on tomorrow's hunt. My feelings were divided between hopefulness that it would be successful and remorse to be facing a creature with the intention of killing it, when I knew it to be intelligent and, in some ways, almost human in nature. Many years ago I had been rescued from drowning in a fast-moving river by a compassionate cow mammoth, and later she had also intervened when I was attacked. She had been killed by hunters sometime after, but not before giving birth to a bull calf. How old would he be now – assuming he had survived? He was likely still a youngster, and it relieved me to know we would not be in pursuit of her calf.

All the same, the cow mammoth's benevolence toward me was not the kind of behavior we generally expected from mammoths, which were understandably wary of men. After all, we hunted them whenever opportunity presented itself. That said, the conditions had to be very specific. The animal almost certainly had to be a bull; while larger and more powerful than most cows, they were also generally loners. Cows congregated in herds with their infants and juvenile offspring, and they were extremely protective of one another. It would be folly to try to cut one of them from the herd as we might a wisent, because the others would rally to the defense of the intended victim. A lone bull, on the other hand, if he could be in some way prevented from using his full complement of size and strength against us – to say nothing of his formidable tusks –

posed far less risk to hunters. The trick was to figure out how to hamper such a beast.

It was not to be discussed this night, however. That would only unnerve our already nervous families, who did not share Hawk and Swift River's enthusiasm for the impending outing. We talked instead of the weather, our lives, the fortunes of our friends, and distant kin. We did not often see many people outside of those who resided here. I found it to be wonderfully diverting to hear news from outside our compound.

I tried not to think about the upcoming hunt and simply enjoy this time with my clan and our visitors, but stray thoughts kept stealing into my head. Had I packed everything I would need? Would we be away from home for only a few days? Would we be able to devise a plan to bring down this creature? Despite my misgivings about killing a mammoth, I knew I would do my part. I was a hunter with a family to feed.

"What say you all regarding our trek to find new lands?" Black Wolf inquired of the assemblage. "Are we still to embark after we return from this hunt?"

"I would say that depends on the results of the hunt," Puh said. "Even half a young adult woolly mammoth would be a huge boon for our families. Between that and the meat we will obtain during the fall hunts, it would substantially lessen the urgency to relocate."

"I agree," Fish Hawk said, nodding at Puh's statement.

"Yes," Bror began. "It would serve us well to stay here as long as we can."

"I am inclined to agree as well," Black Wolf replied. "At least we know what we have here. I am in no hurry to drag our families and everything we own across the countryside to set up housekeeping at some faraway place."

In that instant, I suddenly realized that Gran might well be right – not only about her own inability to make a long journey, but how would Little Fawn manage the journey to a distant place? Most of us admitted to much apprehension at the thought of leaving our homes, but there were those of us for whom the task would be daunting. It would be one thing to carry tiny Great Gran over a rough landscape, but to do the same with Little Fawn would be like transporting a sizable deer.

I then noted Morning Star's change of demeanor. I thought she seemed cheered at the idea that a successful mammoth hunt might mean that I would not have to leave again, and be gone for such a long time.

"Tris, take Lily for me, please." She placed Lily in my arms.

"Yes, my sweet," I said as I held Lily and watched Morning Star walk across the compound to refill our empty drinking gourd with more water.

I was struck that even after all our time together I still enjoyed the sight of her in motion. Perhaps it was because I was often forced to spend time away from Morning Star that I could return home and see my beloved mate with fresh eyes.

Chapter Three

And then they were upon us. They came leaping at us from the deep shadows of the forest, like wild animals on a rampage.

The next morning came all too soon. I was stupid with lack of sleep, having not wanted to waste my last night with my mate by slumbering through it. By the time I had finally settled down to rest, I had vague concerns about whether or not I would be able to awaken early enough to meet with the other hunters shortly after daybreak. But then my pre-dawn Dream startled me from sleep. I then had just time for one more romantic interlude with my mate before it was time to arise for the day.

Morning Star fussed over me, despite being sleep deprived as well, and tried to get me to eat as much as I could while I dressed in our usual late-summer, early-fall attire. I first tied on a loincloth and leggings, then tied a deerskin tunic around my waist by the sleeves. Next, I donned boots, omitting the insulating winter liners we wore in cold weather. As I slipped my pack onto my back, Morning Star stood ready with my wisent-hide cloak, which was tightly rolled with the two ends tied together so that it could be worn over one shoulder across the body.

The children ate their breakfasts, watching the process with avid curiosity. It was unusual for them to be up this early in the day, what with the sun still creeping up over the horizon, but the added noise and activity of my preparations had roused them from their nightly rest. Fox still talked of his excitement at my upcoming outing, jabbering about the triumphant hunts in which he would take part when he was a man.

Finally, I grasped my spear and turned to exit our home. Morning Star did not speak, but she put her arms around me and held me close for a moment. I bent to kiss her forehead, and then she looked up at me, smiling weakly. I tried to give her an encouraging grin.

"I must go now," I said. "The others will be waiting."

"I know," Morning Star replied. "We will come down to see you all off."

Morning Star picked up Lily and I lifted Raven into my free arm, and then with Fox, Pony, and Raena the dog accompanying us, we walked down the hill. As I had suspected, everyone else had already assembled.

In the clans of the Old Ones, traditionally it is the second son who stayed home and watched over the family while the other men hunted. Today, however, even my brother Ty, himself a second son, having inherited the role when our brother Dak was killed, was armed and ready to go.

"Ty, you wish to join us?" Black Wolf asked.

"Yes, I have discussed it with Puh," Ty answered. "We will be away for only three or four days, at most. We have seen no signs of strangers in the area, and large predators have not ventured near in many years. With so many people living here now, all marking our borders with urine, I believe the markings are strong enough to last while we are gone," he added with a smile.

Puh looked around the gathering, "Just so long as those left behind have no objections." After all, those remaining would be left without an adult male to defend the compound.

"I have no objections," Morning Star said firmly. "The more of you there are, the better the chances you will come home to us unhurt, and if you come home with meat, all the better."

* * *

I had had concerns about the wisdom of leaving Black Wolf's hunting dogs behind, but now those dogs would be our loved ones' best defense while we were away. I quickly banished the thought from my mind. Ria was the only woman going with us. She was older now, having survived her fortieth winter this past season, but she strode along easily, keen eyes missing nothing. She and Puh hiked side by side, occasionally sharing a quiet word or pausing to point something out to each other.

I thought back on what Gran had divulged about Ria and marveled at the pluck of this small woman, and the sheer luck that had brought us to her. Snow Leopard, the man Red Bear had mentioned upon meeting me, had lost the bout to win Morning Star in the Challenge Circle and, dissatisfied, he then recruited a group of men to help him abduct her. The abduction also ultimately failed, and the survivors of Snow Leopard's band were left to fend for themselves. They then became raiders and set upon robbing and terrorizing homesteads. Ria's was one of the many that had fallen victim.

Ria was alone and near starvation when we found her. By that time, her mate Bakkae had been gone for nearly four years and a winter of heavy snows had collapsed most of her home. That, and the fact that the raiders had managed to pilfer most of her belongings and stores, had severely diminished the likelihood of her survival. Puh and I could see that she would not make it through the coming winter without assistance, and thus, she left what remained of her demolished hovel and came to live with us.

The gang of roving miscreants were eventually identified and apprehended. I had not spent much time thinking about those raiders in the intervening years since their capture and banishment. I supposed that they had found a way to make new lives for themselves, and being young men at that time, they may have even settled down and started families, hopefully leaving their errant ways behind them.

* * *

The mammoth's last known whereabouts was less than a half-day's walk from our homes. If, as Puh had suggested, the young bull was in search of water, the large lake near Black Wolf's former abode was as good a place to start looking for him as any. We reached the glacier-fed body of water just as the sun was approaching the halfway point to its daily zenith.

We made every attempt to silence our movements, and we did not speak as the glittering waters came into view. It was apparent by the old high-water lines that the lake's level had dropped. This was the biggest lake for quite some distance, and it always drew a considerable amount of wildlife to its shores. Now that we stood at the cusp of fall, the lake itself was dotted with a variety of migrating waterfowl. Songbirds serenaded us from the nearby brush as insects chirped and hummed in accompaniment.

We spotted the tracks of a few deer and an elk in the damp soil. A fox and several otters had also wandered through. Black Wolf waved a hand to signal to us, and he vigorously pointed toward the ground near his feet. There, we saw mammoth tracks exiting the water's edge. We soon found other imprints that appeared to be older, perhaps left a day or two ago, and others that looked as though they had been left only this morning. I noted that Puh was checking the fringes of the forest, so I walked over to join him. His expression was grim.

"What is it, Puh?" I whispered to him.

Puh gestured toward the ground. I then noted the stirred leaf litter. Puh gently pushed it aside, exposing the large circular paw prints of lions. The more we looked, the more we saw. The tracks were fairly large and uniform in size. I thought it likely they belonged to three or four males – brothers – who, like the young mammoth, had probably been ousted from their family group upon reaching maturity. We exchanged glances and then returned to our friends.

"There are signs that lions are in the area," Puh remarked quietly. "There is no blood or suggestion of a scuffle, so it would seem that they have not brought down prey here, but they do appear to be in stalking mode."

"They do not generally shy away from an attack if they think they have a chance," Quiet Foot said thoughtfully. "But then, if they are trying to close in on the mammoth, that is a much larger animal than those they are accustomed to hunting."

"Perhaps they were tracking deer or an elk," I suggested.

It went unsaid that the lions would consider us to be prey as well. We almost never saw any indication that they visited this area; they preferred the tall grasses and brush of the open prairies, where their tawny coats offered the perfect camouflage for their surroundings. This mammoth, however, may have been enough to tempt them to abandon their usual haunts for the woodland. I mused it was also possible that their thirst may have driven them here as well.

"Now I am wishing we had brought a few of my dogs along," Black Wolf said wistfully. "You boys stay close to me," he added to his sons. "If a lion wishes to spring upon us, we will not know about it until it is already happening."

Swift River and Hawk grasped their spears anxiously and obediently moved a half-step closer to their father, wearing small smiles as though they really might like to see a lion, if they could manage to do so without actually becoming its dinner.

"Do you think they are close?" Swift River asked.

"The birds, squirrels, and other animals are not showing any signs of alarm, so I do not think they are near," Puh guessed. "But your Da is right. Lions are incredibly stealthy predators, so we will need to be extremely vigilant. And you . . ." Puh now spoke to Ria, "I will ask that you stay by me as well."

Ria nodded calmly. She was the smallest of us, even smaller than Hawk, which made her a likely target for a hungry lion. Ria was armed with her bow and her little arrows, but they would not stop or even discourage a charging lion.

We fell silent again and continued to follow the mammoth's tracks. Very often they disappeared into the lake. The tracks wandered around the shoreline, presenting the picture of a happy creature that could at last slake its giant thirst. The lion paw prints, on the other hand, almost never left the cover of the brush.

The mammoth seemed to have enjoyed a leisurely saunter along the lake until the landscape opened up to reveal a gap in the forest, giving us a view of an expansive meadow. Even a large lea such as this would not keep a young bull in food for very long. We could see evidence of heavy grazing, and places where the mammoth's tusks had churned up soil to expose the plants' roots. The grasses and flowers, mammoths' preferred diet, were now yellowed and dry, and their roots offered more sustenance than what was more easily accessed above ground.

Under a brilliant blue sky, the mammoth's progress was easily tracked; so too was the lions'. We found a place where several of the beasts had hunkered down in a cluster of small bushes, flattening the undergrowth. One had left a pile of droppings that had attracted a considerable number of flies. It was not fresh. It would seem they had passed this way earlier in the day.

The sun climbed high in the firmament. Hawks and vultures glided overhead in lazy circles, keeping watch on the ground below for a potential meal. The stubs of the heavily grazed grasses were stiff and spiky underfoot, and they poked into the spots where the soles of my boots had worn thin.

Swift River and Hawk were showing signs of becoming bored with the monotony of hiking. We did not speak with one another and we had not yet stopped to rest or take food, but they dared not complain. They knew that if they spoke up, they would likely not be taken on another hunt for some time. Only those mature enough to endure lengthy marches and maintain long stretches of silence could be included.

My stomach was rumbling with hunger. And although I had sipped at my water bag, I was parched now that we were walking in the open, under the midday sun. A welcome breeze blew into our faces, but it was still a very warm day.

When we spied a small grouping of trees ahead of us, Puh motioned to catch our attention, and then pointed to the trees. We all nodded in return. We would break there.

Once in the shelter of the trees, we carefully scouted the area to make sure we were not sharing it with any animals that might provide an unpleasant surprise, or that might be unpleasantly surprised by our sudden arrival. There, we each found a comfortable spot to sit or lounge on the ground, and removed our packs. We wasted no time in quenching our thirst and greedily stuffing handfuls of dried foods into our mouths.

"It seems as though the animals are all hiding, Da," Hawk observed.

It was true. We had seen remarkably little wildlife since leaving the lake.

"You are right," Black Wolf responded. "And my best guess would be that is because the lions came this way not too long ago."

"Our old house is not far from here," Swift River said. "I do not recall that we ever saw any lions when we lived there."

"That is probably because we were there. Or more importantly, because the dogs were there," Black Wolf explained. "Lions are not afraid of much, but they do not seem to like the presence of a bunch of humans and a pack of big dogs. Dogs catch the lions' scent, and then bark – giving warning to all that a threat is near. Now that the area has been free of humans and dogs for some time, large predators will gradually return."

"Like the bears that moved into your old home," Fish Hawk joined in. "The lions will not care much for them, either."

"Where is your old home in relation to where we are now?" Bror asked.

Bror had not been to Black Wolf's former home, nor had he ever been to the Village, which was located some distance beyond that.

Black Wolf pushed aside the debris that covered a section of dirt and then began to draw with a stick. We all crowded around him.

"This is the lake," Black Wolf jabbed the stick into the oblong shape that represented the lake. "This is where the long meadow bisects the forest. My old home was over here. If we had continued along the trail to the Village, we would have passed very close to it."

Bror nodded with understanding.

"And how much farther is it to the Village?"

Black Wolf jabbed the stick into the dirt once more.

"Here." He drew another lumpy circle. "It used to house many people. At least a hundred. Now, there may be twenty or fewer." Black Wolf looked to the three men from the Village for confirmation and they bobbed their heads in agreement. "If we began to walk there right now, we would make it there well before nightfall."

"Speaking of nightfall, we must keep in mind that it might be wise to consider spending the night in the Village," Red Bear said a bit anxiously.

I was sure he was thinking that the number of people and dogs in the Village would discourage the lions from attacking, but I also recalled the stench of the Village, and the piles of rotting refuse.   I wondered if that might actually draw their interest. Lions were not usually scavengers, but they might like to eat the scavengers that came to feast on those scraps. The people who inhabited the place might provide a meal or two as well.

"I do not believe we will need to go as far as the Village," Puh stated.

"Why not?" Bror asked.

"It is a hot day. If, as we have been told, the pond by Black Wolf's former dwelling has dried up, the mammoth will not have found water since early this morning." Puh looked around at the drought-stricken countryside. "If the lions have not yet managed to bring him down, he is going to have to return to the lake very soon. I think we should lie in wait for him. The problem will be that we are currently upwind."

"If he smells us, he will choose some other route to the lake," Horse Tooth predicted.

"He would not be able to get his bulk through that thick tangle of forest," Black Wolf pointed out. "He will have to come through the meadow, whether he likes it or not."

"If he has caught scent of the lions, he may be already distracted and agitated," Puh said.

"Most of us could wait right here," Ria chimed in. "Here, we have cover and shade. But maybe a few of us could go over there and I could send some of my little arrows his way, to draw his attention from those of you who may hope to take him from behind."

Puh seemed to be considering her proposal. He gazed around the grove, searching the limbs overhead.

"If we could get him near the trees, we could thrust our spears down from overhead, and if we can get enough force behind the throw, we may hope to strike his lungs," Puh said.

"What if we lighted fires to drive him toward the trees?" Swift River piped up, eager to make a contribution.

Puh smiled at Swift River.

"You are correct in thinking that mammoths do not like fire," Puh began. "They are terrified of flames. If in close proximity, they are as likely to try to stamp it out as run from it. If they smell fire, and they have an acute sense of smell, they will simply avoid it. But, you are on the right track. We need to attack him without exposing ourselves to his wrath."

"Puh, you did not accompany us on that hunt with the Wolfmen when we killed the woolly rhino," I said, "but they had set up spears against a tree stump in the tall grass and then taunted the rhino to charge so that it impaled itself on the spears. This is a bigger animal, of course, but I wonder if it might work."

The Wolfmen, or the men from The People of the Wolves, as they called themselves, were visitors from a faraway clan. They had been skilled huntsmen and fine companions as well. All the same, that woolly rhino hunt had very nearly ended in disaster. We had no sooner brought down the beast when we were set upon by a large pack of lions. The lions wanted our kill, and they had been difficult indeed to discourage.

"I sometimes think of those Wolfmen and wonder if they made it back to their home," Black Wolf said. "When they left us, they had a long journey ahead of them."

Bror appeared thoughtful. Karno, the leader of the Wolfmen, had been enamored with my sister Ru, and she with him, but ultimately she had become paired with Bror. Karno was at times charming, and at other times brash. However, it was Bror's quiet persistence and patience that finally won Ru's heart.

"I hope they are safely at home," Puh responded rather flatly. He had not been impressed with Karno's wooing of Ru, and he was only too glad to see them – or at least Karno – leave.

"What do you think of the propped-spear idea, Tor?" Fish Hawk asked Puh, since Puh was the only one of us who had been on more than one mammoth hunt.

"Again, there is the problem of getting him to go where we want him to go," Puh said. "I am not sure we could get him to charge in the way a woolly rhino would. Mammoths are not as volatile in temperament."

"Many stings into his backside might encourage him to dash forward," Ria suggested, patting her bow. Her small arrows would not do the mammoth any great harm, but they would perforate the skin.

"If we can find something suitable to prop a spear against, there is no harm in trying," Puh told us. "And, as I said, we can also attempt to get him to walk under the trees."

"And if he does neither?" Horse Tooth asked.

Puh shrugged.

"My ears are open to all suggestions," he answered.

We began to scout the meadow for something we could prop a spear or two against, but we found nothing more substantial than a few spindly shrubs, so we returned to the grouping of trees, where we were glad to get out of the sun's glare.

"Our next problem is to decide from where I can shoot my arrows, to make the mammoth approach the trees," Ria spoke up. "I do not have much range. I will have to be within twenty or perhaps thirty paces, at most."

At that moment, a trumpeting bellow rent the air. We exchanged startled glances and looked up the meadow for its source. The woolly mammoth was trotting into view, issuing deep rumbles from his throat. Suddenly, he wheeled and turned to meet an unseen foe. He tossed his head, swiping at the air with his tusks. He reared for an instant and, upon landing on his feet, he charged in one direction and then another.

"The lions must have chosen to make their attack!" Black Wolf exclaimed.

"But where are they, Da? I cannot see them!" Hawk cried out, impatiently straining up on his toes in an attempt to get a better view. Giving this up as a futile effort, he began to scale a tree. Swift River rapidly followed. They did not want to lose the chance to see their first glimpse of a lion, or a mammoth, for that matter.

"They are there . . . do you hear them?" Black Wolf said to his sons.

By now, we could all hear the lions' impressive roars, intermingling with the mammoth's trumpeting, groans, and rumbles. The fracas covered a surprisingly large area, as the animals fought for advantage. There were not many creatures that could do much harm to a full-grown mammoth, especially a large bull. But this bull was not yet fully-grown. He was old enough to be on his own, but only by a few years. Just like I had guessed, there were four lions, all young males, as their slim physiques and largely unscarred faces testified. I suspected that it was their inexperience that held them back from making their initial contact. Their hunger must have finally overcome their discretion, and now they set upon the mammoth vigorously.

"Do you suppose we could get close enough to thrust in our spears?" Quiet Foot inquired of the group.

"Into the mammoth or the lions?" asked Ty.

We were silent as we pondered this. I thought it was a very astute question. I had been there when the lions tried to wrest our newly won rhino carcass from our possession. There had been a great many more beasts that day, and they were seasoned predators, but I knew firsthand that even a single lion was an extremely dangerous opponent. A large bear had much brute strength, but a lion was even more fearsome. A male lion could be longer than two men lying on the ground end to end and weigh as much as a sizable bear.

There were twelve of us, if you included Black Wolf's two boys. I had little doubt that we could face off against either the mammoth or the lions separately, but it would be a trick to safely engage these combatants. Puh seemed to be deep in thought. His eyes searched the landscape, but they repeatedly returned to the roiling battle that was drawing ever closer to us.

"The lions are fairly new to fending for themselves," Fish Hawk observed. "We could try marching out toward them, arms outstretched and making lots of noise and see if we can frighten the lions off."

"We might be able to scare them off, but as soon as the mammoth was freed from their attack, he would run for the hills," Black Wolf said, shaking his head. "Then we would have to track him for days to catch up with him."

"Perhaps it would be best to let the lions wear him down," Puh responded.

"And maybe I can help wear the lions down," Ria said. "If I get up in that tree . . ." she indicated the one where Black Wolf's boys now perched like a couple of wide-eyed owls as they followed the nearby scene. "Then I can shoot my arrows at the lions. I will not be able to kill them, but I can wound them here and there. The blood loss will eventually slow them down."

"That is a good idea," Puh agreed.

We all nodded. It would help considerably if we could decrease their vigor.

In the meantime, we had not bothered at all to conceal our presence whatsoever. If either the mammoth or the lions had been even the slightest bit interested in us, they surely would have known we were there.

Puh gave Ria a boost into the lower limbs of the tree, and then she climbed up a short way before settling herself on a large branch. I watched her arm her bow and heard the soft twang of the bowstring.

It was an excellent shot. I promptly made a promise to myself that I would devote more time to practicing with the bow and the little spears. We all grinned to see that the arrow had struck one of the lions in the side of his neck. It looked pathetically small against his large frame, but it must have pained him because he turned to bite at it, but he could not reach.

Nevertheless, the stricken lion could not ignore the turmoil around him to concentrate on removing the offending projectile. He returned his attention to more pressing matters at hand, such as not being trampled to death by the mammoth.

Ria's second arrow hit the same lion in the rump. He spun around to gnash his teeth at the arrow's slender shaft and succeeded in biting it in two. At that moment, the mammoth maneuvered to evade the other lions, quickly shifting his feet, and one of the hefty appendages landed on the injured lion's right forepaw.

The lion screamed in pain. It was a frightful sound. One of his companions paused just long enough to spare him a glance, and Ria sent forth another arrow, which struck the second lion in the forehead. He pawed at the arrow, snapping it off, but the point remained firmly lodged in place. He shook his head as though to rid himself of this annoyance, but then quickly had to dance out of the way of the mammoth's stamping feet and sweeping tusks.

The first lion was now limping away, one paw held aloft as he awkwardly slunk from the field. It may have been my imagination, but it seemed as though the other lions were losing heart. Those three puny arrows may have made a huge difference in the outcome of this hunt. I could see Ria closely following the movements of the lions, waiting for one to present a vulnerable target. Fish Hawk seemed to be thinking about Ria's arrows as well.

"It is a shame the beasts are not in a good position for Ria's arrows to persuade them to move closer to the trees, where we can rain down our spears upon them," he said. "Our spears could do much more damage."

One of the lions chose that time to leap up onto the mammoth's back. The mammoth's vocalizations became even more frantic at this unexpected development. The behemoth threw his entire body from side to side to throw off the unwelcome rider. This having no effect, the mammoth suddenly looked toward the collection of trees from where we were watching the spectacle. Then, as if he had had an epiphany, the mammoth lumbered toward us, moving more quickly than I had ever seen a mammoth move. He could not gallop, exactly, but he certainly was capable of a fast jog; the other two lions ran along in pursuit.

The mammoth's long strides soon brought him up to the large tree in which Ria, Hawk, and Swift River were straddling limbs, and he crashed his shoulder into the trunk, scraping the top of his back along the lower-most branches. Those of us on the ground lunged for the shelter of the nearby trees, hoping that Ria and the boys would be able to hang on.

I was incredulous to see the huge lion being swept from the mammoth's back. It fell heavily to the ground, just a few steps from where we stood. Hawk was thrown from his seat as well, and he landed squarely in the middle of the lion's back.

A breathy *ooph* escaped the lion's mouth upon Hawk's impact, and the beast groaned. Hawk and the lion were wearing identical expressions of shock and dismay. Fortunately, the lion seemed stunned into inaction for just an instant, allowing Hawk to scramble to his feet and back away before the lion could regain his sensibilities.

Black Wolf was closest, and he darted out with his spear, lancing the lion behind his left foreleg. Fish Hawk also drove in his spear, right next to Black Wolf's. The lion's head drooped down upon his outstretched forelegs. His breath came in great gasps. The lion was bleeding heavily from the wound, and also from his nose and mouth. He succumbed to his injuries in a matter of moments.

The other lions were now gone from our sight. The mammoth had not faltered in step after he smote the tree, and his ample backside was now appearing smaller and smaller as he put distance between himself and the scene of the attack.

Black Wolf embraced Hawk, who still trembled from his adventure.

"Are you hurt?" Black Wolf inquired of Hawk.

Hawk shook his head. He seemed to be speechless.

"I am all . . . all right," he finally stammered. "I . . . I think the lion broke my fall."

Black Wolf stooped to give Hawk a tight squeeze.

"You were very brave," Black Wolf told him. "And what a story you will have to tell! Not every boy can say that he was knocked out of a tree by a woolly mammoth and then landed on a lion's back!"

"Shall we track the mammoth?" Bror asked.

Puh shook his head in reply as he helped Ria to climb down, encumbered as she was by her bow and quiver.

"He is moving too fast, and it is getting late. I suggest we gut this lion and take him to the Village, where we can butcher him and divvy up the meat," Puh replied. "We will have to act quickly before the other lions regain their confidence."

By now, Swift River had also left the tree and rejoined us.

"Are you all right?" Puh entreated Ria. "The mammoth hit the tree rather hard."

"He did," Ria agreed with a grin, "but I saw him coming and had time to brace for the blow."

Black Wolf now had an arm around both of his sons, but they broke loose to tentatively approach the dead lion.

"Da, this thing is enormous!" Swift River then pointed to its death-grimace. "And look at the teeth!"

Fish Hawk's visage broke out in a mischievous grin, and he snuck up behind the boys. Fish Hawk let free a mighty roar and vigorously grasped both boys by the shoulders as though he were a wild beast taking them from behind.

Swift River and Hawk started and cried out in alarm, but they quickly realized that their uncle had perpetrated a joke on them. We were all quite amused, since it was usually the boys who were playing tricks.

Swift River scowled at Fish Hawk.

"That is not funny!" he insisted.

"Really not funny!" Hawk concurred.

"Of course not," Fish Hawk said simply, but he still smiled and his eyes were creased with mirth.

"Let us get to work," Black Wolf said, bringing us back to the situation at hand.

"But what about the other lions?" Hawk piped up.

"The one with the crushed foot is not likely to survive," Bror predicted.

"Yes," Red Bear agreed, "he also has two arrows stuck in him, but unless one those minor injuries develop a fatal infection, it is his foot that will be his downfall."

"If he survives, he will have a pronounced limp," Horse Tooth added.

"I can sympathize," Black Wolf mumbled. He had suffered from foot pain for many years now. He did not often speak of his discomfort, but after long hikes he limped as well.

The lion was swiftly gutted by Black Wolf and Fish Hawk, while Puh, Bror, Ty, and I went amongst some of the small trees to select a few that could be made into an in impromptu travois sled, and the others stood by to guard against any curious predators.

It was not long before the beast was rolled onto the hastily constructed sled and we began to drag it across the countryside toward the Village. Even gutted, the lion was far too lengthy in body and too heavy to conveniently transport. We all took turns at the pulling, so that each of us had a chance to rest, and we were able to reach our destination in plenty of time for our evening sup.

Chapter Four

As always, I smelled the Village before I saw it. The odor of wood smoke and rotting refuse never failed to announce the proximity of this community, although it seemed to me the scent was not as pronounced as it had been in years past.

The trails that came and went from the Village all led to one of its several gates. The gates were now just a formality, since the log fence erected around the settlement was currently in a state of rampant disrepair, and much of it lay on the ground. But since it was easier to drag the sled along the path, we headed for the closest gate.

Upon arrival, we were greeted by a great many barking dogs. The canines were enraged by the presence of the dead lion. They growled and snarled at it. One lunged forward and grabbed the limp tail of the huge beast to give it a vicious tug. Black Wolf quickly responded to the offender with a loud shout and firm poke with the butt of his spear. The dogs continued to be a noisy escort, but from there on in, they maintained a respectful distance.

The Village residents came forward to welcome us. I heard the word *lion* murmured amongst them, and then *Old Ones*. They did not often see lions, especially not as close as this, nor did they often see Old Ones. Quiet Foot, Horse Tooth, and Red Bear were speaking animatedly with their friends and kin about our adventure, as the rest of us stood to the side with the sled and its burden. I hoped that we would be led to a place where we could hang up the lion, which would make it easier to butcher him. Otherwise, we would have to flip his ponderous bulk from one side to the next to remove his pelt and the meat from his bones. But then my thoughts were distracted when one of the Villagers walked up to me.

"You are Snow Leopard's slayer," he said matter-of-factly.

I had wondered if I would ever be known as the one who had brought about Snow Leopard's demise. Like Red Bear, he was speaking of that time many years ago when Snow Leopard had vied with me in the Challenge Circle to win my mate Morning Star. Snow Leopard had vowed to kill me, but instead, after stealing Morning Star, he was killed by me. This I did not only in self-defense, but to ensure that he would never again come after my mate. Snow

Leopard had not been a personable man, but he was the Village's finest hunter, and he had been well regarded by many.

I merely nodded, and waited to see if he would speak further.

"Tris was offered Morning Star before Snow Leopard asked for her," Black Wolf stated, his voice a deep growl as he looming over the man from his great height. "And yet Snow Leopard still pushed to settle the matter in the Challenge Circle, and there, he lost. Snow Leopard would still be alive if he had honored the results of the Challenge Circle. *But no!* He and his followers abducted her! He forced Tris, Tor, and me to chase after him and his accomplices to get her back." Black Wolf's tone became more forceful as he went on, "If Snow Leopard is dead, it is because of his own folly."

The man blanched at Black Wolf's intimidating diatribe.

"I meant no offense," he said to Black Wolf, evidently hoping to soothe his indignation. "I was just so surprised to see him again . . . I saw the bout with Snow Leopard those many years ago, but have not seen him since. What is his name?"

"My name is Tris," I told him.

"Tris, it has been a long time," the man said, "but I would recognize you anywhere. You are the biggest Old One I have ever seen. And now you have all arrived with a lion! I had heard that you were going after a mammoth; you must tell us the story over the evening meal."

"The mammoth dropped this lion on our laps and then he ran away," Fish Hawk responded drolly.

The man looked confused at this, but Fish Hawk declined to comment further on the subject. However, as a former resident of the Village, Fish Hawk then directed us to a large tree where he knew we could suspend the lion by his hind paws and thus begin work on his carcass.

By now, everyone in the Village had gathered around and was watching as we skinned the mighty beast. When the job was done and the various bits and pieces of the lion were dispersed amongst the hunters and the Villagers, we were invited to sit by a communal hearth and partake in the evening meal.

I sat with my brother Ty, Puh and Ria, and my cousin Bror. Black Wolf and his family and my clan had been close friends for generations, but not all of The People accepted Old Ones so readily, and I could not help but notice that some of The People sat as far away from us as possible. I did not understand disliking a person you did not know, but I did realize that it existed in many humans of all kinds. I also had to acknowledge that perhaps it was my presence, as Snow Leopard's killer, that was offensive to these people, regardless of being an Old One.

All the same, it was an agreeable meal. The night was warm, and the food was hot and filling. I was quite hungry and thirsty, and although the lion's fresh meat was somewhat strong and a bit tough, it was nowhere near as gamey as the boar we had recently killed.

"What will you do with the hide?" one of the Villagers inquired as we ate.

With a prize as grand as this, tradition held that the one who struck the first blow received the pelt.

"Black Wolf, you lanced him first. I believe it is yours," Puh told him.

"I have been thinking on that," Black Wolf said. "I have already gifted almost all my family and various friends – all but my youngest son, Black Oak. He is just a small boy at this time, but I would like him to have something special to remember me by. I am nearing forty winters, and if I do not live to see him become a man, at least he will think of me when he views the lion skin."

"Are you able to see much of Black Oak outside of the annual Gathering of The People?" Red Bear asked.

Black Wolf looked grim. He shook his head.

"No, much to my regret," Black Wolf explained. "I miss him and his mother at all times. I am only able to be with them for a few times a year. I would be with them every day, but I am paired with Little Fawn, and I am bound to take care of her and our children." Black Wolf glanced at the two sons he had sired with Little Fawn, who were solemnly listening to everything he said. They knew of his relationship with The People's Head Elder, Willow Woman, and of their half-brother. Black Wolf gave his boys an encouraging smile. "And, of course, I love all my children, and I want to provide for them. They will each have the best I can give them."

"Da, when will we get to meet Oak?" Swift River asked.

"Not for many moons. Possibly not for some years," Black Wolf replied.

"Mama would not like it?" Hawk guessed.

"That is true. Your Mama would not like it," Black Wolf confirmed. "However, you will doubtless meet Oak when you are old enough to attend the annual Gatherings. But do not fret. Oak is still just a young child. You and Swift River would not be very interested in his company at this time."

The boys fell quiet, and the conversation turned to other matters.

"Speaking of the Gathering," Quiet Foot said, "I am told it will be held in the new Gathering Hall this year."

"I was always in awe of the old one," Red Bear said. "No matter how many times I have seen it, I am amazed at the size of that structure! At the last Gathering the frame of the new hall was under construction, and it seems as though it will be even more impressive! And it seems this one will have . . . um . . . appendage-type things off the sides. Like two halls, one larger and one smaller, but joined at the middle." Red Bear motioned with his arms that the two structures would intersect at their centers.

"I am eager to see the finished Hall," Black Wolf said, smiling in anticipation. I knew that as Willow Woman's paramour and the father of the next Head Elder, Black Wolf was included in many of her decisions. He and Willow Woman had spent much time talking over this grand new building.

"I am curious as to why this Hall is so much larger than the old one," Red Bear persisted. "Are we expected to have a surge in the number of new babies entering the world?"

There was an undercurrent of lighthearted chuckles at this, but Puh and I exchanged glances. We knew of Willow Woman's plans to eventually make the People's Gathering a meeting that included all humans. Because we Old Ones were not always welcomed by some of The People, we expected that Willow Woman's announcement would not be happily received by everyone. But Black Wolf managed to circumvent the question.

"It will not be long before we must embark on the autumn hunts," he said. "I have seen early signs of the upcoming rut. Some of the bucks are starting to parry with one another."

"What about the mammoth?" Fish Hawk asked. "Or do you suppose it would be better to let him settle down a bit before we attempt to go after him again?"

"Yes," Puh said with a nod. "He will be very skittish for some while. There are no other mammoths in this area and, as long as he can find enough fodder, he may stay near the lake, since finding a suitable water source will be his biggest problem here."

"For us, as well," Horse Tooth chimed in. "This Village is all but dead. The stream is down to a mere trickle, and the game animals will scarcely come anywhere near us. We are considering packing up and moving to a new place, possible south of the Gathering Hall. I hear there are open plains down there that are teeming with wisents and horses."

"And plenty of other animals, as well," Quiet Foot added.

"The land can sustain people for only so long, and then we all must move on," Black Wolf said. "And this little plot of land has had to sustain a good number of people for many generations now. It is time to let it rest so that it may heal."

* * *

When the evening sup had concluded, those of us who were not residents of the Village were shown some of the abandoned dwellings so that we could choose a place in which to spend the night. Most of the homes were in various stages of dilapidation, but it was only for a short while since we would be leaving soon after dawn. Bror, Ty, and I would make ourselves comfortable in one small hut, Black Wolf, his sons, and Fish Hawk another, and Puh and Ria, yet another.

I hesitated before following Bror and Ty into the hut. Even from outside the entryway, I could smell its putridly stale interior. We had already discussed a plan to either pull back or remove the tattered hide that covered the doorway, and thus allow more fresh air to flow inside. We chose to tuck the hide to one side, which would allow us to close it in case of foul weather.

I looked up at the sky. It was a clear, cool night. Late-summer crickets chirped and sang. The moon was hidden from sight, making the stars appear all the more bright. A wolf howled in the distance, and then another answered the call. I took one last breath of fresh air and then ducked through the doorway.

Ty and Bror were already lying on the bare floor, using their thick cloaks as under-padding. I chose a spot and spread out my cloak as well. As I settled down to sleep, my thoughts wandered to my family. I hoped that the children were behaving well for Morning Star and that she was not feeling too lonely. I myself missed her and our children terribly. I missed our nightly ritual of putting the children to bed and kissing them as they lay snug in their beds. I was very glad to know that I would be back with them tomorrow, albeit only for a short time before I would have to leave again.

A sudden scream diverted my attention, and then a giant maw appeared before me . . .

I started; had I been dozing? It seemed as though I had just lain down.

"What ails you?" Ty asked irritably. He must have been roused from his slumber.

"Do you have a cramp in your leg or something?" Bror inquired.

"No cramp," I replied, my mind still somewhat foggy. "I must have been dreaming."

"But was it a Dream?" Bror persisted.

"It may have been a Dream," I replied. "I do not know. Perhaps the lions are still on my mind."

"They are still on mine," Ty admitted.

* * *

The next morning we stayed just long enough to break our fast, and then we dragged our sled out of the Village, again accompanied by barking canines. The lion was now reduced to a few hide-wrapped bundles of meat, and the lion's skin. The lion's empty arms now embraced his equally empty head, and the rest of the skin was rolled around it for ease of transport.

After a short distance, the dogs must have decided that they had gone far enough, and they left us to continue the rest of our journey without them. Quiet Foot, Red Bear, and Horse Tooth had stayed in the Village, of course, which meant that there were three fewer men to help pull the sled. However, the burden was considerably lighter on this trip. As before, we took turns in the sled's harness. By midmorning we had passed Black Wolf's old homestead and the lake where we had first tracked the mammoth.

We did not expect to see much game on the well-traveled trail, so we made no attempts at stealth. We talked sometimes, and sometimes Black Wolf sang.

The mighty hunter is bold and brave
He walks a long path and fresh meat does he crave
The mighty hunter must keep his family clothed and fed
And if his mate is large, he must make a big bed

. . .

Puh held up a hand and we all stopped in place. Puh sniffed the air cautiously.

"What is it, Puh?" I whispered.

"I smell poop!" Ria said in a hushed voice.

"Not just any poop . . . I believe it is mammoth poop," Puh responded.

Black Wolf had not yet spoken, but the expression on his face was one of complete revulsion. He shuddered.

"*Ack!* I know that smell only too well!" Black Wolf cried out. He looked around himself as though searching out the pile of excrement, lest it take him unawares.

We began to walk once again, keeping a lookout for the manure. Puh was right. It was just a short way up the trail, and being upwind, the breeze was carrying the odiferous evidence of the mammoth's passage toward us.

"This was dropped earlier this morning," Fish Hawk observed.

"We cannot be too far behind him," Bror added eagerly.

"Will we try to get him again, Da?" Swift River inquired excitedly.

Puh and Black Wolf exchanged glances. We were down to five experienced men and little Ria. Ty would be a good strong hand, but he had not been on many hunts. We could count on Hawk and Swift River to be no more than observers – and observers from a safe distance, at that.

"He appears to be following that swath of grass that lines the banks of the little creek," Black Wolf said, pointing to a barely trickling stream that crossed the trail.

"Yes," Puh agreed. "It is not much to sustain a mammoth, but better than nothing."

I walked along the creek bed. The foliage was greener here, and the trickling water burbled cheerfully. I could see why a mammoth would be attracted to this area. It was a pleasant place to while away the day, grazing on lush plants during a season when little was green.

Then I noticed mammoth tracks in the soft soil by the creek. There were many of them, as though he were moving slowly, being sure not to miss a leaf or blade of grass.

"The wind is in our favor; plus the rustling branches and the sounds of water will help to obscure our presence," I noted.

Puh nodded.

"Perhaps we could track him for a time and see if we can locate him," Puh said. After a pause, he went on, "But my feeling is that he will not be satisfied to stay here long. He will soon need more food and water."

Black Wolf appeared to be deep in thought.

"The creek curves across the landscape like a snake," Black Wolf said. "The mammoth will be following all those bends in creek. If we cut through the forest, we might be able to get ahead of him.

"Then what?" Ty asked.

"We will just have to see where we find him," Bror said with a shrug. "Perhaps there will be something there we can use to our benefit. A huge fallen tree across the stream or something that might present an obstacle for the mammoth."

"It would have to be a tremendously big tree," Black Wolf said skeptically. "But there is a place where the creek veers sharply to the right. At that point it widens and creates a pool with an eddy to the left of the main body of the stream. The water is fairly deep. We may be able to startle him into the deep water, and gain an advantage."

I turned to look at the woodlands we would be cutting though. This would be a challenge, especially with the sled, which we could not afford to temporarily abandon, and leave exposed to theft by either scavengers or predators.

"Ty, would you, Swift River and Hawk pull the sled?" Puh asked, continuing, "and you, Bror, bring up the rear to guard from attack from behind, while Ria guards the front of the sled? Then Black Wolf, Tris, Fish Hawk and I can hasten forward and attempt to reach the widened place in the creek before the mammoth arrives there. You can catch up with us at your own pace."

"Yes, Puh," Ty said.

All but Ria nodded in agreement.

"I understand your plan, Tor," she said to Puh, "but I do not like to be so far from you if you should find danger."

"I will not like to be away from you, either, should danger find you," Puh admitted with a slight smile. "But I am thinking that you are safer with the sled, and the sled will be safer for your presence and your sure aim with your little arrows." After a moment, Puh said, "Besides, you will not be that far behind us."

Then, Puh, Fish Hawk, Black Wolf, and I set off at a quick pace through the trees. There was no path here, so we were forced to break our own trail as best we could. It seemed an eternity, but the sun had still not yet attained its zenith by the time we reached the pool of which Black Wolf had spoken. We peered at it from the cover of brush, searching for any sign that the mammoth had already passed this way.   The foliage appeared largely intact, as compared with the heavily grazed area we had left behind downstream.

The scene was markedly peaceful. Birds sang as the creek whirled in an eddy and then moved merrily along. The dry summer had left the banks broadened by low water levels, but the pool was a dark blue, indicating considerable depth.

"Well, now that we are here, what shall we do to ensnare the mammoth so we can kill it?" Fish Hawk said, taking care to speak just above a whisper.

There were no fallen trees, nothing to impede the mammoth from simply running away rather than voluntarily entering the eddy as we had hoped. The four of us had no chance against a beast this size without something to severely hamper him. Even when the others caught up with us, it would still be no small task to bring the mammoth down.

"The most vulnerable spot on a mammoth's body is right by his anus, so if we want him to bleed out quickly, that is still our target," Puh stated quietly.

"Just like last time," Fish Hawk said.

"Perfect," Black Wolf mumbled. But his tone spoke volumes regarding his true feelings.

I thought on our situation. What did we have at our disposal to use against a bull mammoth? There were not many things they were afraid of except . . . lions.

"What about the lion's skin?" I said, striving to keep my voice down. "He will still be traumatized by yesterday's lion attack, will he not? Can we not use the skin to scare him, somehow?"

Puh turned to me, smiling.

"Tris, that is a very clever idea; the trick is," Puh mused, "to figure out how to use the lion's skin to send the beast into a panic."

"But first, the lion skin has to get here," Black Wolf noted. "However, that will give us time to come up with a plan."

* * *

The sun had crested and was beginning its decline toward the horizon. The rest of our group had caught up with us, but still the mammoth had not appeared. We had briefly discussed having a few of us don the lion's hide and use it to jump out at the mammoth to make him turn and run, but quickly rejected that thought. Mammoths count on their powerful bulk to ward off predators. Rather than run and expose their vulnerable hind end, they face the threat and attempt to mow it down with their heavy feet or brush it aside with their massive tusks. Even a young bull such as this was already sporting sizable weapons.

As we ate our midday meal and drank some water, we devised a plan. We tied together what rope we carried with us, and strung it from a tree across the pool, with the lion's skin hanging in such a way that its body was outstretched and could be set loose to come zipping across the mammoth's path, hopefully making the beast seek haven in the water or turn and flee. The last option was more likely than the first, but I did not hold out much hope that either one would be completely effective. A mature mammoth would never be fooled by this ploy. But a young one might.

We watched the spot where we expected the mammoth to make his appearance – assuming he appeared at all. The creek had a good many twists and turns in its travels, and any creature that came around the bend would not be more than perhaps forty or fifty paces away when he came into view. I listened carefully for any sounds that might betray his proximity, but the trickling creek, the lapping water, and the rush of the wind in the trees masked all but the most obvious noises.

We were about to give up and retrieve the rope and lion skin when at last our prey showed his very large face. At first, all we could see was the mammoth's front half, his trunk raised as he quizzically sniffed the air. I looked to Puh and our eyes met. Puh was tense. There was a lot at stake here. This mammoth represented a tremendous amount of meat, and many other important resources; his marrow, his bones, his tendons, his hide – even his intestines all were extremely valuable. This mammoth could mean the difference between an easy winter and a hard winter.

The mammoth took a tentative step toward us; his little ears were pitched forward as he strained to hear what might be ahead. Mammoths have an acute sense of smell. No doubt he was aware that other beings were present, and he was trying to decide if any of those beings might intrude on his peaceful ramble along the stream. It was a warm day, and the ample greenery around a large pool of water must have been tempting indeed for a huge beast that had been nibbling on what little grass was available and sipping refreshment from a tiny creek.

The mammoth seemed to conclude that any paltry beings that might be in the vicinity were of no consequence to him, and he strode forward, still testing the air with his upraised trunk.

From our hiding place, I could see the marks where the lion, whose skin was now festooned on a rope across the pool, had raked its back. The mammoth's dried blood still striped the creature's sides, but it had not been done any serious harm. A mammoth's hide is about as thick as a man's finger joint, and the layer of fat was usually at least as thick as the breadth of a man's palm. The beast's vital organs are well protected by the sheer depth that must be reached to strike them.

The mammoth was grazing happily, still keeping a watchful eye on his surroundings, and pausing to listen and sniff the air. He drank long and deeply from the pool, but he did not venture far into the water.

We squatted at the edge of the wood, awaiting the time when the mammoth would reach a certain point by the creek. My legs were beginning to ache from crouching for so long. Mosquitoes were a minor annoyance, but most irritating was a fly that was buzzing my face, seemingly bent on driving itself into my right eye. I tried to blink it away, but only succeeded in ridding myself of the pest by blowing it away with a puff of breath.

Suddenly, I sensed the wind shift direction. The mammoth stopped in place and his body stiffened. He must have caught scent of the lion's skin. Black Wolf stood up in a flash, freeing the rope that held the lion skin aloft in the trees. Now that the lion's pelt had been unleashed, it flew out of the tree toward the mammoth, toothy mouth agape and paws held rigidly out front by a pair of sticks.

The mammoth bellowed in alarm and immediately emptied his bowels. He quickly retreated a few steps, almost placing his feet in the fresh pile of dung he had just dropped on the ground. But rather than seek haven in the pool or run away and present a vulnerable target, he reared, tilted his head upward, and swept his tusks back and forth just once. At this time, the lion's flight was nearing the lowest point of its trajectory, and it was close enough to become entangled in our intended prey's tusks and trunk.

We stared in dismay. As the mammoth found himself face to face with his former foe, he also was not at all pleased with this development. He trumpeted repeatedly and rumbled with displeasure. He shook his head to throw off the hated lion, stamped his feet and snorted violently, but the lion's pelt stayed firmly affixed to the mammoth's tusks.

"He is distracted; let us see if we can sneak up behind him," Puh suggested. "If we can launch a few spears into the skin by his anus and the backs of his legs, he may bleed out enough that we can kill him."

We all nodded in silent agreement. Ria had been assigned the task of staying with Swift River and Hawk, and they were now ensconced in the safety of a tree. The rest of us descended upon the mammoth, creeping through the trees and brush until we could come out behind the beast.

The mammoth continued his attempt to shake loose the lion pelt, becoming more and more agitated as the moments went by. My heartbeat was hammering in my ears, but the foremost sounds were that of the mammoth's heaving breaths, his frenzied and angry vocalizations, and his footfalls slapping into the mud by the pool.

As we broke from the tree line, the mammoth must have heard our approach. He wheeled to face us. Although the lion skin, stretched out before his face effectively blocked much of his forward vision, he clearly knew we were there.

The mammoth jerked his great head from side to side as he tried to peer at us from around the impediment, first on one side and then the other, as he gauged the level of the threat before him. During this brief standoff, a new odor reached my nose.

The mammoth seemed to be looking past us. A flash of intuition struck and I turned my head slightly, just in time to see a number of hyenas step out of the nearby brush. The foul-smelling brutes stood there, cackling nervously, their hackles raised. They whooped and growled as they moved forward.

"Tor, behind you!" Ria called out from the place where she and Black Wolf's sons were hiding in the trees.

"Da!" The boys cried, "Hyenas! Hyenas!"

I barely had time to notice that the mammoth had taken full advantage of our momentary inattention, and quickly trotted away. I did note, however, Black Wolf's look of displeasure as the prized lion's pelt disappeared from view with the mammoth as he rounded the bend.

"Stay in the tree!" Puh called back to Ria and the boys.

"Do not come down," Black Wolf added.

We bunched together, spears held at the ready. I was not overly concerned; there were six of us, and there were six hyenas. They must have been attracted to this spot by the smell of blood from the mammoth's wounds and the meat on our sled. They were a mixture of sexes and sizes. Females were the largest of the species; a big female was a force to be reckoned with; she would be heavier than most men. This pack seemed to consist of at least two females;

the rest might be younger females or males. We backed toward the pool, keeping our gaze focused on the hyenas. They were assessing us as potential prey. I hoped a front of strong men armed with sharp weapons would discourage these beasts from actively attacking.

When my foot came down on the slick mud that rimmed the pool, it slipped out from underneath me and I found myself on the wet ground in an instant. One of the hyenas saw her opportunity and she lunged forward. I barely had time to bring up my spear as her jaws snapped just short of my nose, close enough that I felt her fetid breath on my face.

My spear caught her in the belly and she yelped in pain. Puh had lanced her as well, and then Black Wolf followed suit with his spear. The animal was mortally wounded. Her companions did not linger but melted into the forest, whooping and cackling as they went, disappearing as mysteriously as they had arrived.

Bror helped me to my feet.

"Are you all right, Tris?" Puh asked anxiously.

"Yes, I am," I replied. "At least I did not fall there." I pointed at the place where the mammoth had emptied his bowels.

Black Wolf looked down. The mound of excrement was right next to his feet.

"*Ack!*" he cried. "I was so focused on the hyenas I did not even notice!"

"Perhaps you should move away," Fish Hawk said to Black Wolf with a twinkle in his eyes and an affected air of solemnity. "Over the years you have acquired a history with mammoth dung."

Ria and the boys rejoined us, and we stood over the hyena's carcass, watching her twitching legs pedal the air as the rest of her body lay there, lifeless.

"Da, will we take the hyena home with us?" Hawk asked his father. "He would have a lot of meat on him."

"Yes, it would," Black Wolf said slowly, pausing to look toward us to see if we showed any signs of wanting to bring the animal home. Hyenas have both a strong smell and taste, so no one spoke up. Black Wolf broke the silence. "I think it may be best to leave it here. We may have already strained our family's sense of humor and palettes with that rank old boar we brought in. Besides, its presence will attract hungry predators that may otherwise be attracted to us. And it is a *she*, not a *he*."

Hawk seemed confused. He studied the fallen animal for a moment.

"It looks like a boy hyena to me," Hawk said with a shrug.

"Well, that's just the way hyenas are," Black Wolf spoke with a grin. "The females look like males, but they are a lot larger. That is the easiest way to tell them apart."

"Let us go," Puh suggested. "We still have a distance to travel before we reach home."

We all nodded in agreement and retraced our steps along the creek back to the main trail. Here and there we saw evidence of the mammoth's efforts to rid himself of the lion skin and rope. The banks of the creek were littered with broken tree limbs and mangled shrubs; most were decorated with strands of mammoth hair. Finally, we found the front half of the lion's pelt, still attached to a section of rope. Its head was bashed in and jaw appeared broken, but Black Wolf was pleased to have at least part of the trophy back.

"I am grateful to be bringing home our share of this creature's meat, but I am so glad to have recovered even part of the skin for Oak," Black Wolf said as he tried to make the lion's flattened ear stand up again.

Black Wolf gingerly wrapped the lion's forelegs around the head, rolled the rest of the tattered hide around it, and placed it on our sled. We had not gone much farther when we found the back half of the skin and another length of rope. Like the front half, it showed evidence of extreme battering, but other than a few tears and a kink in the lion's tail, it seemed to be all there. Of the mammoth himself, we saw nothing other than his tracks.

* * *

We arrived at our compound well before the nightly sup. Swift River and Hawk were delighted to regale all within earshot about our journey. Morning Star and our children were gathered with the rest of our families at the central outdoor hearth where the evening meal was being prepared. She dropped what she was doing and ran up to throw her arms around me.

"Hallo, my sweet," I said to her, and then I kissed her long and deeply, holding my spear to one side and embracing her with my free arm.

This was the best part of coming home. No matter how long or short the period I had been away – to be back in the arms of my mate, kiss her lips, savor her scent – it made all the trials of the journey suddenly fade away to nothingness.

"I am so happy you are home . . . take off your pack," Morning Star ordered. "And sit! I will have Fox bring you some water . . . I was just about to go check on Gran and the baby. Lily was fussy while I was trying to prepare tubers and onions for roasting, so Gran offered to take Lily to lie down for a while." She turned to Fox, who was approaching. "Fox, go get a drink for your Puh-Puh."

"Puh-Puh, you are back!" Fox said, smiling broadly, but he quickly changed direction as he went to do his mother's bidding.

Morning Star was about to walk away to see about Gran and the baby, but then she stopped.

"Oh, here come Gran and Lily now," Morning Star said, now helping me to pull off my pack. "This pack is so heavy," she remarked as she put it aside so no one would trip over it. "You must be very tired of carrying it."

I was so used to having a pack on my back that I hardly noticed it most of the time. But she was right. I was tired. We had continued to take turns at pulling the sled on the way home, and it had been a long day. And worse, we had come back without any mammoth meat. It must have been obvious to anyone who looked at the small load on the sled that we could not have possibly met with much success on our hunt.

"It is fine," I responded simply as I lowered myself to the ground.

Gran was limping toward us, toting the baby and talking with great animation about the nice nap they had just enjoyed. Morning Star moved to take the baby from her, but Gran declined.

"You have work to do," Gran said cheerfully, "I can continue to hold the baby for now."

"Thank you, Gran," Morning Star replied, "I will get back to work then."

Morning Star stooped to give me another kiss before she left us. Fox returned with a gourd cup of water.

"Puh-Puh, your drink," he announced, holding the cup carefully so as not to spill it.

"Many thanks, Fox," I said to him.

Fox promptly sat beside me, looking at me attentively.

"What happened, Puh-Puh?" he inquired. "Did you get the mammoth?"

"We tried," I told him wearily. "But we could not manage to bring him down."

Fox's expression dimmed.

"Did you bring back something else?" he persisted. "A deer? An elk?"

"We brought back our share of a lion's meat," I answered. "Your Grandpa Black Wolf has the skin. After we eat maybe he will show it to you."

"A lion?" Fox repeated, elated. He sprang to his feet and raced to Black Wolf, begging to be shown the lion.

"You want to see my lion hide?" Black Wolf said with his deep, booming laugh. "Well my Fox, which would you like to see? The front half or the back half?"

Fox looked puzzled at this.

"Grandpa, I would like to see all of it," he answered earnestly.

"I will show everyone after we finish our meal," Black Wolf assured him.

By now, those of us who had just returned were settled down around the hearth, just far enough away not to hinder the meal preparations. We were hungry and thirsty, eating dried stores and drinking copious amounts of water. The sled sat where it had been abandoned by Black Wolf's domicile; we would attend to it later.

Lily was reaching for her Puh-Puh, so Gran passed her to me. It felt good to hold my baby in my arms. She was a solid infant, and she was in good spirits after her nap. She grinned and drooled at me, talking at me in happy gibberish.

"It is good to be home," I said to Gran as I snuggled my littlest daughter.

Gran nodded.

"It was not a good trip?" she said knowingly.

I shook my head.

"It was not a complete disaster, but it was not good," I admitted.

Gran patted my knee.

"You all did the best you could," she said. "No one could ask more than that."

 **Chapter Five** 

It is a green, misty place. Fir trees tower above us, their trunks glistening with moisture. Not a bird sings. The air is eerily still. I am filled with a sense of foreboding.

We had broken our fast and we were now enjoying a few peaceful moments as the mild late-summer day slowly brightened. I relished this quiet time with my family before my labors would begin. I had much to accomplish before I was to embark for our next journey, but for now, I sat with baby Lily on my lap while the other children played.

Fox was poking around the edge of the forest investigating some curiosity that had caught his interest. Pony and Raven were playing "rabbit" and hopped about from one patch of grass to another, saying *hop-hop-hop*. In the meantime, I kept Lily up off the ground. She was old enough to sit by herself, but she was also apt to pick up sticks or clumps of dirt or other such unsuitable items and pop them into her mouth.

All the while, Morning Star was hanging our bedding outside to freshen it for tonight's sleep. This was a task that could be done only during good weather. When next winter's long stormy stretches wore on, it would become obvious that our bedding had grown to become rather pungent, and thus we deeply appreciated the value of this simple chore.

"Puh-Puh," Fox said as he approached me. Raena was close at his heels, watching Fox very keenly. "See what Raena found."

Fox was carrying something mottled in color. It squirmed in his hands and one sparsely feathered wing flapped despite his best efforts to hold on to his unwilling captive.

"What have you there?" I inquired.

A rasping squawk answered my question.

"It is a crow," Fox stated. "He does not seem to be able to fly."

"Fox, set it free," Morning Star insisted.

"But Muh-Muh, it cannot fly," Fox protested.

"No matter," Morning Star countered. "It is a bird, and if it is meant to live, it will fly away. If not, a predator will eat it."

Fox balked at her words, but he obeyed and set the somewhat disheveled crow onto the ground before me.

"It is just a young bird," I noted. "That is why it cannot fly. It does not have all its feathers yet. And one of its wings seems injured. It may have fallen out of its nest."

"And then Raena found it?" Fox asked.

The bird moved a little and tried to regain its feet, one wing poking out crookedly.

"It seems that way," I answered. "I am amazed that Raena did not eat it."

"Well, she might have, but . . ." Fox broke off his sentence. "I saw her carrying it and it pecked her nose, so she dropped it . . . and when she picked it up again I told her to bring the bird to me."

Morning Star paused from shaking out yet another blanket and came over to stroke Raena.

"What a good girl," Morning Star said to Raena. "I know it must have been hard for you to relinquish your snack."

Raena could not have understood the words, but she wagged her tail and panted happily at the praise, nonetheless. However, she was still staring at the crow.

"She is a good girl," I agreed, ruffling the thick fur on her head.

"Good girl! Good girl!" Pony and Raven said, petting Raena, too.

Fox stroked Raena as well, but he had observed Raena's continuing interest and scooped up the crow once again. Fox now held the young bird well to the side, out of Raena's sight. There was no doubt that the dog was not fooled. Raena sniffed the air as though to ascertain the young crow was still in the area, even if she could not see it.

"Puh-Puh, may I have the bird?" Fox pleaded. "Just until it can fly. I will feed it and take care of it."

I glanced at Morning Star for her reaction. A smile twitched at her mouth, but she did not speak. Then, she shrugged. I did not think it likely the bird would survive, and I was afraid Fox would be heartbroken to lose his pet.

"What about its own mother?" I queried. "Do you not think his own mother would like him back? She must be missing her baby."

"Well, I . . ." Fox seemed undecided. "I did not see any other birds. I do not know where Raena found it."

"The crow may not appreciate your efforts to save it," I went on, "It pecked Raena's nose. It may peck your nose, too. It is a wild creature, and most wild creatures do not care to associate with people."

Fox looked at the ground unhappily.

"If I let him go, some animal will eat him," Fox spoke quietly. I thought it was very likely that his own dog would do just that at the first opportunity.

"That is probably true," I agreed. "Sometimes it is sad, but that is the way of things." I added gently. "But if you would like to try to take care of the crow until it can fly, I think it would be all right." I bit off the words I almost spoke that warned of impending failure. Fox was too young not to be optimistic. My words would be lost on him.

"Many thanks, Puh-Puh," Fox exclaimed, a wide grin breaking out on his face. In his enthusiasm, he impulsively pressed the untidy bundle of feathers closer to his chest. The crow reacted in horror; he choked out a somewhat stifled cry and promptly tried to escape.

"Be careful not to squish it," Morning Star cautioned Fox. "Remember, it is just a baby. You must treat it like one."

Fox nodded.

"Yes, Muh-Muh," he responded, and then he disappeared into our dwelling, cradling his charge in his arms. His little sisters Pony and Raven followed him indoors.

I looked up at the sky. The sun was now well over the horizon and creeping its way up ever higher.

"I must get to work," I announced to Morning Star.

"This is the last blanket . . . just a moment and I can take Lily from you," Morning Star replied.

I snuggled Lily as she gave me a drooling smile. Lily's charm prompted me to kiss her plump cheek. I reluctantly rose to my feet. Morning Star then held out her hands for the baby. I gave Lily one last kiss and passed the tot to my dear mate, and then bent to kiss Morning Star as well.

"There you are," I said, "and now I am off to collect more wood. I will be going up and down the hill most of the morning, so I will be easy to find if you need me for anything."

"I have sewn new soles onto your boots," Morning Star informed me. "They had become very thin in spots. Now I will put another coat of birch tar on them to help keep out the damp."

"Many thanks, my sweet." I kissed her once more, gave Raena a pat on the head and said "stay" to her. Leaving my family under the watchful eyes of our dog, I strode down the hill to our firewood cache.

I first passed the home of my sister Ru and her mate, Bror. There was no one outside and the dwelling seemed deserted, so I guessed that they were down at the main compound, where the other households were located. The woodpile was just a short distance from the compound, and it was a communal effort to keep it stocked. Since a wildfire had consumed many of the nearby trees a few years ago, this was becoming an ever more challenging task.

Thankfully, Puh had had the foresight to burn a swath of meadow before the fire reached us, and therefore had preserved our homes and all the trees beyond. However, the forestland we had most often visited to hew our wood had been left blackened and nearly devoid of life. Only the largest trees survived the fire, but their extreme girth presented an onerous target for our axes. Since life had begun to return, the newly sprouted saplings shooting up from the scorched earth were not yet of size to be harvested. This was one of the many reasons that Puh, Black Wolf and I would soon be leaving our families to search out a new homeland.

I sought sections of logs to carry up the hill, where I could hack and split them into smaller chunks. The long summer's drought had made for a thirsty season for many of the Earth's creatures, but one of the few good things about it was that our stock of hewn wood was very dry. I began the first of my innumerable trips up and down the hill. During winter I might regret the necessity of this chore, but on this balmy morning, I did not mind. The day's heat had not yet arrived, and for once, I was alone with my task and my thoughts.

I was about start up the hill once more when Gran found me just leaving the woodpile.

"Pleasant day to you," Gran said, squinting as she looked up at me because the sun was behind me.

"Pleasant day to you as well, Gran," I responded, moving a little to the side to spare her eyes from the glare. I then set the logs down, knowing this chat might last a while.

"What are your Dreams of late?" Gran asked, conversationally. When we were alone, this was very often a topic between us.

"Nothing I can identify," I said with a shrug. "Just fleeting images. And you?"

"I understand," Gran replied with a nod. "That is the way they happen most times."

"Sometimes I sense more than I see," I added. "And many times they appear to have no meaning at all. I may see people I do not know. Places I have never been."

"That, too, is typical." Gran seemed eager to talk, but she wavered as she stood.

"Gran, would you like to sit?" I inquired. I arranged the logs like a seat and guided her to them and then sat down on the ground beside her, legs crossed in front of me.

"Many thanks, Tris," Gran placed a thin hand on my knee. I noted the dark veins standing out against her pale skin and the swollen joints of her fingers. Hands that had cared for so many children and accomplished so much work over the years. I placed my comparatively cumbersome paw over her withered extremity and gently squeezed it. Gran returned the squeeze and looked at me fondly.

"You are troubled about something," she stated.

"I can keep no secrets from you," I said with a weak smile. "I wish we had brought back more meat yesterday. And, as always, I worry about how my family will fare while I am away."

"You brought back something," Gran reminded me. "If hunters were successful all the time it would be called *slaying* rather than *hunting*. The lion will provide several good meals for the entire group. And besides, Black Wolf is so proud of that lion skin. He has Petal working on it so that he can take it to his son with Willow Woman when he sees them at the next Gathering.”

“Petal has her work cut out for her,” I noted. “That skin was rather battered by the mammoth.”

“*Battered?*” Gran repeated, “It was torn in half! One side of the skull was flattened.”

“Yes,” I replied simply. All she said was true, and there really was not much more I could add regarding the condition of the lion’s hide. But then I said, “Fox has found a fledgling crow that is in pretty sad shape, too. I think its wing is damaged. He begged me to let him keep it until it can fly, and, in spite of my better judgment, I told him he could. I do not know if it will live very long under his care, and even if it does survive, I wonder if it will ever be capable of flying.”

“It is possible it was deemed unviable by its parents because of its bad wing and thrust from the nest,” Gran mused.

“I suppose, but Fox took it from Raena’s mouth,” I informed Gran. “It is my guess that the dog broke its wing, but you could be right.”

“Hmmm,” Gran said with a nod. “That could be true. Crows push their fledglings out of the nest to make them learn to fly. This one may have been on such a mission when Raena found it. In any case, whether or not it lives, this will be a good learning experience for Fox.”

“It will, indeed,” I agreed, adding to myself, *and probably for the crow, as well.*

"I know you have much to do," she began anew. "I hoped to find you here so I might have a word with you before the evening sup, since it is so much more peaceful here. But I do not want to keep you from your work."

"I have some time, yet. You have not told me of your Dreams," I reminded her. I was always eager to hear of her visions.

"Oh, yes," Gran took a moment to gather her thoughts. "I saw a big toothy creature snap at your face. I worried while you were away. But then you came back with your face intact, so I was happy to see that all was well this trip. Returning home with a huge kill does not matter; coming back safely does."

I had heard enough of Gran's Dreams to know she often saw incidents I had or would experience.

"A hyena did come at me," I said to Gran. "But as you see, it did not harm me."

Gran smiled at this.

"Keep your handsome face while you can," she said with a grin. "You already bear a few scars, but it seems inevitable that in time each man will accumulate evidence of his misadventures on his face and body. Your Puh, my mate, Gareth, all good huntsmen, all were marked by many of their victims."

I nodded at this. Again, her words were all true.

"I have seen much of my deceased mate in my Dreams," Gran continued. "He tells me things; nothing important, just things. And then when I awaken and I . . . well, I miss him. I miss him so much that I did not know it was possible to feel this much pain and still be alive. Then I think I must reach deeper into myself and find more strength, as we all must sometimes. Find the will to live, even without those we loved so much." Gran hesitated. "I have been trying not to regret reaching this old age. I used to think it a curse, but now I realize that I have been fortunate to have so much time with my family. I know I can be terse and even a little short-tempered sometimes, but you are all kind to me, regardless. As time passes I am able to do less and less, and yet you all smile and do my chores for me. Then I realize how lucky am I to have this life. To have had a man who loved me too, a caring family whom I adore, and good friends as well."

"Who could help but love you, Gran?" I said to her. "And with luck, we will have you with us for a long time yet to come."

Gran gazed at me skeptically.

"I know you say that from the goodness of your heart, and who knows?" Gran shrugged. "I may still be here for a few years yet. My eyesight is failing, but I can always see clearly in my Dreams, and even they have not shown me where my days end. But I have taken enough of your time. I must go."

Gran moved to stand up. I immediately rose to my feet and helped her straighten up.

"I will walk you home," I said, taking her arm.

"Your words bring back memories," Gran told me.

"Do they?" I asked.

"Yes," Gran responded, looking past me as though the sights in her recollections were coming into view. "Ever so many years ago, even before I was paired with your great-grandfather, he used to say those words to me after we had been out walking and it was time for me to go back to my family."

I smiled to think of Gran as a young woman, hardly more than a girl. I wondered at how much life she had seen and wisdom she had gained over her long years.

"Those must have been good days," I said to her.

"Yes, good days," Gran agreed.

* * *

Bror soon joined me. We spent the day bringing wood up and down the hillside and chopping the log lengths into manageable fuel for our fires. Morning Star fed us during a midday break, and then we returned to our work.

Fox made a sling that he wore crossways around his body so he could carry the crow with him wherever he went. I was impressed by his patient and gentle handling of the frail bird; he had taken his mother's words to heart, and he was indeed treating the crow like an infant, coddling it and trying to entice it to take morsels of food.

Before long the fledgling was taking tiny slivers of meat from him and drinking water from his cupped hand. The fight had gone out of the bird, and while I would not hazard a guess as to whether or not it was enjoying Fox's attentions, it was at least submitting to his loving care.

That evening we gathered at the center of the family compound for our nightly sup, and Fox insisted on bringing his bird. It rested quietly and unobtrusively in the sling. I was surprised to see that it did not attempt to escape, but rode in the sling, apparently contented. Fox continued to feed the bird during the meal. It was no longer tentative about taking tidbits from his hand but gobbled them down greedily.

"Fox, what are you feeding?" Black Wolf spoke. He was sitting across from us, and he could see Fox slipping tiny nibbles of food to an unseen animal.

"It is my crow, Grandpa," Fox said, his voice tinged with pride.

"A crow? Is it hiding in a bag?" Black Wolf asked with avid curiosity.

"Yes, Grandpa. I have made a sling it can sit in, so it can be with me always."

"I have not known crows to be so amiable," Black Wolf mused. "Is it injured?"

"I think so," Fox replied. "And it is too young to fly."

"Well, that would explain a lot," Black Wolf said as he smiled at Fox.

"Will you give it a name?" my sister Saree inquired. "It should have a name."

"I was thinking I might call it Kaw," Fox told Saree.

"All crows say *caw*," Saree pointed out. "When the crows cry out it will think they are calling for it."

"I will take care not to say Kaw like a crow says *caw*," Fox mimed a crow's raucous cawing. "I will say it like *Kaw*." Fox emphasized the *k* sound and drew out the *aaaa* so that there was a subtle difference in the pronunciation. This seemed to settle the subject.

The conversation then drifted to talk of our day's activities and what we would do on the morrow.

"The weather seems to be stable for the time being," Black Wolf said to the assemblage. "Tor, Tris, what do you say to embarking on our trip soon after sunup?"

Puh nodded thoughtfully. I too had expected this subject to come up tonight.

"Yes, the sooner we leave, the sooner we will return," Puh remarked quietly.

"Tris?" Black Wolf prodded me.

"I will be ready to go whenever required," I answered.

"We have not had a story in some days," Hawk piped up, "Bror, would you tell us a tale this night?"

Bror was the son of a Keeper of Stories, and although he had not officially taken over the role upon his father's death, he knew all the tales by rote and would tell them if asked.

"I will tell a tale about a crow, to honor Fox's new friend," Bror said, and then he launched into his story.

There once was a crow that hatched early one spring. He had a large family, and they lived in a nice wood. There was lots to eat and a sparkling blue lake that provided plenty of fresh water. Sometimes a gentle rain brought a pleasant shower and puddles to bathe in.

But one day after this crow had learned to fly, he became restless. He longed to see more of the world. Surely there must be more to it than just these trees and fields. The other birds and animals with whom they shared their wood all seemed so ordinary and boring.

The crow's desire for adventure eventually got the best of him. He broke away from his kin and went off to see what he could discover. He was enjoying many new sights. As he rode the friendly breezes under sunny skies he was delighted to see a river, wide meadows, and many creatures that he had never seen before. In comparison, his home seemed drab indeed.

Then strong winds began to buffet him, and the crow settled down to shelter in the protective branches of a large tree. Heavy rain and booming thunder rolled in. Bolts of lightning blazed across the sky. The terrified crow had never seen anything so horrifying. He longed for the comfort of his family.

When the sun came out at last, the young crow immediately flew for the familiar safety of his woodland home and his welcoming kin. They questioned him about his travels, and he regaled them with stories of all he had seen and of the frightening storm.

The crow was surprised to hear that they had experienced the storm too.

"You did? The whole while it raged overhead, all I could think was that I should have stayed home where I would be safe with my family," the crow said.

"Oh yes," said his wise old father. "We all experience storms. But we can choose whether to experience them together or alone."

There was a lull in conversation as everyone digested this story.

"I miss our friends the Wolfmen; might we hear a story of them?" Hawk again spoke up.

Bror appeared to ponder Hawk's request. This was different from reciting one of our traditional stories, which had been passed down through the generations.

In the not-too-distant past, a group of men who called themselves The People of the Wolves visited our clan. They were unlike anyone we had ever met before. They wore wolfskins on their backs, with the wolf's head worn atop their own pates. They spoke a language unknown to us, but they gradually learned our words and soon we were able to converse with them. We learned that although they might be different from us, they were good men and they impressed us with their many skills. They were

. . .

"Tell about their hunting," Hawk broke in. "About when Karno rode on the deer's back."

"Um – yes – they were very proficient hunters," Bror continued. "And very brave. I was not there when the Wolfmen's leader, Karno, went on that unexpected gallop through the woods, but as I understand it, he thought the buck was dead, so it came as a surprise when the animal suddenly leapt to its feet . . ."

"And then there was the woolly rhino!" Hawk interrupted again.

Bror laughed silently as we Old Ones do.

"Are you telling this story or am I?" Bror asked good-naturedly. Then he resumed.

The woolly rhino was a challenging beast, but the Wolfmen were instrumental in bringing it down. Karno darted right under the belly of the beast . . . that would not have been my first choice . . . but the hunt was fairly uneventful until the rhino lay on the ground, passed from life. It was then that a number of lions emerged from the tall grass and attempted to drive us away from our kill . . .

Bror continued to tell the tale, but I felt my blood run cold as I thought back on that ominous day. The lions were confident, but so was Karno. He could not be dissuaded from his determination to fend off the beasts. Not even after his two closest companions had been grievously injured. No matter how long I might live, I would never be able to forget the gut-wrenching sight of the lion as it stood there, a helpless man dangling from his jaws. Karno himself survived only because Bror slew the lion that had charged him. Bror, modest as always, did not mention his own heroics.

In the end we were successful, and we brought home a huge amount of meat. But it had been at great cost. We did not typically engage in such risk taking, but the Wolfmen took it in stride. They were jolly, adventurous, skilled craftsmen and, above all, fine company. Karno could be somewhat boorish in nature, but he was good-hearted and a loyal friend. He had hoped to win the affections of my sister Ru, but much to everyone's surprise, perhaps Karno's most of all, she had chosen the stolid and steady Bror, who had patiently wooed Ru for quite some time. I often thought of Karno and his men and wondered what became of them.

"Tris, it grows late, and the children are weary," Morning Star said to me as Bror completed his remembrances of the Wolfmen. "And you must be ready to depart early in the morning."

"Yes, my sweet," I replied, nodding.

Chapter Six

The woodlands are dark, dank, and silent. Something feels wrong ... off ... I cannot fathom what it is. Then a sharp crack rends the air from somewhere within the depths of the forest. We are not alone.

Puh, Black Wolf, and I departed soon after sunrise the next day. As was often the case when we were leaving for a long trip, I stumbled along half asleep, having preferred to spend most of the previous night awake with my mate. I could catch up on sleep while we were away. Besides, it would not be long before the fresh air and sunshine would awaken my senses and bring me to life. And if that did not work, Black Wolf's full-throated singing would do it.

The mighty hunter is bold and brave
He keeps a cool head and never does he rave
As he walks the trails the mighty hunter has not a care
So long as his stomach is full and he has clothing to wear
The mighty hunter has power and speed
And at home he has many mouths to feed . . .

Black Wolf's song went on and on. He seldom repeated a line, and he never seemed to run out of things to sing about the Mighty Hunter.

We stopped at a fast-running stream to top off our water bags and eat a quick midday meal. Due to the drought, many of our water sources might have either dried up or seriously diminished, so we were required to refill our bags at every opportunity. Since this stream was the best source of water for some distance, we thought it prudent to scour the immediate area for tracks to see what animals were in the vicinity as we chewed mouthfuls of dried foods. The gravel banks did not offer many clues.

"Something has knocked away the moss from these stones," Black Wolf announced, pointing to the slick rocks; the dampness attested to the recent baring of the stone surface.

"Yes," Puh said with a nod, "and there are some deep imprints in the moss over here. These may be claw marks . . . it is something heavy with soft feet. A bear, perhaps."

"Speaking of something heavy," Black Wolf started, "I wonder where our young mammoth has gone to."

"I would not be surprised if he was headed north, as well," Puh replied.

"To the Lake Region?' I asked.

"Yes," Puh said, "there is plenty of water and fodder there. But there are also plenty of mammoths. He will have to find his place in the hierarchy of the resident bulls . . . if he can."

We continued to laboriously chew our meal as we looked about.

"Deer droppings here," I announced, having spotted a few collections of the pellets.

Puh and Black Wolf joined me to have a look themselves.

"Not very big," Black Wolf said. "Perhaps yearlings?"

"Small yearlings, at that," Puh mused. "Possibly fallow yearlings or even roe deer."

We nodded in agreement. We also found the places where smaller animals halted to drink from the creek, and a single muddy patch where it seemed many animals of all sizes stopped to partake in a luxurious wallow in the muck.

We soon concluded that there was not much else to see, so we resumed our hike, eager to cover as much distance as possible before nightfall.

When the sun neared the horizon, we began to search for a place to spend the night. We settled on a spot where there were a number of saplings that we could bend toward one another until their tops met, and then lashed them together. We then quickly lopped off as many fir tree boughs as we could quickly gather and used them to cover our sapling frame, starting at the bottom and working our way up.

This traditional shelter was not completely weatherproof unless we chose to add more layers to the structure, but it was not unduly windy and there was no sign of imminent rain, so we simply hoped to have a place in which to escape the night's chill.

As Black Wolf and I finished laying the pine bough floor in the shelter, Puh began to gather deadwood to make a fire. We could see our breath in the cool air. The fire was crackling and throwing off plenty of heat by the time we were set to get off our feet. We sat with our newly constructed hut at our backs and the fire warming our fronts. The blaze was welcome indeed. More dried foods made up our evening sup. We sipped at our water judiciously, hoping to conserve as much as possible so it would last until we located our next water source.

After my hunger was satisfied, I found I could barely keep my eyes open.

"I think I will retire for the night," I stated, rising to my feet.

"You look as though you are ready to close your eyes," Puh said with a smile. "I will not be far behind you."

"Me either," Black Wolf replied.

"Yes, it has been a long day," I responded. "I will see you on the morrow." And I turned to enter the shelter, fervently hoping I could get to sleep before Black Wolf came in and began his habitual snoring.

I ducked into the entryway of our little hut and, standing hunched over, spread my cloak over a section of the fir-branch floor. As I lay down, some of the branches creaked a little, and I could smell the fragrant piney scent as the boughs were crushed under my weight.

I must have fallen asleep almost instantly. I was awakened by dreams of lions that stood just out of reach, roaring at me. I was unarmed, and they did not charge me, but they just roared and roared repeatedly. I was unnerved until I realized it was just a dream. Not a Dream, which differed in its striking clarity and sense of foreboding. As my awareness increased, the lion's roars dissipated into the sounds of Black Wolf's hearty snores. I tentatively poked Black Wolf in the middle of his back until he rolled over and the beast-like sounds issuing from his mouth became a bit more muted.

I craned my neck to look out the entryway of the shelter. I could not view the moon from where I lay, but I could see the stars as they made their nightly circuit across the firmament. Morning was still some time off. I rested my head on the crook of my arm and longed for home and the presence of my mate.

At times such as these I enjoyed curling up against Morning Star's warm flesh, feeling the comfort of her nearness, or, if the mood struck, stirring her to wakefulness. I closed my eyes and willed myself back to sleep.

* * *

The sun had just begun to brighten the eastern sky when next I awoke. Puh was already outside, poking at the remains of the previous night's fire. I crawled out of the shelter with my cloak wrapped around me.

"I hate to rouse Black Wolf by striking up some sparks, but the coals are cold," Puh said.

"I think he will pardon the interruption to his sleep if it means he will have a nice fire to warm himself by," I responded with a grin, shaking my cloak a little to dislodge the many fir tree bits that still adhered to it.

"I suppose that is so," Puh said as he arranged tinder in a pile and then gripped his pieces of flint and iron pyrite. Puh sharply struck them together several times, causing sparks to fly in little arcs in all directions. He paused to see if any of the sparks had caught, and we soon saw a telltale whiff of smoke rise from the tinder. Puh blew on it gently and then backed away to let the fire grow. As it gained strength he blew on it one more time, and at last it was burning strongly so that he could add more fuel without snuffing out the fragile flames.

"*Ack!*" Black Wolf exclaimed from inside the hut.

An instant later, a drowsy Black Wolf appeared on all fours at the entrance to the shelter.

"*Ack!*" He said once more, "It is daylight. And it is cold!"

Black Wolf crawled out to join us and groaned as he stood upright. He was far too tall to sleep stretched out at full length in the hut, so this was his first opportunity to straighten out since the night prior. Black Wolf rubbed his back for a moment and then massaged one of his shoulders.

"Are you all right?" Puh questioned him.

"*Ack*, I forgot my cloak," was Black Wolf's only answer.

Black Wolf turned around and reached into the shelter for his cloak, but as he attempted to drag it out it snagged on the fir tree branches inside.

"Oh, come now!" Black Wolf fretted aloud at his cloak, as though it were a reluctant dog that did not want to leave the warmth of its home. Finally, a good yank freed his cloak and it came loose, although a few odd limbs still clung to it, like cubs clinging to the back of a mother bear. Black Wolf wordlessly removed the limbs and tossed them on the fire, where the green branches smoked and spat, and he then placed the garment around his shoulders.

It was indeed a chilly morning. A low mist hung over the land, and each word we uttered was accompanied by a little cloud. However, we knew that as the sun rose and filtered down through the trees, the mist would evaporate and the late-summer temperatures would return.

After a brief breakfast by the small fire, we snuffed it out and covered it with dry earth. It was a chore to stab the ground with the butts of our spears until the dirt was broken into chunks that we could further break apart and place atop the smoldering remains of the coals, but we had seen what a wildfire could do, and in no way did we want to risk another.

A second day of hiking brought us to our next site. We came across an uprooted tree and used nearby deadwood and more fir boughs to create a lean-to. We had not found water that day, and although we were thirsty, we carefully rationed our water. We hoped to find a creek or stream on the morrow, before our water bags ran dry.

The woodland's foliage was already starting to show the first bright colors of autumn. We could see where the bucks were stripping velvet from their antlers. The rutting season would be upon us in the next moon or so. Our fall hunts would start soon afterward.

The forest was thick, but even so, it showed signs of heavy grazing. Thanks to Black Wolf's constant torrent of song we did not actually see any animals, but it was plain that there were at least a small number in the area. This was encouraging. We hoped that the farther we traveled from home, more the more game we might meet.

The sun had begun its decline when we finally found a bounding stream. The water level appeared to have dropped considerably from its high-water mark, but it careened down a stony bed, splashing against the larger rocks and creating a green bank of lush plant life. We lingered just long enough to fill our water bags. We also drank as much as we could. The water was wonderfully cool and refreshing.

"Two days out from home and we have water, wood, and at least a smattering of prey animals," I said. "I think we are going in the right direction."

"And sweet water at that," Black Wolf agreed. "I drank so much it is fairly sloshing in my stomach, but it was so good I could not stop myself."

Puh nodded in agreement. I could appreciate his sentiment as well. Our thirst had been great, and we were buoyed by this discovery as we hit the trail once more. The sun was just setting when we found a couple of dilapidated shelters that someone must have constructed some time ago. Either one was easily roomy enough for the three of us, but it would need a little work to restore its roof and walls. We chose one of the huts and promptly busied ourselves with stripping the old branches off the frame and collecting new fir boughs to cover the structure. We then piled deadwood near our hut for the night's fire.

Puh built our fire in a spot where someone had already created a fire pit, while Black Wolf and I finished the final touches to our temporary home. We crouched by the flames, warming ourselves in frigid air that had tiptoed in as the sun set. After momentarily basking in the heat, we drew out our food bags and began to gnaw on dried stores.

"How odd to find these old shelters here," Black Wolf said uneasily. "I did not know there were any people in this area. Even if these are just a pair of huts, it would appear that a group of people stayed here at some point."

"Yes," Puh agreed. "By the looks of the site, they must have stayed here sometime between now and last winter. There must have been at least twelve occupants, considering the size of the shelters."

"Perhaps they were traveling to find a better place to move to as well," I suggested.

"Perhaps," Puh said thoughtfully. But I did not sense that he thought it likely.

"What do you think?" I asked Puh.

Puh shrugged and was silent as he considered this.

"They are too few to be a clan, but too many for most hunting parties," Puh started. "However, just as we did recently, we have sometimes joined with others to form a larger hunting party. It is my hope that this is the case."

"But you suspect something else?" Black Wolf guessed.

Again, Puh shrugged.

"I do not know," he answered. "But they were here some moons ago. It is unlikely they are still in the area, or they would be using these huts themselves."

"We might journey up to see Uncle Inlee and Uncle Trae and inquire about who has been hunting around here," I said, thinking it would be pleasing to visit my late mother's older brothers. I had not seen them in several years.

"I think that would be a good idea," Puh said as he added more fuel to the fire. "What say you, Black Wolf?"

"Yes," Black Wolf chimed in, "if there has been any activity up this way, they would know about it. It will be a slight detour for us, but I think it would be prudent. And they may have a few good thoughts on where we might relocate, without impinging on their hunting grounds."

* * *

That night I was awakened by a slow drip from overhead. It was still dark out, but a soft rain was falling and it was leaking through the fir boughs. I pulled my cloak up to cover the spot where the drip was landing and went back to sleep. The rain had not stopped by morning, and we awoke to a cold gray day. We did not bother to light a fire, as it was too wet to sit around it and warm ourselves anyway. So we simply gathered up our gear and set out, cloaks wrapped tightly around us. We would have to hike for several more days before we would reach the homes of my uncles.

As the days and nights wore on, the rain did not cease. In fact, it seemed to increase in strength, and we found ourselves to be on a very cold and wet trudge indeed. My newly soled and sealed boots kept my feet dry at first, but the rainwater that came down from above eventually ran down into my boots and still managed to soak my feet. The path that had been dusty and dry now squished underneath us with every step.

When we were still one day out from my uncles' place, we came upon something unusual. Bleached bones lay in the ground litter by the trailside. It was not unusual to see bones, but these were not the typical sort of remains we often saw.

Puh, Black Wolf, and I paused to study them in the drizzling rain. Suddenly I remembered where I had seen bones like this before. I believe Puh and Black Wolf came upon the realization at the same time, as we three had all been there.

"I believe these are human bones," Puh said quietly.

"Um ... yes," Black Wolf responded. "And I suppose there is more of him somewhere about. However, I do not see any butchering marks, so I would guess that this is not a victim of cannibals, like those we saw at the Cave of Bones."

"It looks as though animals have been at them," Puh observed. Then Puh pointed into the forest. "There are more here."

We walked over to another grouping of bones, which led to more groupings of bones, all of which seemed to belong to one individual. Scavengers seemed to have spread his remains over a large area.

"He looks to be a man of The People," Black Wolf observed. "He has not the thick heavy bones of the Old Ones."

"I think so too," Puh replied. "And he has been out here a long time. All summer, at least, for his bones to be this clean."

I felt a chill that was not due to the damp conditions. My Dreams of the wet forest came back to me, along with the eerie sense of foreboding that accompanied them.

"But why is he out here alone and unburied?" I asked, perplexed.

"It is possible he was buried and animals . . . um . . . retrieved him from his resting place," Puh said.

"That is likely," Black Wolf responded. "Well, he is beyond help now. Let us move on."

"I hate to leave someone lying all about like this," I said regretfully.

"I do as well," Black Wolf agreed, "but we have a long way to go yet, and it may well be that even if we take the time to bury him, hyenas will come along to get what is left of him and dig him up once more. Let us go."

We resumed our trek, but the grim discovery we had left behind stayed on my mind.

* * *

The rain was letting up as Uncle Inlee's and Uncle Trae's homes came into sight. Puh whistled long and loudly to announce our arrival. Black Wolf followed up with his own *halloos*.

Another piercing whistle met our ears and then Uncle Inlee appeared from around the far side of his woodpile. He dropped his armload of firewood and rapidly strode up to meet us.

"Tor!" Inlee cried, his arms outstretched toward us. He embraced Puh with feeling and then came to me. "Tris, how good to see you!" Inlee hugged me as well. Like most of Muh's family, he was a tall man, as tall as I. Then he faced Black Wolf, who took Inlee by the forearms, in the way of The People. "Black Wolf," said Inlee, "I am so happy you are here! What brings you all the way to the North Country?"

"We have been trying to find a place to move our families since the wildfire," Puh told Inlee. "We thought we would see what the lands are like to the east of you. But first we wanted to discuss the possibility of being so close to you, and also to ask you about the presence of other people in the area."

A conflicted look crossed Inlee's face.

"I would be most pleased to have you close by," Inlee told us. "Come say hallo to the family. They will be eager to see you. Come. Come inside."

I pondered the significance of Inlee's look, but then Inlee waved us to follow him, so we did as bidden and ducked into the doorway of his earth-bermed dwelling.

"Inlee, I thought you went to get wood. . . ." Inlee's mate said, but she abruptly broke off her sentence and rushed over to greet us. "Tor!" She exclaimed joyfully, hugging and kissing Puh. "It has been ever so long! Can you stay with us for a while?"

The family was very welcoming; Inlee's mate, Soosha, insisted on divesting us of our wet cloaks and footwear, which she draped by the hearth to dry. As the dripping articles heated, I was sorry to note that they lent a rather rank quality to the air in their household.

Inlee went back out to retrieve his wood, but when he returned he brought his younger brother Trae and his family, too. They lived in another earth-bermed home next to his. Trae was nearly as tall as his brother, but he now had a marked limp, and I wondered what misadventure had occurred. He seemed cheerful, but it was obvious that his leg pained him a good deal.

We were fed a delightfully hot and hearty meal and we enjoyed a nice chat, catching up on the events of the past several years. As the day stretched into evening, the various children in the families had to be put to bed, so we men were now left alone around the hearth, talking quietly so as not to disturb the bedtime rituals.

"I do hope you can stay with us for a few days at least," Inlee said.

"I would like that as well," Trae agreed. "I am pleased to see you all and I look forward to enjoying your company . . . but I know you must have noticed my bad leg. Around the last new moon Inlee and I set upon a young cow wisent. She was not very big, but she did not go down easily and she kicked me in the knee. We finally managed to dispatch her, but it was all I could do to make it home."

"Carrying half a gutted wisent, too," Inlee said, shaking his head. "Even a small wisent is quite a load. We made it, but we have not been able to get out hunting ever since. I have been hoping that we might be visited by our older children and their families so that I would have other men to accompany me on a hunt or two until Trae has recovered, but they have not come."

We all knew that it was extremely unwise to venture out alone. Even the most skilled hunter was not likely able to fend off any of the numerous large predators that lurked about, ever on the prowl.

"We would be happy to hunt with you," Puh said immediately.

Inlee and Trae exchanged relieved glances. But then Inlee became sober.

"We are grateful for that," he said. "I did not want to speak of this earlier, but you asked about other people in the area and I must tell you, the raids have begun again."

Black Wolf, Puh, and I were silent for a moment as we absorbed this news.

"The raids?" Black Wolf repeated. "They are happening again? When did it start?"

"This spring," Trae replied. "There was a raid on our homes just as the days were warming, but there was still a little snow on the ground. We managed to repel the attackers who came at us in several groups of five or six men. I am not sure of their numbers. We tracked them into the forest some distance to make sure they were not doubling back for another try."

"Is it the same sort of raids as they were carrying out the last time? The same men, do you think?" Puh inquired, referring to Snow Leopard's former associates.

"I believe it is the same men," Inlee responded. "But of course I cannot be certain. However, the attacks are not quite the same as before. As I understand, before they were only after what goods they needed and destroying anything not needed, as a way of either driving us Old Ones off of these lands or starving us out. This time it is worse; they have killed."

"We found the skeletal remains of a man, about a day's trek from here," Black Wolf stated.

"A man of the Old Ones?" Trae asked.

Puh shook his head.

"A man of The People," Puh answered. "Have they killed Old Ones?"

"Yes," Inlee said, nodding. "They taunted us that they had killed a clan of Old Ones nearby. That could only be your mate Ria's kin."

I felt a lump of sorrow grow in my throat, and I forced it down. Ria's conniving brothers had not been particularly likable, but I had never wished them dead. And their innocent families certainly did not deserve such a fate. I grieved for them and poor Ria, for they were the last of her original clan. I looked at Puh and I could see that he too was shaken by this news.

"Willow must hear of this," Black Wolf said firmly. "These men must be dealt with before they wreak more havoc ... and it now it would seem, murder, as well."

Black Wolf was right. As Head Elder, Willow Woman must be told of this new development. She had banished those men on pain of death should they return. It appeared that they were willing to risk her wrath. I shook my head at the thought. I knew Willow Woman to be a very warm and generous person, but I had no doubt that she would take decisive action to rid our lands of the perpetrators of these transgressions.

"We would be pleased to have your families close by," Trae told us. "There is plenty of game to feed us all. But if you choose to make your homes here, it may put you in harm's way. We cannot be sure that the raiders will not return."

"They have come twice now," Inlee said. "I do not think they will stop until they have killed us all. We were lucky last time. We had more people in residence for the spring migration hunts; two of my daughters and their families were here, plus one of Trae's sons and his family were also visiting. We had enough force to drive them off. We may not fare as well the next time."

"Do you have any notion where they are now?" Puh asked urgently.

I was eager to know as well. Should the raiders head south, our homes and families would be vulnerable to attack, and they knew where we lived.

"I believe they withdraw to the north after each raid, but that is only a guess," Inlee answered. "They seem to retreat from whence they came."

"It would make sense that they would slip south from their place of exile to do their misdeeds and then slip back over the northern border into exile again," Black Wolf speculated.

"I agree," Inlee said, and then added, "The last report I heard was that they were making forays up by the mountains. I believe you have a cousin there, do you not, Black Wolf?"

"Yes, I do," Black Wolf replied. "My cousin Gray Elk. But I do not believe they can do him much harm. He has his many dogs to see to the protection of his home."

"Gray Elk has more dogs than ever, so I hear tell," Trae piped up. "As someone who breeds and trades dogs, he must be doing very well these days."

"Yes, partially thanks to Tris," Black Wolf said with a grin.

My dog Raena had contributed many young dogs to Gray Elk's menagerie. She managed to get with pups at least once a year, and it seemed that every spring we would have to take them up to Gray Elk's mountain home while we were on our way to the plains for the wisent hunts.

"Not me, but my Raena." I said, adding, "Your dogs also may have had something to do with it, Black Wolf. I am just glad to know that Gray Elk benefits from receiving the pups." Black Wolf's dogs were all males, and they were as friendly with Raena as she would allow.

"If we are fortunate the raiders will satisfy their needs with all the game animals that can be found up there," Puh said. "But I would not count on it."

"Yes," Black Wolf continued. "They do not only seek meat. I had brief thoughts of waiting until the fall Gathering to bring this up with Willow, but I think she should be told as soon as possible. We should leave for the Fen of Falls tomorrow."

Inlee and Trae looked somewhat crestfallen, and then Black Wolf seemed to remember that we had agreed to help them bring in a few animals.

"I mean, after we go hunting. I got a little ahead of myself," Black Wolf said, appearing momentarily abashed. "I have not seen Willow and my boy Oak in many moons, and I was forgetting about the hunt. We will get a few deer or elk and then set out to see Willow at her summer lodgings. She should remain at the Fen of Falls for at least another moon or more until she leaves for the Gathering Hall."

 **Chapter Seven** 

In our haste to reach the Fen of Falls as quickly as possible we cut across the landscape rather than taking the more well-used trails. Patches of forest that interspersed the open grasslands consisted largely of conifers and thickets of richly varied undergrowth. The parched surroundings we had become accustomed to were now pleasantly refreshed after several days of rain. It was almost strange to be in a place that had ample food and water. We had the luxury of bypassing the less desirable water sources, knowing that sooner or later there would be a better option. We carried fresh meat from our successful outing with Inlee, in which we took down an elk and a young red deer. The meat was cooked, unlike the dried stores we had been consuming on our travels, and that was a very nice change indeed.

The closer we drew to our destination, the harder Black Wolf pushed. He still sang in a rather breathless bass as Puh and I strove to keep up with his long strides. If his feet pained him, as they often did, we could not tell.

The sun was low in the sky as we neared the end of our journey, but no one suggested that we halt for the night. We knew this area well, and although little light filtered down through the heavy canopy of evergreen boughs overhead, the pine needle path was fairly free of obstacles.

When we could hear the roar of the cascading falls and smell the smoke from the fire pit at Willow Woman's lodge, Black Wolf broke into a run. Without a word, he left Puh and me behind. We were not concerned. Puh and I knew how desperately he had yearned for his other family, impatiently awaiting the day when he would see them again. It was nearly dark when Puh and I entered the clearing that surrounded the lodge. A few lighted torches illuminated the area around the fire pit, where I could see a group of men milling about.

One of them walked over to welcome us as we slipped from the shadows of the forest into the halo of light surrounding the fire. The falls were louder here. I had forgotten how they thundered, even though they were yet a distance away.

"Tris! Tor! Pleasant evening to you both! Your visit is a wonderful surprise!" Slow Bear said, smiling broadly as he grasped our forearms. Slow Bear was the head of Willow Woman's household and one of her foremost advisors. "We were taken aback to see Black Wolf come running out of the woods; he certainly is spritely for a man his age! He nearly bowled over White Cloud as he entered the lodge."

"Pleasant evening to you, Slow Bear," I said, returning his greeting.

"Pleasant evening," Puh followed. "We are happy to be here, and we hope our presence will not be an inconvenience to you."

Slow Bear waved aside Puh's remark. He was an older man, rather heavyset, with a calm and good-natured demeanor.

"It is no trouble at all," Slow Bear assured us. "We are still in the quiet lull before we begin to pack for the fall Gathering, and we have plenty of meat just now. White Cloud assumed that Black Wolf would have been accompanied by others, and he is now preparing a meal for you."

It was apparent that everyone at the lodge had already consumed their evening sup.

"That is very kind of him," I said. "Most appreciated. I am indeed hungry."

"Please sit. Have you journeyed far?" Slow Bear inquired. "Ah! Here comes White Cloud with the food now."

We thanked White Cloud as he set before us a birch-bark tray laden with an assortment of roasted meats, cooked eggs, late-summer fruit, and tubers.

Everything was served cold, but to me it was still a feast. Puh and I began to eat immediately.

"We came from the North Country region, where my uncles reside," I answered.

"That must be about four days' travel from here," Slow Bear responded. "So what has inspired the trip to see us?"

"While we visited with my first mate's brothers, they imparted some rather unsettling news," Puh replied. "Black Wolf thought that Willow Woman should know as soon as possible."

Slow Bear appeared to be thinking. He absently reached for a piece of meat and began to chew thoughtfully.

"Have they heard reports of raids taking place?" Slow Bear inquired.

"Yes," Puh said with a nod. "Did you already know of this?"

"Just rumors," Slow Bear started, "no firsthand accounts. We did not know whether or not they were true. We have been concerned that those exiled might chance a return."

"It would seem as though they have," I said. "My Uncle Inlee's home was attacked last spring, and he told us that the raiders claimed they had killed everyone in a nearby clan."

"I have met Inlee," Slow Bear stated. "A most impressive man. He must be getting on in years. . . . I believe he is older than I am. But his word is as solid as a rock." Slow Bear sighed. "So the rumors are true. But you must be tired. We can wait until tomorrow to discuss this further. Willow will want to hear everything you can tell her. She has foreseen that this might come to pass and has dreaded the possibility."

The conversation remained subdued as the evening wore on. Black Wolf and Willow Woman did not come out to join us, but then, no one expected they would. Slow Bear mentioned that Willow Woman was just putting her son Black Oak to bed when Black Wolf arrived, so no doubt he was enjoying a happy reunion with Willow Woman and their four-winters-old son, Oak.

After Puh and I had been fed, we were shown to the same room in which we had stayed during previous visits. As Puh and I settled down to sleep, I realized that I too was looking forward to being with Willow Woman. I had not seen her in some time. While I had found her rather intimidating upon our first meeting many years ago, I now instead found her to be warm and engaging. I had become quite fond of Willow Woman.

The sound of the rushing waters of the falls soon lulled me to sleep.

Men crouched over large stones near a campfire. They chanted with deep harmonized voices while striking the stones in a measured cadence. The men wore wolfskin cloaks, with the wolf's head perched atop their close-cropped skulls. I recognized Karno's face amongst those in the group. He sang out with a strong voice, and yet he seemed uncharacteristically somber.

* * *

We broke our fast as an orange sun hung low in the morning sky; there was no sign of Black Wolf or Willow Woman. However, their son Oak came out to join us for breakfast. I was amazed at how much he had grown since I had last seen him. He was a tall boy with a sturdy build. Oak had his parents' black hair and dark eyes. I had once noted that when he played with my son Fox I saw that he could be just as lighthearted as any child, but here in the company of adults, he was somewhat serious for one so young. The only time I saw Oak speak with animation was when he excitedly announced to Slow Bear that his father had come to see him.

"Yes," Slow Bear began, "your father will stay with us for only a few days, but you will have a good long visit with him during the Gathering."

Oak's face lit up with a smile.

"I will like that," Oak answered. "Mother will too. Mother was so happy when Father arrived last night! He came in just as Mother was putting me to bed. Father told me a story about Wolfmen . . . you know, Slow Bear, the men of the Wolves you sometimes talk about?"

"Yes, I do know the Wolfmen," Slow Bear replied. "They were lively fellows. It must have been a good story."

"It was a funny story; it made me laugh," Oak said, giggling a little at the memory.

It pleased me to see the warm rapport between Oak and Slow Bear, who must have been much like a grandfather to the boy. I pondered that Oak should be so formal as to call his parents *Mother* and *Father*. Most children of The People simply referred to their mother as *Mama* and father as *Da,* but then again, when and if Oak should attain manhood, he would inherit the role of Head Elder from Willow Woman, so it was likely that his life would be quite different from that of most children.

Oak was the only child in a large household of many adults, and while everyone looked out for him, he was not treated as a youngster. I think the only times he was able to indulge in any kind of rambunctious playtime was when a few children from my clan came to visit, most especially Fox and Mror, Puh and Ria's son.

"Tris," Oak said, addressing me, "will you bring Fox next time you come? And Tor, will you bring Mror? They are my best friends, and I have missed them."

"I will certainly try," I said with a smile, surprised that he had been thinking of Fox and Mror just when I had. "I know that Fox misses you, too. He speaks of you sometimes."

"And Mror as well," Puh added. "Mror always asks when he will see you next."

Oak beamed with pleasure at this.

"I will ask Mother and Father if we might travel to see your home," he said brightly, "You have always come to me. It should be our turn to travel to see you now."

I just smiled at him. I did not have the heart to tell him that it was unlikely he would ever see our home. Little Fawn had resigned herself to the notion that after her long and bitter coexistence with Black Wolf he had found a new relationship elsewhere, but I did not think she would gladly suffer Willow Woman's and Oak's presence at her place of residence.

Slow Bear cagily changed the subject. He cleared his throat before speaking.

"Have you seen the Great Hall since its completion?" he asked Puh and me.

"Not since it was finished," Puh replied, shaking his head. "But we have been by the new Hall during its various stages of construction."

"It looks to be a marvel," I said. "Will the old Hall be repurposed?"

"The thought is that many of the Gathering's attendees can stay in the old Hall while the Gathering is underway," Slow Bear answered. "They used to strip the countryside of all the wood in every direction to erect their little shelters around the Hall; now they can just stay in it, or at least some of them can. I suspect most will want to stay in the new Hall. Who knows? The new Hall is so much larger, perhaps they can all stay within its walls for the duration. That is, if we can keep them from fighting."

Slow Bear sighed. I understood his reservations about the ability of the attendees to behave in a civil manner toward one another during the moon-long Gathering. I had been to a Gathering some years ago. It was at the time when the raids against Old Ones had broken out, and Black Wolf took us to the Gathering so that we might testify before the Head Elder. At that time, Willow Woman's father, Standing Oak, had been Head Elder. However, just prior to the Gathering he had passed suddenly, leaving Willow Woman to assume leadership in his stead.

This had been our introduction to Willow Woman, and, for those of us Old Ones, our introduction to The People's Gatherings. I found them to be noisy, crowded, and rather unsettling, especially considering that approximately half of the men there obviously did not appreciate our attendance. They scarcely got along with one another; adding Old Ones to the congregation made for a volatile assemblage.

A large number of the men also contested Willow Woman's right to take up her father's seat as Head Elder, but she would not be deterred in any way. In fact, she soon cowed the opposition into a resigned if somewhat disgruntled silence.

As the sun ascended bright blue skies, we continued to converse while we waited for Willow Woman and Black Wolf to exit the lodge. It was a pleasant and unhurried conversation. We were eventually joined by Gray Owl, Willow Woman's healer. He was a slight man with a staid nature who seemed to be perpetually preoccupied. I imagined that a man as wise as he must have a lot to think about. Gray Owl, too, seemed to have a close relationship with Oak. The two wandered off together when Oak became restless with all the idle talk.

The sun had almost reached its zenith when the sounds of Willow Woman's chatter reached my ears. She and Black Wolf ducked though the doorway of the lodge and approached us as we sat by the hearth, whose fire was now reduced to crumbling coals. White Cloud sprang to his feet to collect fresh food for them, and Willow Woman, guessing at his errand, thanked him as he hurried past them into the lodge.

Puh and I stood to greet our hostess and took a few steps toward her to close the distance between us. I could not help but notice that Willow Woman had diminished in girth since our last meeting. Her tattooed skin hung off her, giving her the appearance of a partially filled water bag. She was still a very large woman – as tall as I – and she still outweighed me by a considerable amount. However, Willow Woman was smiling broadly; in fact, she was glowing with happiness.

Willow Woman's outstretched arms embraced me in a heartfelt hug.

"Tris!" she exclaimed in a voice that would have halted a woolly rhino in midcharge. She then planted a kiss on my cheek. "Oh, how I have missed you!"

"And I, you," I told her. "Thank you for having us." I gave her another squeeze to reinforce the sentiment, but then she released me to throw her arms around Puh.

"Tor! Welcome!" Willow Woman boomed heartily.

"Many thanks," Puh gasped, crushed as he was by her strong arms.

"It is I who must thank you for coming to see me and bringing my dear Black Wolf, whom I have not seen in such a long time!" Willow Woman gushed.

She turned to Black Wolf, who smiled down at her adoringly.

"Let us sit and take sustenance," Black Wolf said to her, his deep bass taking on a tender quality. He guided her to a place where they might sit together. "Here is White Cloud now with some food and drink."

The conversation resumed, interspersed with light anecdotes and laughter. I tried to enjoy it, but I knew that soon the tone would change when we must speak of the raiders. When Willow Woman and Black Wolf had finished their meal, Willow Woman's easygoing smile dimmed and she exchanged glances with Black Wolf, who gave her a grim nod.

"I know the purpose of your visit was not just to allow Black Wolf an opportunity to be with those who have been longing for him," she began. "Black Wolf has told me that the attacks on homes of Old Ones have started again. We had heard tales of raids that occurred when no one was home, so there were no witnesses; but this is the first substantiated report we have received."

"And a report that includes reasonable confirmation of the identities of the men and a definite time and location," Black Wolf added.

"Yes," Willow Woman agreed. "What with the fall hunts looming in the not-too-distant future, we do not have much time to investigate, but I promise you, we shall."

"We must make time," Black Wolf said firmly. "You are the one who banished those men, who deemed them to be Outsiders who cannot return to this territory on pain of death. They may seek to take their revenge on you and . . . and. . .." Black Wolf seemed hesitant to finish his sentence. I was sure it occurred to him that Oak would also be in danger.

"If they are after revenge, then we are all potential targets," Willow Woman concurred. "But if that is so, they will not find us to be easy prey."

"We have dealt with them once; we can do it again," Black Wolf assured her.

"Do you want us to seek out those who have suffered attacks, just as we did before?" Puh questioned. The last time, we had been charged with finding others who could provide practical information we could use to track the miscreants.

"So far as we know, they have been striking homes not far from the northern border. Who else lives up that way other than your kin, and Ria's unfortunate family?" Willow Woman replied. "I know of no one else up that way. But you may be better informed than I."

"I know of no one else, either," Puh said. "But that is what worries me. That means if they are determined to make attacks on unwary clans, they will have to travel to other areas. My brothers Kror and Zor have moved their homesteads since the last attacks. I know not where they are now, but I believe they are somewhere southeast of here. We met a large clan of Old Ones who live by the coast, but that is a very long way to journey, and they are plentiful in number, so I would guess that they are probably safe. But I am most concerned for you and those who live at our family compound. If the Outsiders want to take out their anger on those of us who had a part in their capture and exile, our families will be endangered by their association with us."

"I believe you are correct, Tor," Willow Woman said solemnly. "I wonder if the raiders have managed to sustain their numbers, or even increased in number while they have been exiled. It could be that they have met up with other criminals who have also been banished, and joined forces with them."

"The skeletal remains we found in the forest . . . perhaps that was one of them?" I suggested.

"It would not surprise me to know that at least one of them had been fatally injured when they attacked Inlee's and Trae's homestead," Puh answered.

"I think it would be prudent to question all we can to find out what they know about the comings and goings of the raiders, even if they themselves were not victims," Willow Woman stated. "Some of The People may not even realize that these men were banished. It would help if we could recall the names of all the perpetrators so that we can spread the word. Black Wolf, you said you knew some of them."

"I knew only a few of them by name," Black Wolf replied. "But Petal's mate Fish Hawk resided in the Village for most of his life, and they were his neighbors and friends of his brothers'. He would be able to tell us who they are."

Willow Woman nodded thoughtfully.

"The first step is to make as many people as possible aware of who these men are," she said. "And we need to go after them. Hunt them down. And this time, they will not walk away."

* * *

Much to Black Wolf's sorrow, we departed for home the next day. He disliked leaving Willow Woman and Oak because he would miss them, but he also worried.

"I hate leaving Willow and Oak, knowing that those men are marauding again," Black Wolf lamented. Then he went on, "I am also concerned that Willow is growing so thin."

"*Thin*?" Puh repeated. "She has lost some of her . . . bulk . . . but I would not say she is exactly thin. I thought she looked fine."

"I fear she has not been well and is hiding it from me," Black Wolf went on, still very much concerned.

"Do not worry yourself, my friend," Puh said soothingly. "She appeared quite robust to me. She gave me a farewell embrace that was worthy of a bear. Willow is a strong woman, and not just in physical strength. She can handle anything that comes her way."

"I agree, Puh," I added. "Black Wolf, although she is a bit slimmer, I thought she seemed very happy and healthy."

"I hope you both are right," Black Wolf. "It tears at my heart to leave them knowing that those

Outsiders are back, murdering people and pillaging homes. I try to tell myself that she and Oak are surrounded by plenty of men, but I want to be there to ensure their safety. *Ack*, but then my other family must be defended as well. And I cannot be two places at once."

* * *

We were eager to return to the family compound and reassure ourselves that nothing untoward had occurred during our absence. We hiked swiftly, leaving camp each day as soon as there was enough light to see and trekking each evening until darkness began to overtake the forest.

When we returned home, we knew we faced a dilemma. The fall hunts had to start soon. Autumn foraging had already begun and must continue until the harvests were complete. It was vital to collect as much food as possible before winter set in. And yet it was imperative that we also deal with the raiders. Fish Hawk would have to tell us the names of the men, which would then have to be relayed to as many people as possible – most especially, to Willow Woman.

The more information we could gather about the Outsiders, the easier it would be to find them. I was troubled at the thought of possibly facing them again. I had killed many animals during my life, and other than trying my best to make a good kill and keep my family fed and clothed, I did not think much about it. But when those men abducted Morning

Star from our pairing ceremony and Puh, Black Wolf and I had to go after them to get her back, we had had to slay several of them. The thought made me feel ill. They were the only humans I had ever killed, and now, it would seem it might happen again. All the same, I would not hesitate to do what I must do to protect our families and friends.

* * *

We reached home just as the sun was midway in its descent to the horizon. The fire had been lighted in the central fire pit so that it would burn down to coals in time to cook our evening meal. Morning Star and our children were there with the rest of our families, the adults still busy with their chores and the older children minding the younger ones. The dogs were the first to sense our arrival, and they barked a joyous and noisy greeting.

"Tris! You are home!" Morning Star cried out in surprise at our unexpectedly early arrival.

My tiredness and hunger and thirst were momentarily forgotten as I leaned my spear against the nearby wall of Petal and Fish Hawk's dwelling and I wrapped my arms around my beloved mate and kissed her. Raena pranced in circles around us, barking happily, wanting to welcome me, too.

"Yes, I am home," I said. "And I am so glad to be here and hold you again."

Fox, Pony, and Raven had all trotted up, too, and they hugged my legs, although Raven soon let go and silently held up her arms in a wordless request to be picked up. I stooped just long enough to scoop her up and was gratified to feel her plump arms around my neck and her head on my shoulder. Morning Star had not yet released her grip on me.

Gran approached toting Lily, who whined and fussed as she longed to be returned to her mother. Morning Star obligingly took Lily from Gran.

"Thank you, Gran," Morning Star said, "I hope Lily has not worn you out."

"No," Gran replied. "She has kept me company. But I think she is hungry now."

Gran squeezed in closer to me, which was a feat when one considered that there were a bunch of children, a large dog, and Morning Star between us. But Gran managed to get close enough to touch my hand and give it a pat.

"I hope it was a good journey," Gran said to me with a grin. "We did not expect you men to return so soon."

"It was productive," I replied. "We visited Inlee's and Trae's homes while we were up north, and they said they would be pleased if we relocated to their area."

Morning Star smiled hopefully.

"Do you think it would be a good move?" she asked.

"I think we would have everything we need there," I responded. "But I will leave it to Puh and Black Wolf to decide if it will be our best option."

"Take off your pack. Come and sit," Morning Star instructed. "I will bring you some water and a little something to eat before the evening meal is served. I know you must be famished."

"Yes, I am," I admitted, "but I would like one more kiss first."

Morning Star tiptoed up to kiss my lips and then we all moved as a group, Pony still clinging to one of my legs, toward the fire pit. There, an inviting array of matting was laid out, and I gratefully sank down on the closest one.

Morning Star walked away with Lily on her hip and soon returned with a gourd cup of water. She placed the cup in my free hand. Raven wanted a drink as well, so I gave her a sip before downing the rest in one long gulp.

"I will get more water for you," Morning Star volunteered.

"Many thanks, but no," I said shaking my head. "My thirst is quenched for now."

"All right." Morning Star turned on her heel as she spoke. She was back a moment later with a birch-bark platter that was loaded with a tempting variety of foods. At this time of year, we had a broad selection of fresh fruits, greens, mushrooms, and tubers from which to choose. Additionally, Morning Star had included a handful of roasted nuts and thinly sliced slivers of roasted boar meat. It was the same boar we had brought down many days ago, and it still had a very strong flavor, but it was filling, nonetheless.

The children hung about, sampling some of the food from the tray as well. Morning Star tried to shoo them away.

"Let them be," I said gently. "I have missed them, and I am glad to be back amongst my family again. Besides, there is enough here for all."

Morning Star just smiled and left us once again to resume her meal-making preparations, adroitly managing with Lily still perched on her hip. Lily often became irritable at this time of day, and could be soothed by no one except her mother.

"Puh-Puh," Fox started. "Look at Kaw. Is he not looking so much better?"

Fox opened Kaw's sling slightly so I could view the bird as it lounged comfortably. I could see only Kaw's head, and his eyes blinked at me as though he had been disturbed from a nap. Kaw grabbed the edge of the sling and pulled it closed again, apparently not pleased by this intrusion.

"Kaw looks fine," I told Fox. "He is eating well?"

"Yes, Puh-Puh," Fox said, nodding. "But he does not fly yet. He has more feathers, but he still has not flown."

"It is possible he may never fly," I speculated.

"I guess he would probably like to fly." Fox shrugged his shoulders. "But I would not be sad if he cannot. That would mean he cannot leave me."

"We want Kaw to stay," Pony piped up. "We like Kaw."

"Well, we shall see what will happen," I said noncommittally.

I continued to enjoy the chatter of my children until they began to get restless and wandered off to play with the other resident youngsters. When I had consumed enough food to take the edge off my hunger, I began to feel drowsy.

* * *

"Tris, do wake up." Morning Star's voice stirred me from the depths of sleep.

I was startled to find that I was curled up on the mat like an animal. I raised myself to a sitting position and rubbed my face. Darkness had set in, and I could smell the wonderful aromas of cooking food. I looked up to see stars dotting the firmament overhead.

"I must have fallen asleep," I said, my mind still foggy.

"You and Da both," Morning Star said with a giggle. "Da nodded off on the mats just like you, and he was snoring like a beast. I am surprised his noise did not keep you awake."

"I heard nothing," I admitted. "I must have been more tired than I thought."

Black Wolf apparently had caught his daughter's words.

"I was not sleeping," he said indignantly from where he still reposed with his many dogs. "I was just resting my eyes."

"Your eyes make terrible sounds when they are resting," Fish Hawk replied, grinning.

"It was the dogs," Black Wolf responded. "The dogs snore something awful."

"They learned it from you," Little Fawn said dryly.

Black Wolf narrowed his eyes and he stared balefully at Little Fawn, but he refrained from commenting.

"The food is ready. Let us eat," my sister Ru announced.

I still had a good appetite, and I tackled another platterful of food with gusto. The group had many questions about our journey to the North.

"It is good land," Black Wolf told them. "There is a lot of open prairie, but also a lot of woodlands, and plenty of water. When we saw Inlee and Trae, they said they would be happy to have us nearby."

"It must be a lonely place," Ria said. She appeared downcast; Puh must have told her of the sad fate that had befallen her brothers and their kin. "And now that the raiding has started in that area again, I am sure they would welcome the presence of more armed men."

"I believe you are right on both counts," Black Wolf agreed.

"If we relocate up there, are we not putting our own families closer to potential danger?" Bror asked. "Or do you intend to … um …." Bror's eyes scanned our assembled families, noting the many children in attendance, "… eliminate the problem before we make our move?"

"There is risk no matter where we live," Puh pointed out. "While the Northlands are closer to where some of the trouble has taken place, the location is not the issue; it is the people who reside there."

This was soberingly true. The Outsiders seemed to be determined to complete their original mission to rid all Old Ones from our long-held territories. We could only assume that they would also take out their malice on all those who caused their banishment.

"So what are you thinking, Tor?" Black Wolf asked Puh. "As discussed with Wi … *the Head Elder*, we will need to get the word out about these men." Black Wolf was careful not to mention Willow Woman in front of Little Fawn, who was understandably sensitive about it.

"Yes, and after that I think we will need to track them, just as we would any game," Puh replied. "Some of us will have to stay here to look out for those left behind. And we can count on the dogs to help take care of any intruders."

"Yes, between the dogs and the arrows from Ria's and Ty's bows, that should be enough to discourage any uninvited guests," Black Wolf agreed once more.

"I am going, too," Ria said firmly.

"You want to go with us while we pursue those men?" Puh inquired of her, somewhat incredulously.

"If any are willing to look after Mror while we are away, then yes, I want to go," Ria said. "Before I came here, they watched for opportunities to pilfer almost everything I owned anytime I was not home. And now they have done away with the last of my clan. I want to find them. I will make many arrows. They will know me when I loose my weapons upon them . . . ." Ria trailed off, as she seemed to realize that her words might frighten the children.

"Mror is always welcome in my home," Little Fawn was quick to offer.

"And with us, as well," Morning Star chimed in.

"Of course Mror may stay with us, too," Ru added.

"Mror can stay wherever he likes," Gran said with a chuckle. I noticed that Gran was looking at Ria with a warm smile. I wondered if she was recalling how wild Ria was when she first came to us: the little huntress with her bow and arrows. Ria might have settled in with Puh and motherhood, but we sometimes saw flashes of the old Ria at moments such as these.

"Then come with us you shall," Puh said to Ria. "I am sure they will remember you."

"At least one of them ought to," Black Wolf acknowledged with a hearty laugh. Years ago, Ria had launched one of her arrows into the buttocks of the lead raider. "In the meantime, we need to go on another hunt so that our families will have meat while we are gone."

Puh nodded. "That is true. Maybe in a few days or so."

Morning Star was sitting close enough to be touching me, and I felt her stiffen beside me. I knew she would not be pleased that I would be leaving again so soon.

"Tris, I think we should put the children to bed," Morning Star stated. Lily had already nodded off in her arms.

"Yes, my sweet," I responded.

We bid our families a pleasant evening and, with Raena padding alongside, walked up the hill to our home.

There, I built up the fire as Morning Star started to wipe down faces and hands and get the children onto their sleeping platforms. Lily was awakened so that she could nurse before she was placed into her little nest-like bed. Pony and Raven willingly put themselves under their blankets and quickly fell asleep. Fox fussed over Kaw, wanting the bird to sleep in his embrace, but Kaw preferred to make himself comfortable up by Fox's head. Fox gave up trying to reason with Kaw and soon was dozing, too.

I looked in upon them and kissed each of my children on the forehead. They barely stirred.

Morning Star looked down at Lily as she suckled. Lily's eyelids were drooping. She had not really become fully awake when she was roused, and she was nursing half-heartedly. I saw a single tear run down Morning Star's cheek. I quickly bent to gently wipe it away.

"Why do you weep?" I asked, concerned and even somewhat alarmed at her upset. Morning Star was not one to indulge in frivolous displays of emotion.

"There are many reasons," she said in a hushed voice, so as not to disrupt our children's rest. "It is a horrifying to know that those terrible men who abducted me from our pairing ceremony are back. They are not like any men I have ever known. Snow Leopard proved he was a lout when he would not abide by the results of the Challenge Circle after you won me, but then when he stole me; it was he who made sure those men did me no harm. Without him, I shudder to think . . ." Morning Star paused. "And then there is the fact that you must go after them. I am afraid. I am so afraid."

Morning Star rose to place Lily on her pallet, and as she turned toward me I saw tears in her eyes once more. I gathered her in my arms and kissed her until I felt her relax against me.

"We will make sure that the families are protected at all times," I promised her. "And we will not be careless when we go after them. I do not relish the thought of hunting down men as we would an animal, but I do not see how else we can prevent them from either starving out our clans or eliminating us altogether."

"I know you will do all you can," Morning Star said quietly. "This feels as it did when we were at the coast and that storm blew in as we sheltered in the cave. I was terrified that the waves washing into the cave would either drown all of us or carry us away, out to sea. Only this time, it is a wave of men who seek to snuff us out."

I stifled my own fears about our situation as I sought to comfort her.

"Fortunately, waves of men are much less powerful and much more predictable than the ocean," I said, tightening my embrace and kissing her several times. "Try not to worry, my sweet," I whispered, and then I took her to bed.

 **Chapter Eight** 

We are in the forest. The setting sun glimmers near the horizon, throwing long shadows across the darkening landscape. Suddenly, strange beings appear in the gloom.

I awoke from my Dream glad to find myself at home, nestled against my warm mate. We had enjoyed a long romantic interlude before finally drifting off to sleep. It had been wonderfully pleasurable, but this puzzling and somewhat disturbing Dream was a grim reminder that we faced an uncertain future. The nearness of Morning Star drove all such dire thoughts from my mind. I kissed her hair and caressed her back, and she responded by pressing up against me. We knew we would have precious little time together before I would have to leave again, and we breathlessly ushered night into morning.

We were agreeably entwined and talking softly to one another when we heard the children begin to awaken. Fox was speaking to Kaw as though chatting with an old friend.

"Pleasant day to you, Kaw! Come now, hop into the sling," Fox instructed.

"He would rather ride on your shoulder," Pony pointed out.

"*Kaw!*" Raven said with a giggle. She was still too young to laugh silently as we Old Ones did, or perhaps she would laugh aloud like The People. She was, after all, from both cultures. We Old Ones believed that to make laughing and crying sounds would attract predators; our only sounds were to speak or, on occasion whistle a signal.

"I must get up," Morning Star said to me, and she rose and began to dress in the dim confines of our small chamber.

"I will too," I said, feeling around for my clothing as well.

I heard the sharp raps of stones striking against one another, and I peered out into the main room of our dwelling. There I saw that Fox had propped open the door-flap to allow a little sunlight to enter the room and he was now attempting to light the tinder he had arranged in the fireplace.

Raena caught sight of me and she woofed softly, her tail wagging furiously. Fox turned to see what had captured Raena's attention.

"Pleasant day, Puh-Puh," Fox said when he saw me observing him. Kaw was perched by the edge of the hearth and he seemed to be watching Fox, too.

"Pleasant day to you, too," I answered, and I withdrew back into our bedchamber to finish tying on my loincloth.

When I came to stand by Fox, the tinder was already smoking. Fox lifted the smoldering bits of wood shavings and gently blew onto them and then held them up to see if flames would arise. Seeing no results, he then blew again.

"Fox, watch your hair does not light too," Morning Star warned as she ducked into the hide-covered doorway to our storage area.

Fox pushed his long curly hair back with one hand.

"Yes, Muh-Muh." Fox grinned to see the fire come to life and he set the bundle onto the fireplace, where he had already placed an assortment of small sticks.

I smiled to see how proficient my son had become at making fire. It was not an easy skill for a child to master, but Fox seemed to learn most things quickly.

"I did it, Puh-Puh!" Fox exclaimed.

"Yes, and you did very well," I told him, crouching beside him and patting his back.

Fox beamed happily and picked up Kaw to move him away from the fire as it grew in strength. Kaw had a pebble in his beak, and when Fox held out his hand, Kaw placed the pebble on his palm. Fox then studied me for a moment.

"Puh-Puh, you hair is sticking out all over the place," Fox said.

Fox's hair, thick and bushy like mine, was a bit mussed, too.

"I will ask your Muh-Muh to fix it for me," I replied.

"I will fix it, Puh-Puh!" Pony volunteered. She approached and stretched up to reach my head as I knelt by Fox. Pony attempted to tame my hair by gathering up fistfuls of the loose locks and squeezing them together, to no avail. I wrapped her in a hug.

"Many thanks, my little one," I began, "but your Muh-Muh has spent many years learning how to bind my hair. She may have to be the one to make it right."

Morning Star had just emerged from our storage area, toting the foods with which we would break our fast.

"I will, indeed," she said lightheartedly, having regained her spirits after last evening's somber mood. "Fox has been practicing making sparks with the stones; he wanted to surprise you by making fire when you returned home."

"It was a great surprise," I said, "and it has been a very nice homecoming."

In truth, it was. I was pleased to be home, perhaps even more pleased than usual after being away for a time, although I could not say why. My family was content: my mate busied herself with preparing our first meal of the day, the children playfully tumbled about, the dog happily placed herself in the midst of it all, and Kaw squawked in accompaniment.

Bright early-morning sunshine slanted through the doorway, portending a mild day. It would be a good weather to go foraging, something we did nearly every day at this time of year. The fire quickly took the chill off the little room. We broke our fast with fresh berries and roasted nuts as shell bowls of swelled grains were heated up on the cooking stones by the fireplace. Raena caught a mouse as it tried to sneak past her into our abode and swallowed it whole, scarcely pausing to chew, and then I gave her a few slabs of dried seal meat to gnaw on, as well.

When our meal was through and the children were once again wiped down and clothed, Morning Star and I finished dressing as well, and we all ventured outdoors to start our day. Morning Star carried a forked stick she used to untangle hair. She asked me to be seated, so I sat on a chunk of wood from our woodpile, and she placed Lily in my lap as she set to work on my unruly hair.

Meanwhile, the older children kept themselves amused; Pony and Raven drew in the sand and Fox sat with Kaw. The bird would retrieve little items and bring them to him. Fox had accumulated quite a collection of these gifts, which he kept on a ledge by his bed. Kaw sometimes flexed his wings and flapped them a little, but he did not seem inclined to do more.

Morning Star had become well acquainted with how we Old Ones arranged our hair. Once she had worked through the knots, she sectioned my hair and twisted it into cords, turning the hair in the direction of the curl until my hair was a series of coils that were then gathered into one bundle and lashed into a single rope that hung down my back to past my waist. This was usually done about once a moon, but after the boar hunt, the trek to the North Country and back – and the previous night might have had something to do with it as well – it really needed to be done again.

While Morning Star was tending to my personal care, she also carefully trimmed my mustache, which had grown annoyingly long. My beard would be left alone, since winter would be upon us in a few short moons and its insulation would help to keep my face warm.

"Now my handsome mate looks as he should," Morning Star said as she brushed away stray bits of mustache hair from my chest.

"Many thanks, my sweet," I replied, rising to give her a kiss. "And just in time. Lily is becoming very bored with sitting with her Puh-Puh."

Lily had become increasingly vocal about her growing displeasure. She was not outright squalling yet, but she soon would be.

"It is not you she objects to," Morning Star told me. "She is teething. See how she chews on her fingers and drools? Poor girl! Let us go down the hill to see what our families are doing. It would be a good day to pick grapes. They should be ready by now. If we wait too long, the other animals and birds will eat them up, and, besides, overripe grapes attract bees."

"Bees sting!" Fox stated. He had been stung by bees several times. Despite the pain of the sting, Fox was still fascinated by the insects. He would study the creature's dead body and marvel at its tiny features. Fox had pointed out the place where the bee's stinger had been before it was torn from its body when he was stung. He did not begrudge the bee the right to defend itself, but he was amazed that the bee did so, even though the act brought about its death.

"All the more reason to pick those grapes now," Morning Star responded. "I will retrieve a few baskets and sacks."

As Morning Star and Lily disappeared into our home, the eldest children clamored about in anticipation of our grape harvest. Grapes were a favorite of Fox's, despite their tangy flavor and the necessity of spitting out seeds. His younger sisters might not remember previous harvests, but they shared Fox's enthusiasm nonetheless. Morning Star soon distributed a bag or basket to each one of us, even little Raven, who shook her bag wildly. I lifted

Raven into my arms as we began to walk down the hill to the main compound, Raena loping easily beside us.

"Keep your bag still," I said to her gently. "You will put fruit in there and they will be smashed if you rattle them about."

"*Gapes*, Puh-Puh," Raven repeated, not quite able to say grapes. "Get gapes?"

Moments later we were standing amongst our families, who were also readying to go about their day. It did not take long to interest many of the others to join us. Unless animals had cleaned out the grapevines, it would take many hands to pick all the fruit; there was plenty to be gathered at this time of year.

It was just a short hike to the thicket of vines. As we had hoped, the grapes were now a lustrous deep purple and they were fragrantly ripe. Kaw was still riding on Fox's shoulder, hanging on as Fox moved about. Fox offered an occasional piece of grape to Kaw, who ate it with enthusiasm.

Raena sat in the shade of a tree, watching over us dutifully, Puh's dog Auchs at her side. Morning Star and I picked one-handed, since we each carried one of our youngest daughters. It was a happy outing under cheerful blue skies. Birds sang from nearby branches, and we chatted as we worked. I too was tempted to try a few of the grapes, but I found them a bit tart for my liking. Raven wanted to try one, so I bit a grape in two and took out the seeds before giving half to her. The other half, I ate; gulping it down hastily before it could impart its flavor to my tongue. Raven made a face at her piece of grape but swallowed it down with a shudder.

"It is a bit sour," I said to Raven. "Would you like some water to wash away the taste?"

Raven nodded, so I set down my basket and took a small water bag from where it hung at my side and offered her a drink, wiping the drips from her chin when she was through. I had just bent for my basket when suddenly Kaw spread his wings and fluttered to the ground at Fox's feet. Kaw's beak was open, and as he extended his wings, his feathers poked out from his body at all angles.

Everyone stopped picking fruit and stared at Kaw in amazement. Kaw began to squawk noisily and he hopped about vigorously, as though he were doing an energetic dance. All at once I had an epiphany; Kaw sensed something we could not.

"Fox, step back!" I commanded.

Fox seemed to be frozen in place. He looked confused at the situation, but then he took a backward step. Kaw's beak darted out and he stabbed it into the leaf-littered ground. Then, I knew for certain that something was wrong. I dropped my basket and came up behind Fox to drag him several steps farther from Kaw.

Kaw continued his agitated dance, his feathers all askew. He repeatedly jabbed his beak into the carpet of dead leaves until finally Kaw lifted something into the air. It hung limp for all to see.

"An adder! Stay away from it, just in case it is still alive!" I exclaimed. I had not seen an adder in this area for many years. "Those snakes are very poisonous. It must have been hunting the small creatures that have come here to eat fallen grapes."

Kaw's duty done, he flew back up onto Fox's shoulder, and Fox affectionately stroked his feathers back into place. I wondered if he realized that Kaw had probably saved his life. If Fox had stepped on the snake it surely would have bitten him. We adults exchanged glances. Morning Star looked pale and frightened.

"Let us take a rest," Puh said. "Perhaps you all should sit in the shade by the dogs."

I realized that Puh was trying to move us away from the vines so he could poke around the debris that lay on the ground to look for more snakes before we continued picking. Puh searched for and found a long piece of deadwood.

"Yes, Puh," I agreed, trying to keep the mood light so that our companions would not be too unnerved by Fox's close call. "It would be nice to sit down for a bit."

As we found comfortable spots on which to lounge, I noted that Fox appeared downcast.

"Are you all right?" I asked Fox.

Fox shook his head. Tears glinted at the corners of his eyes.

"Kaw flew, Puh-Puh," Fox answered. "Did you see Kaw fly? Now that he knows he can use his wings, he may go away."

As if Kaw understood what we were saying, he fluttered down from Fox's shoulder to the ground, where he picked up a light-colored pebble and gave it to Fox.

"I am sorry, Fox," I said, putting an arm around him. "It is true that Kaw may decide to go and live the life of a crow, but he is still here now. Enjoy him while he is with you, and know that while he stays, it is because he likes you and he chooses to be with you."

Fox brightened a little at the thought.

"How long do you think he will stay, Puh-Puh?" Fox asked.

"I do not know," I said. "But if he decides to leave, you must be brave and let him go."

When Puh deemed it safe to continue foraging amongst the vines, we returned to our task, but we warily kept an eye on the leaf litter for any potential movement. When we brought home our grape harvest, the children were excited to tell the story of Kaw's heroic actions. Kaw himself had ridden home on Fox's shoulder, and the crow seemed to take all the praise and admiration in stride. Kaw showed off his new skill as he flew across the compound, where he collected an empty nut husk. Kaw then flew back to Fox and offered him the husk.

Despite Kaw's evident fondness for Fox and his constant gift-giving, I felt that soon Kaw would leave us. He had always seemed to be rather undersized, but Kaw was a wild thing, and he could not help what he was any more than Fox could help being a little boy.

* * *

The day did not end with the grape harvest. We also made several short excursions to gather mushrooms, dig up various tubers, and pick berries. We finished in time to help prepare the evening meal, during which we discussed our plans for the following day's hunt.

"What would be our best course of action, Tor?" Black Wolf asked Puh. Just then it occurred to me that in matters concerning animals, we generally deferred to Puh, while in matters concerning people, often Black Wolf was the one who was consulted.

Puh appeared to be thinking as he chewed. We were still consuming the old boar, and it required much tedious chewing.

"I have been considering that," Puh replied. "While we were out foraging today I saw a buck's scrape on a tree. It looks fresh. I could see where it had scraped the ground as well. If a few of us are in place early tomorrow morning, we might be able to take him."

"There have been so few deer in the area, it is almost a shame to hunt them before they can build up their numbers again," Black Wolf mused. "But we do not have the luxury of wasting time. We must take the first animal we can bring home."

"I agree," Puh said with a nod. "That was my thought as well. I suggest that Tris and I go by ourselves. The fewer hunters, the less evidence there will be for the buck that trouble awaits him. Tris, what say you?"

"I will be ready at first light," I told Puh.

* * *

I left before the children awoke the next day, but Morning Star made a hearty meal to break my fast. Then after a few lingering kisses, my sweet mate bade me to take care as I walked out the door.

The sun was just peeking over the horizon, making a pale swath of sky that extended to the upper branches of the trees. Birds sang and flitted about in the misty morning air. It was cold enough to see my breath.

Puh was waiting for me. After he said his farewells to Ria we slipped away, the silence disturbed by only a few halfhearted woofs from Black Wolf's dogs. We marched steadily through the fog-shrouded forest; the air was absolutely still. There was no wind to whisper through the tree branches or rustle the desiccated leaves that covered the trail. Despite all efforts to walk as quietly as possible, each step made a slight but audible crunch. I could feel the moisture accumulating on my face. It dripped off my eyelashes and ran down my nose, and I could see the droplets as they rested on Puh's skin, hair, and clothing.

The murky gloom persisted until we reached the tree trunk the buck had marked. Puh pointed at the spot on the tree, making sure to stand as far from it as he could and still indicate the place. Bucks scrape their antlers on trees not only to rid themselves of the putrid shreds of velvet as it slowly rots off their antlers, but it is also a way of attracting does to them. Between the tree scrapes and scrapes made on the ground, the does pick up their scent and then decide if this buck is a potential mate or not.

Bucks check their scrapes every day to sniff at them in hopes that they might include the aroma of a receptive doe. With luck, we would be able to encounter this buck as he made his daily rounds. However, if he picked up our scent and did not like it, there was a chance he would not approach at all. We could only conceal ourselves in the nearby brush and stay very still and wait.

Puh and I stood motionless as the sun rose higher in the sky. Small gnats flew into my eyes and up my nose, and yet I did not flinch. To do so might mean that my loved ones would not eat. I grew thirsty, but I dared not drink.

Puh and I had done this often enough over the years that we did not need to formulate a plan. We simply awaited our prey and, assuming he appeared, we would then dart out from our hiding places and lance him with our spears behind the forelegs, where we might hit the heart and lungs.

At long last we heard the sounds of snapping twigs. Something was coming. I could smell his musky odor as he neared. At first, we could see only a shadowy outline of the buck, but he came into focus as he drew nearer. He was a young red deer buck with a modest antler spread, but he appeared to be well nourished. I could see that his tongue was out as he tasted the air for the scent of does. A few bits of miscellaneous foliage decorated his antlers. As he walked partway past Puh and me, I also noted his mud-caked body; he must have created a large wallow somewhere, where he had rolled to liberally coat himself with urine-tinged mud.

The buck paused to renew the place where he had pawed the earth with his hoofs and then deposited a steaming stream of urine into the shallow trench. There, he did a brief dance, splashing the muddy liquid onto his forelegs. Next, he stepped up to the mark he had carved into the tree and sniffed, his upper lip raised and pink tongue protruding. The buck positioned himself to freshen the scrape on the tree, and at that moment I saw Puh lift one finger very slightly. This was my signal. I nodded to show I understood and I was ready.

Puh and I burst from our positions, thrusting our spears into the buck with all our might, twisting the shaft as it went it to widen the wound as much as possible. The buck was so startled by the dual attack that he cried out and reared on his hind legs in confusion, not knowing which way to turn to escape.

He struck out at us with his forelegs, but as we were standing at his sides and still grasping our spears, he was unable to reach us. Blood began to drip from his mouth and bubble from his nose, but he still sought to free himself. I could see the crimson fluid now pumping from the wound where my spear had entered the buck's body. The spear's shaft flexed in my hands as the buck continued to thrash, and I fervently hoped the fire-hardened wooden shaft would not fracture. If either Puh or I was unable to keep the buck pinned in place with our spears, he would no doubt break free. If that occurred, we would be forced to track him and hope that we could find him before another predator decided to steal our kill for itself.

The buck's frantic struggles had already dragged us a short distance from where we had ambushed him, but he was tiring. He had lost a significant amount of blood, and he was panting with his tongue hanging out like a dog's. At last he slumped to the ground. Puh and I looked across his body at one another.

"I am grateful he finally went down," Puh said in a croaking voice. He must have been thirsty, too.

"As am I," I said, reaching for my water bag to take a swig. "We must have missed his heart. It took longer than I thought it should for him to pass."

Puh brought out his water bag for a drink as well.

"Yes," Puh concurred. "He was young, but he was a fighter. But no matter; he is large enough to provide many good meals for our families."

We quickly gutted the animal and then selected two sturdy saplings from which to attach his body for the trek back to the family compound. He might not the biggest buck we had ever seen, but he was a large animal for two men to transport by themselves. We ate various dried foods as we worked, to fuel us for the trip home. Finally, we took one last swig of water before we hefted the buck between us, the two saplings resting on each shoulder.

We maintained a swift pace and arrived at the compound soon after midday, where we briefly greeted our family. As I embraced and kissed Morning Star, our dog Raena sniffed at me and then licked at the blood and sweat on my leggings.

"You were away longer than I expected," Morning Star said. "I was beginning to worry."

"We had to wait for the buck, and he took his time coming to us," I informed her. "But it went well. He was too distracted by his mission to care much about anything else. He did not seem to know we were there; we were almost close enough to touch him by the time we struck."

"Well, I believe he is the dirtiest deer you have ever brought home," Morning Star said with a small laugh. "But it looks as though he is a robust animal.

He may be a tad musky, but he will give us a good deal of meat."

"And there should be a nice hide under all that dried mud, plus a decent set of antlers," I added. It was true the hide would need an extra good scrubbing, but the buck would yield a number of useful materials besides, such as bones and sinews.

"You may want to wash and change into other clothing before we eat," Morning Star pointed out, her nose wrinkling a bit as she spoke.

"Puh and I are nearly as filthy as the buck," I said, laughing silently. "Yes, I will go home and wash and change." I leaned down to give Morning Star a parting kiss and began to walk away.

Fox trotted up to me, Kaw bouncing along too as he hung onto Fox's shoulder.

"Puh-Puh, you are back!" Fox exclaimed, but he stopped a step short of reaching me. "Oh, Puh-Puh! You smell!"

"Indeed I do!" I agreed, smiling at his youthful candor. "I am going to wash and change. Why do you not watch your uncles Ty and Bror as they butcher the deer?"

Fox nodded with a grin and ran off to do just that. Ty and Bror had taken possession of the buck almost as soon as we'd arrived, and they had begun to work on it immediately, no doubt eager to consume something rather than the old boar's meat.

Raena accompanied me up the hill to our home, where she watched me gather a scrap of hide and a fresh loincloth and belt. Then she walked with me to the stream, where she sat on the bank as I stripped and began to scrub myself first with handfuls of sand, and then with the dampened piece of hide. The water was cold, but given the buck's pungent aroma and muddy coat, there was no alternative but to wash away as much of the odor, blood, and grime as could be removed.

I had worn only a loincloth and leggings during the hunt, and after cleaning myself I took them from where I had left them on the bank, first removing Raena, who had rolled on top of them and then laid down over the soiled and odiferous clothing. Thankfully, she had not managed to transfer much of the dirt or scent onto herself. Like most dogs, she had adopted a curious habit of rolling on dead animals. And that clothing now smelled like a very musky dead animal.

I placed my clothes in the shallows of the stream and, one by one, washed and wrung out each item and placed it back on the bank. After donning the clean loincloth, I returned to our home, where I hung the wet items to dry on branches of a few nearby bushes.

The temperatures were now cooling as the sun sank lower in the sky. My wet hair was still dripping down my back, despite my having wrung out the rope of coils that Morning Star had so carefully arranged just the day before. I added a little wood to the smoldering coals in our fireplace and quickly dressed in dry leggings and a tunic before returning to my family at the main compound. The evening meal would soon be ready, and I was quite hungry.

When I rejoined our clan, I could see that Puh had cleaned up as well. The deer's organ meats were being roasted over the coals in the fire pit, along with an assortment of additional foods, including – much to everyone's regret – more of the old boar. That boar would probably accompany nearly every meal until the animal had been completely eaten.

"That is much better," Morning Star said when she saw Raena and me returning. "Now you are clean enough to hold the baby." Morning Star tiptoed up to give me a kiss and placed Lily in my arms.

"All right," I responded. "Lily and I will find a seat by the fire. It grows cool."

"Is it?" Morning Star seemed surprised. "I have scarcely left the hearth, and it is quite warm there. I thought it seemed refreshing when I have had a moment to step away."

Morning Star went back to her work while Lily and I found a vacant spot on which to be seated, where I could lean against the outer wall of my boyhood home. Lily was in reasonably good spirits for this late in the day. She jabbered at me and at times clapped her hands, a new trick she had recently learned. Her sister Raven sat down next to us and leaned against me, so I put an arm around her.

"Are you tired, little one?" I asked her.

Raven nodded and put her thumb in her mouth as she sometimes did in quiet moments. But when Kaw launched himself from Fox's shoulder and flew across the compound to alight in a tree, Raven took her thumb from her mouth just long enough to point and say, "Kaw!"

Fox ran after Kaw, calling for him. Kaw stayed in the tree for a short time, but soon returned to Fox, much to Fox's relief. Each day as darkness came Kaw sought out his sanctuary within the sling.

It was not long before the food was ready. Morning Star, Fox, and Pony sat down beside us, carrying our food and drink between them. It was a sumptuous dinner; the buck's heart was large enough to give everyone a small serving of the delicacy, and I enjoyed my portion greatly, savoring each bite. In contrast, the boar's meat I ate mechanically, strictly because it filled my stomach and offered nutrition.

"I have been pondering our dilemma regarding the need to relay to... *the Head Elder* ... the identities of the Outsiders, and also look into the location of the Outsiders, and still manage to hunt before the rut is over and the next Gathering begins," Black Wolf stated. "I believe we should combine those errands. We can return just in time for me to make the trip to the Gathering. And also you, Fish Hawk, if you should choose to attend this year."

"I have expected that you would want me to go with you to the Head Elder's," Fish Hawk replied. "I would have to speak with Petal before I commit to anything more." Petal smiled at Fish Hawk and took his hand to give it a squeeze. She was pregnant with their second child but barely showing any sign of that impending event.

"I will let you decide," Petal said demurely. "I would miss you, of course, but I trust you to know what is best. It sounds as though we could be facing a serious situation, and it may be important to go to this Gathering. That would be a good place to gather news about the Outsiders whereabouts and discuss what should be done about them."

Petal, in her soft and gentle way, was quite astute. Fish Hawk grinned at her.

"As usual, you are smarter than I," Fish Hawk said good-naturedly. "Yes, you are right. While I would not like to be away from you either, even if I never attend another Gathering, I should probably go to this one."

"We will have to leave enough men here to protect our families," Puh pointed out. "And all those who live up the hill should probably come down to the main compound while we are away so they will not be off on their own. I know it is only a short distance, but you will be safer here."

"It is twenty-eight steps up the hill to Tris's house," my littlest sister, Mi, said matter-of-factly, "I have counted each step. If I take bigger steps, it is only twenty-two steps."

"You have become very good at counting," Puh said to Mi, affectionately snuggling her as she sat by his side.

Morning Star was listening intently. In the past she had come down to join the families when I was off hunting for an extended period, but not since we had begotten so many children. Nonetheless, I would feel better knowing she and the children were staying at one of the main compound's households. My eldest sister, Ru, her mate, Bror, and their children would have to come down the hill as well.

"I think that Bror and Ty should stay here," Black Wolf answered Puh. "And I think you are right in saying that everyone should stay at the main compound while we are gone."

"And," Puh went on, "no one should leave the compound unless it is absolutely necessary. As long as everyone stays close by, no one can be caught off guard by themselves or in a small group."

At this statement, all in the assemblage traded glances with one another. This would mean no foraging for as much as an entire moon cycle.

"So we cannot go out to collect foods?" Little Fawn asked.

"Not for a while," Puh answered. "We can harvest as much as possible over the next few days. And we can hold off on picking apples until after we return. They can stand a little cold weather before they are gathered."

"When do you want to leave?" I asked. That was one of my biggest concerns. How much time did I have with my family before I was to leave them for a very long time? My other concern was for their safety while we were away.

"I think we should depart on the morning of the third day from now," Black Wolf replied. "That will give us a little more time to bring in what we can. I think that will be enough to see us through the winter and spring. As Tor said, we can wait to pick apples and we can still dig up onions throughout the winter. It seems as though we have already brought in all the other fruits. We can concentrate on mushrooms tomorrow; they will not last much longer. We should check to see if there are any more grains to be harvested. Nuts, too, since they will be either devoured by squirrels or shaken off the tree by the wind to rot on the ground. The day after that we can dig up roots, onions, and tubers."

"Yes, combining all that, what remains of the boar, today's buck, and what we bring in during the fall rut, we should have enough stores," Puh agreed.

"It is a shame we curtailed our outing to the coast," Bror said. "We might have dried much more fish and seal meat."

"Well, we do have some left," Black Wolf responded. "But I feel as though we should continue to save it for the depths of winter, since it keeps so well without spoiling."

"Yes, I understand," Bror said with a nod. "It is just that previously we have taken so much meat there; but I remember the storm that came during the summer of the red skies. The coast is not a good place to be near the end of summer. I will just look forward to the fall hunts."

"Da, what about Hawk and me?" Swift River queried his father. "We could go with you to help find the raiding men."

Black Wolf seemed surprised at this. The boys were so keen for any adventure that I had expected them to ask to accompany us well before this. Black Wolf must have been so preoccupied with our dilemma that he had not thought of including his sons. He smiled at them.

"I know you are brave enough to face them," Black Wolf began. "But I need you to be home to help protect the family here. I would feel better about being away if I knew I could depend on you two to help your mother and to watch over everyone."

If Hawk and Swift River were disappointed at being left behind, they did not show it. In fact, their chests swelled at the implied praise. They may have realized on some level that their father was placating them, but I was sure it was true that Black Wolf would feel more at ease with his sons at home rather than with us.

* * *

The next days passed quickly. Stores were gathered and dried, placed in baskets, layered in straw, and left in our various storage rooms to wait until it was time to make use of them. Gran and all the children old enough to assist took care of laying out the fruits and mushrooms to be dried while the rest of us foraged. Thankfully the days were sunny, and heated rocks from the fire pit helped to speed the drying process.

I was sorry that I did not have more time with Gran to tell her of my recurring Dream. It was always in a damp, dark forest. Nothing untoward seemed to be happening, but I was consumed with a feeling of dread and watchfulness. A strong sense of impending trouble. Even if Gran could not offer any insight, she could at least console me; she understood the weight I carried because of the Dreams. Morning Star knew I was uneasy, but other than occasional concerned glances, she did not pursue the matter. She was busy with the demands of our children and preparing a winter's worth of food. I did not want to delve into my worries with her and add to her burdens.

Besides, I wanted to keep this time with my family as happy as possible. I took pains to give both Morning Star and our children, and even Raena, as much attention as this little time allowed. When the time came for me to leave, I did not know when I would see them again.

 **Chapter Nine** 

Fire erupted into the nighttime sky. Tongues of flame licked the air, crackling and sending bright sparks arching into the surrounding darkness. My heart ached. I had a sense that something was leaving me. Leaving me forever.

Puh, Ria, Black Wolf, Fish Hawk, and I hiked swiftly. The morning was quite cool. Sunny days were still comfortably warm, but nights could be downright frosty and the rising sun had not yet taken away the chill. Although Black Wolf sang as always, it was not with his usual enthusiasm. Black Wolf's songs meant that we seldom saw any animals, but we did spot several hyenas that stared at us from positions of safety near the edge of the brush. We got a whiff of their strong odor as we neared them, but it was their cackling laughter that truly gave away their presence. Black Wolf looked annoyed at first but then he grinned.

"When I hear their mocking laughter I have to remind myself that they are just animals," Black Wolf said. "For an instant I thought they were laughing at my song, and I was about to throw in an insulting line about stinking hyenas."

"Go on and throw it in if it will make you feel better," Fish Hawk spoke lightly.

The mighty hunter is clean and neat
The mighty hunter even washes his feet
Unlike the nasty smelly hyena
Who if he took a bath would be a lot cleaner

Fish Hawk snorted and guffawed.

"How many hunters – mighty or otherwise – do you know who are clean and neat?" Fish Hawk asked.

"Well, not many," Black Wolf admitted. "Tor may have been while his first mate Awna was still alive. That woman, as kindly as she was, was a fanatic about cleanliness."

"That is true," Puh said after a brief pause, no doubt concerned to injure Ria's feelings. "But for her, it was not just for the sake of keeping clean. She never said as much, but by my understanding, it was because she worried so about everything. Would I survive each hunt? Would we bring in enough wood and food to get through each winter? Would our children live to adulthood? As you know, three did not. Nothing was sure. The only thing she could control was how well she took care of her family. So we all were scrubbed and dressed in carefully constructed and mended clothing and footwear; she fussed over each meal, and she cleaned incessantly. That was her way of coping."

I felt a lump of grief grow in my throat, and I swallowed it down. I often thought of my mother and mourned her absence. I had never considered why Muh had been so meticulous in her care of her family, but now that Puh had spoken of it, it all made sense.

"It is a hard life for women," Fish Hawk observed. Like Puh, he had lost his first mate in childbirth. "Sometimes I think they have a much more difficult existence than do we."

"And then there is little Ria here," Black Wolf pointed out, "Who manages to take care of her mate, mother children, keep a household, and bring in game as well." Black Wolf smiled down at Ria. They had always been good friends.

"I am very grateful to have a mate, children, and household to care for," she said simply.

* * *

We kept watch for any signs of men who might have passed this way before us. However, we saw no human tracks that we did not recognize as our own from our trip home after visiting Willow Woman's lodge. These tracks were easily recognizable, as they consisted of our three sets of footprints, made by Puh's average-sized feet, my big feet, and Black Wolf's huge feet. Some were faint, some were partially obscured, but many of our tracks were still plain to see.

As always, when we felt the change of humidity in the air, we knew we were nearing Willow Woman's lodge. There, the fir trees grew tall, and there was a pervading dampness. Not long thereafter, we grinned at one another when we heard the dull roar of cascading water from the falls. We would soon reach our destination.

This time, Black Wolf did not run ahead of us. We had to quicken our pace to keep up with him, but we entered the clearing that surrounded the lodge together. Black Wolf hallooed loudly to announce our arrival.

A number of faces appeared in the main entrance of the structure, which almost immediately parted like a herd of wisents at the sudden arrival of a pack of wolves in their midst. Oak ran out to meet us, quickly followed by Willow Woman. Both greeted Black Wolf fondly.

"It is such a treat to have you back with us so soon," Willow Woman said after receiving a long kiss from Black Wolf. "And I see you have brought Fish Hawk, Tris, Ria, and Tor with you. Please remove your packs and sit by the hearth. The coals are nearly ready to cook our nightly sup, so you have arrived at a good time."

"Thank you, Willow," Puh said to her, taking off his pack and sitting next to it. Fish Hawk, Ria, and I did the same.

I approached Willow Woman and was welcomed with a hearty hug and a kiss on my cheek. Willow Woman received all of us warmly. She did not know Fish Hawk very well, so she was more formal with him and greeted him by grasping his forearms in the way of The People, as he thanked her for being our hostess.

Slow Bear and some of the others also joined us. We chatted easily as they questioned us about our journey and Oak told Black Wolf about the things he had done since his last visit.

"I made something for you," Oak told him.

Oak had been sitting on Black Wolf's lap, but he rose and dashed into the lodge, and then reappeared holding something in both hands. When he stood before his father, he proudly held the gift before him.

"Slow Bear helped me," Oak said, casting a grateful glance toward Slow Bear, "but I did some of the work all by myself. It is for you."

Black Wolf took the proffered item with great care.

"Why, thank you, Oak," Black Wolf said. "It is very fine." Black Wolf smiled broadly and displayed his present to all.

Oak had made a piece of twine and strung a mysterious dark object on it.

"It is for wearing around your neck," Oak explained, just in case there was any question about what to do with the present. "I found a stone by the river that had a hole in it. I showed Mother and she said it was a lucky stone. I told Mother I wanted to give it to you, and she said I should ask Slow Bear to help me make a string from which to hang it."

"I see," Black Wolf responded. "Well, this is a wonderful gift. A man can never have too much good fortune, and a stone with a hole in it is indeed lucky. Even luckier when it is given to you by your son. Thank you, Oak." Black Wolf embraced Oak and then put the pendant around his neck. The twine was barely long enough to slip around Black Wolf's head, which was tricky business at any time, given the many braids that stuck out at odd angles from Black Wolf's skull. But Black Wolf paid no mind, and he seemed genuinely pleased with the gift.

"It is very fine, is it not?" Black Wolf asked Willow Woman, turning to show it to her.

"Indeed," Willow Woman replied. "Oak worked very hard on that twine. He demonstrated remarkable patience."

Just then, White Cloud came out toting baskets of various food items. He greeted us cheerfully as he set down his load and then checked the progress of the fire. He nodded at the coals with approval. They were a uniform red, with just a few small flames flaring up here and there.

"White Cloud, would you like assistance?" I offered. I had sometimes helped him in the past. I was somewhat weary from our long walk, but I was willing to lend a hand nonetheless.

"Thank you, Tris," he said. "Perhaps later, when all the food is ready, you might hold out the trays for me while I pile them up."

"Of course," I replied.

When the time came I did as requested, and I salivated to see all the sumptuous food heaped before me as I held out the sturdy birch-bark platters.

The meal was satisfying, as always. There was much talk about the Outsiders and their activities. At home, we customarily downplayed any discussion of danger if children were present. Here, Oak sat through the very frank assessments of what was happening and what was likely to happen. I suspected that Willow Woman wished to begin his training early; after all, she anticipated that one day he would take her place as Head Elder.

Willow Woman asked Fish Hawk to repeat several times the names of each of the raiders he knew, and to tell whatever he could recall about them. They had been close associates of his older brothers. I had seen them on two occasions, once when we caught up with them after Morning Star was abducted from our pairing ceremony, and again when they started carrying out attacks on homes of Old Ones. This time, they seemed to have a far more serious agenda.   If they could not drive us off, perhaps they meant to kill us off.

They may have had early success by murdering Ria's two brothers and their families, but those two men had nothing like Ria's intelligence or competence handling weapons. They would have offered little opposition. Inlee and Trae, on the other hand, with help from their kin, had repelled the men and then chased them through the forest.   If homesteads were raided while the men were in residence, they could expect more of the same.

However, we had no indications that the raiders had returned to this area for some time. Had they given it up as a futile endeavor? Were they hoping we might suppose that they had given up so they could later catch us when our guard was down? There would be no knowing until passage of time revealed their strategy – if any.

"The question remains how best to find their location and to learn their plans," Fish Hawk said. "While I did not know these men well, they were regular companions of my brothers. There was something about them – they could be difficult . . ."

"How so?" Willow Woman asked.

"They taunted anyone they did not believe would retaliate," Fish Hawk replied. "If they did not like you, they might knock down your smoking racks when you were not looking. That sort of thing. If you dared to speak up, they would demand to be met in the Challenge Circle to fight it out – but only if they knew you would decline. Many people left the Village because of them."

"I am amazed that your Village Elders did not exile them themselves," Willow Woman said. "Or bring it to my attention at the Gathering."

"They feared them," Fish Hawk answered with a shrug. "And they feared what retribution that might bring."

"The Elders should have feared the result of not taking the problem in hand before their bad behavior became so ingrained," Willow Woman spoke heatedly. Then she went on, "Well, there is no help for it now but to take action as best we can. Rumors of attacks have already begun to spread, but we must warn everyone so they may see to the protection of their own families. And, keep us informed of any roving bands of men . . . men who are not hunting."

"The best way to reach as many people as possible in a short time would be to address the assemblage at the Gathering," Black Wolf stated. "I believe we should tell everyone about what has been happening, but the problem is that we see so few people outside of our families in our day-to-day lives. I do not know any other way to spread the word quickly other than to do it at the Gathering."

"But it is not the attendees who are being attacked," Puh pointed out. "It is the Old Ones who need to know that we are being singled out by the Outsiders again. We can get word to Bror's family, and we can try to find the place where my brothers and their kin have relocated, but while there are not many of us, that is just a start."

"You are correct, Tor," Willow Woman said. "Do your best to get word to all you can and we will do the same at the Gathering. As you know, I would like to work toward including Old Ones at every Gathering, but I have seen that there are many who are not receptive to that notion. I hope to gradually introduce the idea so that when the time comes there will not be as much opposition."

"I understand," Puh told Willow Woman. "It is not just some of The People who are reluctant to go along with that idea. There are some Old Ones who will not wish to take part. Not only because of a general distrust, but because they fear mistreatment – that they will be greeted with suspicion, derision . . . as loathsome interlopers."

"I am sorry to say that is true," Willow Woman said with a deep sigh. "But it grows late. I must put Oak to bed. Black Wolf, you will join us? Pleasant evening to you all."

Willow Woman stood to leave us, lifting Oak into her arms. Black Wolf stood as well.

"He is heavy, let me take him. Come to me, Oak," Black Wolf said as he slipped a tired and droopy Oak into his embrace.

We wished them a pleasant evening as well. I was sure this night would be idyllic for them; they had so little family time to be together that they must make the most of every moment.

Given the rigors of our past days' hiking and my full stomach, I began to feel sleepy. It was not long before we all were ready to find our beds. Fish Hawk and I shared a small chamber within the lodge, while Puh and Ria bedded down in another. Our room was dimly lighted with a single lamp. Not being an in-ground or earth-bermed structure like our homes, it did not have the ground to insulate from the cold and heat, and the chamber was cool. We wrapped our cloaks around us and made ourselves comfortable on sleeping platforms covered with matting. I was soon sound asleep.

* * *

A shout brought me to wakefulness, just as the smell of smoke drifted into my consciousness. In my sleep-fogged state, I wondered if it had been a dream, but then Puh burst into our room, with Ria at his side. Their arms were loaded with their belongings.

"Tris! Fish Hawk! Wake up!" Puh called out to us. "The lodge is on fire! We must get out now!"

I had removed all but my loincloth prior to bedding down, but I quickly snatched up my leggings and tunic and grabbed my pack and spear. Fish Hawk did the same. Our room had an opening that led to the outdoors; it was not a doorway, but a movable panel that created a place where fresh air could be allowed into the chamber. The smoke was beginning to enter the room around Puh and Ria, so we all headed toward that panel, which Puh quickly thrust aside. Without a word, he picked up Ria in one sweeping movement and passed her through the opening. The rest of us also passed our belongings through to the outdoors, letting them fall to the ground, where Ria hastily collected them. Then, one at a time, we climbed through ourselves.

"Tris, you go first," Puh had said, shoving me toward the opening.

My initial thought was to argue, but I realized that we all could be standing outside in the time it would take to dispute our order of departure. So I had simply nodded and sat on the sill and, swinging my legs outside, dropped to the ground. Fish Hawk came next and, finally, Puh. We then backed away from the structure, staring in horror as flames shot up from the back of the lodge, where Willow Woman and Oak resided.

Billowing smoke rose up into the star-speckled sky. We were relieved to see that it appeared everyone had made it out. We gathered in a group, still grasping our gear, and eyes round with shock.

The flames threw a great amount of heat, but as soon as we stood away from the fire, the air temperature dropped rapidly and our breath came in foggy little clouds. I then noticed that Puh and Ria, apparently having more presence of mind than I, were donning the rest of their clothing. With shaking hands and trembling legs, I tied my leggings to the belt that held up my loincloth and then shrugged into my long-sleeved tunic.

I had barely popped my head through the neck hole of my tunic when a flash of movement caught my eye from the darkness outside the circle of light cast by the flames. I felt a terrible sense of foreboding.

"Over there," I shouted, pointing.

As the others turned to see what I was pointing at, a band of men broke from the shadows and raced toward us, spears poised for attack. I had already taken up my spear, as had many of my companions. Puh, Fish Hawk, and I were closest, and we rushed out to meet them before they could inflict harm on those who were relatively defenseless. Black Wolf, Slow Bear, and some of the other armed men joined us a moment later. We parried thrusts with them briefly until we heard the sounds of another attack occurring from the other side of the lodge.

I was busily engaged with the men opposite me, using my spear to block their jabs and pushing them back, but on some level, my brain registered the sound of an enraged scream, followed by many more cries. The raiders suddenly changed demeanor. They turned and fled.

* **

I was stunned at this unexpected development. What had made them retreat? Keeping our eyes on the place where they had made their hasty exit, we rejoined our friends. The lodge was now an inferno. There would be no extinguishing that fire. We stood as close to it as we dared for its light and warmth.

"The audacity!" Willow Woman exclaimed, chest heaving and long braids swinging as she spoke. "They came after me and my darling Oak! *Well!* Some of them are now sporting a few new holes!"

"You were very impressive," Ria said to Willow Woman. "I doubt many men could have done any better. I have never seen a woman actually throw a man like that before. And then you impaled a few more with the unlit torch you pulled from the ground! Indeed, I am sure you have given them a sobering lesson." The torch bases were tapered so they could be more easily planted into the soil. Willow Woman still brandished her weapon, whose point now glistened with blood.

"And you put your arrows to good use," Willow Woman said, looking down at Ria with affection. "I shall never forget how bravely you came to our defense. Tor, you should have seen her! Ria placed herself in front of Oak and me, and she launched those arrows with such swiftness! I have not witnessed a bow and arrow in use before, and now I believe we must learn more about them. Once they saw her pull out her bow and start shooting, they did not tarry."

"I can well imagine," Puh answered her, pulling Ria to him in a one-armed embrace.

"Thank you, Ria," Black Wolf said to her, "for protecting my family. And you," he said, turning to Willow Woman and bussing her cheek, "you are a wonder!" Black Wolf peered around Willow Woman. "Where is Oak?"

"I am here, Father," Oak said, emerging from behind his mother. "Were those men the bad ones you have been talking about? The ... *the Outsiders*?"

Black Wolf picked up Oak and hugged him.

"Yes," Black Wolf answered him. "I think I recognized some of them. Fish Hawk? You are the one who would know for sure."

"It is them," Fish Hawk said. "And I am sure they knew me as well. They will not be pleased to know that I have sided with you."

There was a brief silence as we absorbed this news.

"We cannot stay here," Slow Bear stated firmly.

"We can temporarily relocate to the Gathering Hall," Willow Woman said decisively. "There are still some supplies at the old Hall. Let us pack up whatever we can and leave."

"Yes. That is our best option," Black Wolf agreed.

"We will need to take as much as we can from our food caches," pointed out Gray Owl, Willow Woman's healer. "Perhaps we can fashion a few sleds to help transport the load."

Most of the tools had been lost to the flames, but one full-sized axe had been left at the woodpile, and Puh, Fish Hawk, and Black Wolf and I each carried small hatchets. We cut down saplings for the construction of the sleds while the food caches were emptied. It was a considerable amount of stores, even taking into account that this was just their summer home and they would soon be abandoning it for the Gathering Hall before finally going to their winter abode.

As this was a place mostly forested with tall fir trees, there were not many saplings from which to choose, but we eventually found enough to build three travois sleds. The sun had now risen over the horizon. At its peak, the fire had reached the height the treetops, but now I thought it was burning itself out. Nevertheless we had to keep watch: red-hot embers that drifted down on all sides might easily start a forest fire. We were fortunate that the wind was mercifully nonexistent just then, but even so we were often compelled to stamp out smoldering patches of ground litter and assorted small fires.

With such a blaze at close proximity, it seemed ironic that White Cloud would start another fire over which to make breakfast. We had completed the sleds and were lashing down the loads when White Cloud announced that our first meal of the day was ready. I was more than willing to fill my stomach and quench my thirst. Most of us ate while still on our feet, keeping our eyes on the surrounding forest – not only because of the risk of a forest fire, but out of worry that the raiders would attempt another assault. We would need to be vigilant at all times.

No one spoke as we chewed, until Puh broke the silence.

"I think there is an opportunity, should we choose to take it," Puh said.

"What do you mean?" Willow Woman asked.

"Some of us could track the Outsiders," Puh replied. "We could put an end to this."

Willow Woman appeared to be thinking.

"That would mean dividing our forces," she said at last.

"Yes," Black Wolf responded. "Some to accompany you and Oak and the supplies to the Hall, and some to go after the raiders."

"Your men could accompany you and Oak to the Hall," Puh said. "The rest of us can track the Outsiders. Many of them were injured, possibly fatally. This is the time to go after them. Their trail will be fresh, and they will have just come from an armed encounter."

"An armed encounter from which they withdrew," Black Wolf added. "Their morale will be low."

Again, Willow Woman seemed to be deep in thought.

"I have come to care for you all very much," she said, looking at Puh, Ria, and me. "I do not like to ask you to do this thing. I fear it is dangerous."

"I fear that is so," Puh said quietly. "But this is a problem that is not going to go away until we see it to its conclusion. And we may not get another chance – a chance as good as we now have – to go after them. I suggest we – Tris, Black Wolf, Fish Hawk, Ria, and I – go as soon as we finish eating.”

“I think you are right, Tor,” Black Wolf said. “It is my guess that they are not well led. I do not think they expect to be pursued. They believe themselves to be the hunters. Well, now they will be the *hunted*.”

* * *

A quick search revealed the location where the raiders had made a fire, which they presumably utilized to light the small torches they had used to set the lodge ablaze. Clearly, they had planned to take us unawares and force us out into the open where we could be attacked. We also found the path they had taken to make their escape, made plain by the splatterings of blood that marked their trail. It was not a real path, but one identifiable only by the signs of their passing through the forest. By now, Willow Woman and her household were ready to begin their trek to the Gathering Hall. We left on our separate journeys, each hopeful that we would see one another again before too long.

* * *

Footprints on bare patches of earth and trampled undergrowth seemed to indicate that we were following a group of possibly as many as eighteen or twenty men. If so, that meant that they had managed to increase their numbers since we had last encountered them. Just as when we tracked game, we did not speak; we communicated only through facial expressions and hand gestures. We moved at a slow trot, hoping that we would gradually gain ground on our prey and thus catch up with them.

As the day wore on, we saw fewer drops of blood on the path. Clouds blotted out the sun, and a heavy mist descended over the land, soon turning to a slow drizzle. A cold wind began to blow, and we leaned into the stinging rain as we walked. I expected that eventually we would see tracks that had been left while the ground was damp. Wet leaves on the trail often adhered to the underside of the boot and as the person strode on, small amounts of leaves would flake off and be deposited a step or two farther down the path. But so far, I had seen no signs of this. That meant they had passed this way before it had started to rain, and we were still some distance behind our quarry.

The gloomy skies made it difficult to gauge how much time had gone by, what with no visible sun for reference. Brief cloudbursts drenched us now and then and washed away many of the signs on which we relied to follow the raiders. Steady breezes shook the trees and caused the colorful autumn leaves to flutter down amongst us. This, too, would help disguise our foe's trail. Nonetheless, we continued, occasionally finding subtle clues that told us we were on the right track.

At last, the gray skies and rain had blown past and a setting sun burnished the landscape in warm shades of gold. The cold wind had not relented, and the temperature was raw indeed as the sun sunk lower in the sky.

"This is discouragingly familiar," Black Wolf muttered when we stopped to slake our thirst.

"What do you mean?" Fish Hawk inquired.

"When they stole Morning Star from her pairing ceremony, we chased them for over a day before we caught up with them," Black Wolf replied. "I had rather hoped it would not take so long this time. I would have thought that their injuries would have slowed them down more. *Ack!* But instead it is I who is slowing. My feet are aching."

"I am sorry about your feet," Puh said. "It is late in the day, and it will be dark before long. After all that rain we will never be able to track them when we lose the light. We can set up a camp and resume tracking the men on the morrow."

We all nodded in agreement. I understood Black Wolf's frustration. I had hoped to catch up with the Outsiders by now, as well.

"They are moving more quickly than I would have thought," I said.

"I half expected that we might find a body or two, given the injuries that some of them had sustained," Ria piped up.

"They seem amazingly ..." Black Wolf seemed to be searching for the right word, "... motivated."

"I agree," Puh said. "I would guess they are eager to get over the northern border, where they have a chance of finding sanctuary. So long as they are in our territory, their lives are forfeit."

"That is quite true," Black Wolf observed. "Their lives will be certainly forfeited when I get hold of them!"

Now that we were standing still, I began to shiver. We were still wet, and the biting wind was relentless.

"Let us move away from the trail for the night," Puh suggested. "We can put up a couple of quick shelters and build a little fire to warm and dry us."

This sounded like a sensible proposal. We located a small opening between trees and began to erect two lean-tos from fallen deadwood and live fir tree branches. The lean-tos would be barely large enough to sleep in, but they would help trap our body heat and keep out some of the wind.

Ria made a digging stick from a sturdy length of fallen branch and using it, she chopped a hole into the loam, until it was just big enough to use for a fire pit. The hole was designed to be big enough to hide the fact that there was a fire until you were close enough to be almost upon it. But the smoke would be another matter. Ria poked around under trees to find the driest wood available, but it was bound to still be wet enough to send up a moderate plume. We could only hope that it would not be too noticeable. She then returned to us and asked to borrow Puh's hatchet. I soon heard chopping. A short time later she returned with an armload of wood, grinning.

"I found a dead pine," Ria said triumphantly. "It should be full of resin; I brought back all I could carry, but I will go back for more. This should make a good hot fire, and there should be enough to chase the chill away before we go to sleep."

My spirits soared at the thought of settling down by a fire, despite the frightening spectacle of Willow Woman's lodge aflame that still lingered at the back of my mind. I had never seen anything like it. It was one of the most terrifying sights I had ever witnessed. Not just the fire itself, but the knowledge that all those personal belongings – tools, clothing, weapons, everything so laboriously amassed over the years – had been lost in that inferno. To purposely set fire to a home was unconscionable.

We settled around our modest blaze just as the sun was nearing the horizon. It would be dark very soon. We dug into our packs for the dried stores we carried with us. We would not bother to heat our food. I, for one, was famished, and I just wanted to fill my empty stomach and to warm and dry myself by the flames.

Just then a sharp crack, like that of a stick of wood being snapped in two, made us look toward the forest.

"We have been looking for you," a voice said as a group of men stepped into our camp, spears poised for battle.

We rose to our feet, our own weapons in hand. I could not help but think that Black Wolf was right when he had said they were not well led. They might have had the advantage of surprise, yet they had apparently given that up to gloat over their success at sneaking up on us. Ria quickly armed her bow.

"And we have been looking for you!" Ria answered, her arrow speeding toward the speaker. It hit him squarely in the throat. The man did not seem to anticipate this, despite the group's having had several encounters with Ria and her arrows. It strained credulity to think that someone would continue to expose himself to the same situation and expect a different outcome, and yet here we were.

The men charged into our camp, and again we struggled to fend them off. We were outnumbered. Ria selected her targets as best she could; arrows were most effective at even a short distance, but they were almost useless in close quarters. As a spear slashed my forearm I renewed my resolve to fight harder, to block thrusts and to stab my spear as hard and as often as I could. Another spear jabbed my thigh. I must have been cut and bleeding in countless places, but I forged on. A raider pushed past us to Ria. I was sure that he sought to slay her to end the barrage of arrows, but Puh and I both fell back toward Ria, who had stepped back so that she could continue to shoot as opportunity presented itself. Puh struck the man in the back with his spear and, with one fluid powerful motion, pulled the lanced man around in front of him and then, freeing his right hand to unsheathe his knife, plunged the blade into the man's neck. The man dropped in an instant, and Puh loosed his weapons from the body.

Another raider had flung himself into the gap before me as Puh and I retreated to aid Ria. I traded spear thrusts with him, but Puh joined me and the man did not seem to know which of us to strike first. Just as when hunting a deer, Puh and I came at him from opposite sides and buried our spearheads into his torso, aiming for his heart, habitually twisting the shaft as it went in.

Black Wolf and Fish Hawk were similarly occupied. I had a brief instant to think that as hard as we fought, more and more men kept coming at us.

A series of sharp yaps and howls rent the air. Suddenly, the woodland around us came alive with furry creatures. The howling became mad barks as the creatures descended upon us. It was not until they had come within the light of our fire that I saw they were not animals – they were men! Their wolfskin cloaks, complete with wolf heads still attached, had obscured their identities until we saw their upright stances and dark faces.

The Wolfmen joined the fray, attacking the Outsiders from behind. We let none escape.

Chapter Ten

Darkness had set in. We built up the fire so we would have more light with which to see our friends. They were indeed our former visitors from years ago, the men from The People of the Wolves clan.

"Tris! Karno thought that you!" Karno exclaimed, throwing his arms around me in a bone-crunching embrace. "*Back Woof!* Tor! Funny Little Woman!" Karno greeted them. But then he came to Fish Hawk. "Karno not know you."

"I am Fish Hawk," he told Karno, grinning, "and I am very glad to meet you."

"*Ish Awk*," Karno repeated as best he could. "Me, Karno. These Karno's men."

We exchanged happy greetings, but Puh interrupted.

"Let us remove the bodies from our camp before it grows too late," he said, indicating the various slaughtered men that now lay all around us. "I think we should get them as far from here as possible so as not to draw predators to us.”

“Karno say yes. Good idea,” Karno concurred, thumping Puh on the back heartily. “We make fire sticks to light way, take dead men far into wood.”

Just as before, the Wolfmen were cheerful and willing workers. We toiled together to complete this task and hoped that the pile of miscreants was distant enough to keep any interested carnivores over there and not over here. The last chore was to cover the blood-soaked ground with a thick carpet of leaves and pine boughs, and create several additional lean-tos to accommodate the Wolfmen.

Once the rush of fracas was over, soreness set in and I was then aware of all the places I had been cut and my clothing damaged. Puh, Black Wolf, Fish Hawk and I were all battered; only Ria had escaped mostly unscathed, having had the luxury of striking her opponents from afar. Without being asked or calling attention to what she was doing, Ria tended to us one by one, gently cleansing some of our hurts and applying a salve. Despite Karno’s never being able to remember her name, she took care of him as well, wrapping his right hand with a scrap of hide where his knuckles had been flayed open.

“Many thanks,” I said to Ria after she had seen to my injuries.

Ria seemed unusually grim. I thought it was perhaps due to the gruesome confrontation we had just survived.

"This was my fault," Ria said, speaking hardly above a whisper.

"Why would you think that?" I asked, shocked that she would believe this.

"I was so pleased to find that resinous heartwood, I did not think of the noise I made as I hacked at the dead tree," Ria said, hanging her head. "But as soon as the Outsiders revealed their presence, I knew they had heard. I drew them to us."

Some of our companions turned to look at us, apparently having heard her words.

"Ria, my love," Puh began as he drew her to him and put a consoling arm around her, "as the man said, they were looking for us. They had been quite a distance ahead of us. They must have circled back to see if they were being pursued. They would have found us one way or another. I am just grateful that the Wolfmen found us as well."

"We look for you, too," Karno said with a grin.

"Yes," Bewok agreed, "we were on our way to the encampment where you live when we saw signs of a large group of men. We had heard of a band of raiders, and we suspected that a group of this size comprised solely of men would mean trouble, so we tracked them."

"I am glad you caught up with them before it was too late," Black Wolf stated.

We all nodded in agreement. I hoped that Ria was comforted by Puh's words.

The moon was high in the sky and it must have been quite late. Normally I would have been asleep or at least very tired at this time, but I was wide awake. Maybe it was the excitement of the fight or the reunion with the Wolfmen, or perhaps both. My thoughts swung between two extremes: the incredible revulsion I felt at killing fellow humans, to elation that we had succeeded in removing the dire threat those men represented.

I strove to drive the hideousness of the battle from my mind and concentrated on the current conversation. After thanking Karno and his comrades for coming to our assistance, we chatted excitedly, speaking of our recent shared experience and of many older, more pleasant remembrances. Karno was seated next to me as we each gnawed on dried stores and sipped at our water bags.

"I thought you would be home by now," I said to Karno. "You left us years ago. Did you not go home?"

"Start go home," Karno began. "But then we have stop. The land ... the land turn to ash. Like fire, but no fire. Tree, rock, animal, all there but no burn. All dead or soon dead."

"What?" Black Wolf queried. "I do not understand."

"Karno not understand," Karno shrugged. "We walk long time. Long time. More ash. Much more ash. All dead. *Gah!* We turn back. We think we have friend here. We come back to our friend." Karno smiled at us warmly. "You our friend."

"How long ago did you start back?" Puh asked.

"Two year … little more," Karno said, shrugging again.

"For a time, we stayed with a clan about a moon's hike from here," added Mino, one of Karno's closest companions. "But then they asked us to leave."

I thought this a curious revelation. However, it occurred to me that a number of young men, while they might be skillful hunters and hard workers, might disrupt some of the social construct of the clan, such as creating competition for nubile women. But I did not want to delve into that subject just now.

"How much ash was there?" Puh questioned.

"At first, there was not much," Mino replied. "But the farther we went, the deeper it was. And it was an odd ash. Hard to describe. It did not look as though it came from a wood fire. The farther we went, the fewer animals we saw. We had no choice; we had to turn back. There was nothing to eat."

"It sounds terrible," I said. "I cannot imagine what might have caused that."

"And it was not like that when you first traveled from your home?" Black Wolf asked.

"No," Karno said, shaking his head emphatically. "Land alive at that time. Now it dead."

"And that was a few years ago?" Puh persisted. "Was it during the spring or summer?"

"Yes, a few years ago," Mino confirmed. "It was summer. The ash lay all over everything like snowfall. I have never seen anything like it."

"Sky become angry," Karno said. "When sun rise and set sky turn to blood."

I thought back on the year of the blood-red skies. Had it portended some cataclysmic event?

"But you say it was not like wood ash?" Puh was trying to understand what they were describing.

"Not exactly like the ash I am used to," Mino responded. "But perhaps it was some other kind of ash that was carried on the wind from other lands."

"I am inclined to agree with you," Puh said, nodding absently as he thought it over. "But if that is true, it must have been a tremendous fire."

"Not want to think on that," Karno said glumly. "That mean home, family, everything gone. Karno wanted to go home to show father that he change. He ready to be leader of his people. Now all gone."

"We do not know that for sure," Mino said comfortingly to Karno.

Karno just shook his head again.

"Karno know," he said. "Karno know."

I was not sure how Karno could be so certain. At that time they would still have been a long way from their home. It seemed to me it was possible that whatever disaster had befallen one area did not mean that it had necessarily destroyed his homeland and all its occupants.

"Perhaps they were not affected. Perhaps they are well," I said, hastening to dispel this gloomy notion.

"Karno like to think that," Karno admitted. "But in Karno's heart, he think no."

* * *

The next morning we packed up our camp and again located the sparse trail we had been following as we tracked the Outsiders. Now we had to catch up with a different group of people. We had to inform Willow Woman of this latest happening. I was sure she would be tremendously relieved to know that the Outsiders had been vanquished – for good this time.

The weather continued to be cold and breezy, but at least the sun shone brightly as puffy clouds scudded across a crisp blue sky. Cutting across the landscape, we hoped to reach them not too long after they had arrived at the Gathering Hall.

I had not yet seen the new Hall in its completed state. I was astounded at the view as we stood atop a knoll looking down across the surrounding grassland, which was studded with tree stumps that must have numbered into the thousands. Even at a distance the long structure looked huge. At its midsection, two short additions sprouted out each side. Smoke exited the chimney holes at one end of the building, where Willow Woman, Oak, and all the lodge's former occupants must have set up residency. As with the old Hall, Willow Woman's quarters were at the far end. There, she had some degree of peace and quiet, and privacy.

If I was surprised at the grandeur of the place, Karno and his men were momentarily stopped in their tracks. Their eyes bulged and mouths hung open in shock.

"*Gah!* What this place?" Karno asked. "Karno never see place like this! Men build this?"

"This is The People's Gathering Hall," Black Wolf informed him, grinning broadly at the sight. Then he let out a lung-bursting, "*Hallooo!*"

Puh also whistled loudly to announce our arrival. As we drew nearer, Oak and Slow Bear emerged from an open doorway and came out to meet us. Oak ran the distance, arms outstretched for his father.

"Father!" Oak cried out. "I am so glad to see you! Mother will be so glad to see you, too!"

"I am so glad to see you, as well!" Black Wolf said as he lifted Oak off his feet and easily carried him as we walked.

"What news?" Slow Bear panted as he came up the hill. "We did not expect to see you so soon! Did all go well? What news?"

"All went well," Black Wolf assured him. "Thanks to the timely appearance of the Wolfmen. You remember Karno and his men, do you not?"

Slow Bear nodded to Karno and his followers.

"Of course I remember Karno, Bewok, and Mino. I do not believe I have met the others," Slow

Bear replied. "But I am grateful for their help, and certainly happy to renew my acquaintance with them." Slow Bear looked at the Wolfmen, picking out the ones he recognized. "Bewok, you have healed? And Mino, you are well?"

The two men had been brought to Willow Woman's healer, along with Karno, many years ago after they were seriously injured during the rhino hunt. They replied that they were well.

"I am amazed that your group has survived the years intact," Slow Bear marveled.

"Not quite intact," Mino said, suddenly serious. "We lost one of our number; it must have been over three years ago, now."

The rest of the group became somber, too.

"It was Rattah," Bewok told us. "He was accidentally elbowed in the mouth during the woolly rhino hunt. He was in much pain; he developed a fever and never recovered."

"Karno could not save him," Karno said sadly. "Karno try."

"I am sorry that you have lost a friend," I said. "I remember Rattah. He was a fine man. You must miss him."

"Yes," Karno agreed, nodding. "Much miss him. Friend since boy."

By now we had come to the Hall's main entrance, where Willow Woman stood waiting for us. I thought I saw her smile falter for just an instant as she realized that we were cut and bruised, but she quickly rallied. Willow Woman first greeted Black Wolf with a long hug and kiss; then Fish Hawk, Puh and I were favored with the same welcome, although perhaps not as lingering as Black Wolf's. She next regarded the Wolfmen.

"Karno," Willow Woman began. "Welcome! I can guess that I owe you and your men thanks. Let us go into the Hall where we can sit and you can tell your story."

Willow Woman moved aside so that we could enter the Hall. Again, I was awed at the immensity of the structure. The great room where the Gathering attendees would assemble was nearly twice as large as the original Hall's room. The ceiling rose to a height that rivaled only the tall chambers of Black Wolf's cousin's Gray Elk's cavernous home in the mountains. Just a few torches were lighted, so the area was sparsely illuminated other than bright shafts of slanting sunshine that created columns of light under each chimney hole. Willow Woman quietly made a request of Slow Bear to have her healer join us in her quarters. Slow Bear nodded and left.

We stared at our surroundings, struck mute by the novel sights. Like the former Hall and Willow Woman's summer lodge, it seemed to be constructed with a wooden frame that had saplings and branches woven into the walls, which were then mudded over until the building was weather-tight. Willow Woman motioned for us to follow her to her personal chambers.   When she led us through the structure's midsection, I could see that a large hearth filled the center of that area. Off to one side, a short addition seemed to be used as a storage area. The addition on the opposing side was currently empty.

Willow Woman's rooms were already filled with most of the comforts of home. A fire warmed the first chamber, and matting and pelts covered most of the floor so that we did not have to sit directly on the ground.   At Willow Woman's invitation we leaned our spears against a wall and took off our packs, and then gratefully sank down onto the matting. I had barely rested my bottom on the mat when Gray Owl the healer appeared at my side.

"Tris, would you come with me?" Gray Owl queried.

"Of course." I stood and accompanied Gray Owl to another chamber.

This room was obviously Gray Owl's own quarters. There I saw a small sleeping platform, baskets of plants, bunches of plants hung up to dry, stones that looked as though they were used to grind things, and dried gourds presumably filled with salves and tonics and teas of one sort or another. Several lamps lighted the space, and an unused fireplace was situated at one wall. Gray Owl asked me to remove my tunic and my leggings, and then requested that I sit in front of the sliding panel that opened to the outdoors. I did as instructed and Gray

Owl then opened the panel to make use of the day's sunshine. The cold air that accompanied the sunlight was bracing. Gray Owl motioned for me to turn slightly. Now he looked down on me from his standing position and moved my straggling bits of hair aside to better examine my head. I noticed his face stiffen.

"Is something wrong?" I asked.

"You have lost a part of your left ear," Gray Owl answered flatly. "But it looks as though it was a clean cut. Part of the top and outer edge was sheared right off. Did you not notice that your ear hurt?"

I involuntarily moved to touch my ear, but he held my hand back.

"Do not touch it, you may start the bleeding again," Gray Owl warned.

"Well, no one said anything to me about my ear, and a lot of things hurt, so I guess I did not worry about it. After the fight was over Ria looked at each of us briefly, but it appears she did not see it," I said, now concerned that Morning Star would fret over the missing flesh.

"Your hair covered your ear, so no one was likely to notice," Gray Owl explained. "It was the remnants of blood on the side of your face and on your shoulder and chest that gave me the notion that something must have dripped down from higher up. The slash seems to have lopped off a little bit of hair as well, behind where your ear was. But the hair will grow back."

I wished the same could be said for my ear. Gray Owl carefully assessed my other injuries. There were many cuts, abrasions, and contusions, but of those Gray Owl was not much bothered.

"I am going to dab this salve where your ear was damaged," Gray Owl said. "And then I will do the same in a few other spots."

"Many thanks," I replied.

Gray Owl did not speak for a few moments as he worked.

"Tris," he said, breaking his silence, "I must thank you for what you and the others did. I am keenly aware that those men meant to kill everyone in Willow Woman's household, and our visitors as well. I worried that when you went after them you would be facing greater numbers than your own. And while I realized that your father was correct in wanting to hunt them down while there were fresh tracks to follow, I have to say that I harbored more than a few reservations."

"As did I," I admitted. "Our plan was to catch them unawares. Unfortunately, it seems it happened the other way around. If the Wolfmen had not come along when they did, I am not sure what the final outcome would have been. I appreciate your thanks, but I feel as though the Wolfmen deserve it more than we do."

Gray Owl surrendered a rare smile.

"Karno's bravery is his biggest strength. He has no ear for language, no sense of numbers, and he is almost entirely lacking in social graces, but he has no fear," Gray Owl stated. "I will be sure to thank him and his men."

After Gray Owl had seen to our injuries, we feasted to celebrate our victory. I soon forgot about my ear and was reminded only later that night when I lay down to sleep and felt a twinge of pain when I rested my head on my arm. I turned to my other side, wrapped my cloak more tightly around me and promptly fell asleep.

* * *

Flames! Flames engulfed the clearing! Red-hot embers swirled up a wide plume of smoke into the nighttime firmament. People watched the fire solemnly from the shadows, not speaking. The only sounds were those of the roaring flames amid the crackling, popping, hissing wood as it was consumed by the inferno.

The following morning I awoke with an unsettled feeling. Why was I still Dreaming about fire? I had Dreamt of fire before, but now that the lodge had burned, I had thought those Dreams would stop. Perhaps it was such a traumatic event that my brain was still replaying the scene in my head. I would be sure to ask Gran about that after our return home.

We planned to leave that day. As we enjoyed a delightful breakfast of fresh roasted wood grouse, cooked tubers, and a few roasted apples, we talked of our upcoming plans. The fall hunts would have to start almost immediately after our homecoming.

"And then I will be coming back here for the Gathering," Black Wolf announced happily. "I cannot wait to return, already." He looked to Willow Woman. "I hate to leave you, even if it is just for a moon. It has been so wonderful to be with you and Oak these recent days."

"Yes, it has," Willow Woman agreed. "But you will be busy, and that moon will pass quickly. And I have the Gathering to prepare. As much as I hate to give you up, I know you have a responsibility to your first family to make sure they are amply provided for."

"Why not stay here?" Fish Hawk asked.

No one spoke for a moment.

"But the hunts . . ." Black Wolf faltered.

"We hunt for you," Karno offered, waving his concern aside. "Now plenty of men to hunt. Like *Ish Awk* say, stay here with family. Come back after *Gaddering*."

"There really is no reason for you to come back with us at this time," Fish Hawk added. "So why not stay here and enjoy the time with Willow and Oak? You can help them ready for the upcoming

Gathering, as well. I am sure they could use the extra hands to make the new Hall ready for the onslaught of people who will be arriving within a moon's time. Besides, we will need to go to Inlee's and Trae's homesteads at some point to let them know that the Outsiders are no longer going to be bothering them. Do you want to subject your poor old feet to that journey, too?"

Black Wolf and Willow Woman traded joyous smiles.

"I would respect any choice you make, my dear," Willow Woman told Black Wolf, "but I would be so happy if you were to spend this time with us."

"Then it is decided," Black Wolf said, his deep bass even louder than usual with elation. "I will stay!"

It felt a little odd to be leaving Black Wolf behind as we departed for home. I was sure that his other family would be at least somewhat upset that he had not returned with us. With luck, the Wolfmen would provide enough of a distraction to soften the blow.

Puh had not said much through all this. I wondered at his silence. I knew that Puh had not approved of Karno when he had clumsily attempted to court my sister Ru. But now Ru had been paired with Bror for some years and they had two children. I doubted that Karno would be much interested in Ru these days; she was no longer the young, nubile girl she had once been. She was devoted to her mate, and she could usually be seen with two children clinging to her; this did not exactly present an image that would inspire feelings of romance in a man like Karno, who craved excitement and adventure above all.

I also suspected that the Wolfmen would not stay with us for very long. They might camp with us through the winter, but come spring I expected they would be off to discover new lands and look for mates. Were it not for winter's impending arrival, I would not have guessed them to stay even that long. But the seasons were already changing, and fall was upon us.

The strong winds eased during our trek home; however, the days were cold. A few flakes of snow fell from the sky, but it was not enough to cover the ground. As the days went by, we watched flock after flock of migrating birds winging their way south. When we passed a pond, a multitude of geese took to the air at our unexpected presence, and Ria's quick actions with her bow and arrows brought several down. Again, I marveled at the efficiency of the weapon and I yearned to be more proficient with it. The geese were roasted that night for our evening sup and did much to improve our usual trailside meal of dried stores.

Dreams of fire visited me again each night. I could not understand it. Why were these Dreams so persistent? What did they represent? Were they trying to tell me something? Was this about what had happened at the lodge? Was this a past event? The Dreams offered few clues. I was unable to recognize the people or any details the landscape might provide in these Dreams, since all was hidden by darkness. I was always eager to return home to my family, particularly now to give them the good news that the Outsiders were no more. But I was also impatient to consult with Gran.

* * *

The last night of our journey was undisturbed by Dreams of fire. I dreamt of being with my family. It was a peaceful dream of mundane things: holding children on my lap, embracing my sweet mate and sharing our love . . . it was a good dream. I was eager to be home once again.

As we neared the compound, our dogs must have heard our approach, and many of them rushed down the trail to meet us. Raena reared on her hind legs as she strained to reach my face with her long tongue. I stopped just briefly to ruffle her fur and then continued on. The dogs barked, but it was not entirely a welcoming bark. Some of the dogs knew the Wolfmen from their prior visit, but those that had arrived since that time snarled and growled at the newcomers. We shushed them and the dogs settled down, but only grudgingly.

"Do you smell smoke?" Puh suddenly asked.

I sniffed at the air. Especially since the burning of the lodge, we had come to carry so much smoky aroma on our clothing that sometimes it was hard to distinguish what was fresh and what was on our persons. It would not be unusual to smell smoke from our cooking and hearth fires, but Puh was had picked up on something else. This smoke smelled different.

"I do," I replied. "It has an odd odor."

We quickened our pace.

As we strode into camp, our families were all gathered near the central fire pit. A low fire was burning within the pit and everything seemed to be in order. I let out a long sigh of relief to see that all was well. Then I noticed that the faces present were markedly subdued and strained. My children smiled when they saw me and ran to greet me – all but Lily, who was in her mother's arms. Morning Star also gave me a wan smile and walked behind the children to close the gap between us. I feared she saw my condition and my tattered clothes and would thus be distressed.

Amid cries of *Puh-Puh! Puh-Puh!* Morning Star and I embraced as best we could, each of us encumbered as we were, me with my gear and Morning Star with the baby. Additionally, the children and dogs bounced around us and Kaw fluttering excitedly on Fox's shoulder.

"I have good news," I said to Morning Star after giving her a long kiss. "As you see, the Wolfmen are with us, and they helped us make sure that the Outsiders will never harm anyone again."

"That is very good news," Morning Star said, brightening somewhat at this. "Let us go up to our home and light the fire in our own hearth to warm up the rooms."

I was startled at her suggestion. It was usual to relax around the fire pit and enjoy a bit of respite from the trail with food and drink, but I simply nodded and followed my family up the hill, smiling at family members and friends as we passed and hoping our abrupt departure did not seem too impolite.

Once at home, I set my spear aside and took off my pack, and then went out to bring in more firewood while Morning Star settled the children back into their home.

"It is good to be back in our own house," Fox announced. "Is it not, Kaw? Do you not like being here best of all?" Fox asked his crow.

"I liked being home, too," Pony piped up. "I like my own bed and having my own toys."

Most of the toys Pony used were actually Fox's worn and outgrown playthings, but he had no qualms about sharing with his younger sisters.

I thought that Morning Star seemed weary.

"Did you not sleep well while I was away?" I asked Morning Star as I lay tinder in the dark, cold fireplace. We would have only the light that came in the doorway until I managed to make a fire.

"I never sleep well while you are gone," Morning Star answered.

I struck up some sparks and watched for the telltale smoke, but as I saw none I struck up a few more. This time, the tinder caught. When the tinder was burning well enough, Morning Star reached in with a strip of bark and used it to light a few lamps.

Now our little abode was starting to look more like home. When the fire was well established and could be left alone for a few moments, I began to empty my pack and put away its contents. Morning Star looked around at our children as they amused themselves, and then looked at me.

"Tris, I must tell you something," she said earnestly.

She was so serious it frightened me. A myriad of thoughts ran through my head; did she have a miscarriage in my absence? Had someone become ill or been injured? Had someone . . .

"Gran?" I said on impulse, "is Gran all right?"

Morning Star shook her head and tears appeared in her eyes. She turned her back so as not to alarm the children.

"Let us go into our sleeping chamber," Morning Star responded. "Fox, keep an eye on your sisters, please. Do not let them play near the fire." Morning Star followed with a hand motion to Raena instructing her to keep watch, and the dog obediently moved to her usual spot by the doorway to ensure that no one came in and no one got out.

"Yes, Muh-Muh," Fox replied. "Raena and I will take care of them."

Like the dog, I silently obeyed. In truth, I was speechless. My mind rebelled at the thought that something might have happened to Gran, but at the same time, I knew. I sank down on our bed and held my head in my hands as tears coursed down my cheeks. Morning Star wrapped her arms around me, weeping quietly.   I did not know how long we stayed that way.

"Tell me what happened," I said, when at last I could speak.

Morning Star sniffled and wiped her eyes. She had known Gran all her life; this was a blow to her as well. I gently brushed away a few of her stray tears.

"Two days ago Twie discovered that Gran had passed in her sleep," Morning Star told me in a choked voice. "I am so sorry to tell you this. I know that you and Gran had a special bond. I believe that you were always her favorite. She loved you dearly."

"And I loved her," I said. "Gran taught me much."

"She taught all of us many things," Morning Star agreed.

"It just will not be the same without Gran." As I spoke, fresh tears flowed from my eyes. "Every homecoming, after I had greeted you and the children, my next thought was always to see Gran. I was waiting to see her this time as well. I had been Dreaming of fire and I wanted to ask her what it might mean."

Morning Star then sat back and looked at me with widened eyes that could not be missed even in the semidarkness of our sleeping chamber.

"What is it?" I asked her.

"The fire," Morning Star replied. "We had to burn much wood to thaw enough of the permafrost to bury Gran. Bror and Ty did not want to burn through the aged wood we would need this winter, so they cut down a lot of saplings, and once the fire was going good and hot, they burned those. The smoke was tremendous! And so was the fire. The fire burned on all day and all night. We buried Gran just this morning." Morning Star wiped her nose and sighed. "I can still smell the smoke."

 **Chapter Eleven** 

I did not go down to the main compound for several days. I could not bear to go there, knowing that I would not find Gran. I did, however, venture to the burial grounds. The morning after our return I took our water bag to the stream to refill it. Raena accompanied me, trotting along by my side and I was glad for her comforting presence. It was a frosty morning. White crust covered the undergrowth and any remaining foliage that still clung to the brush. I was not eager to immerse my hands in that painfully cold water. On a whim, I set the bag down at the edge of the stream and continued walking along its edge until I came to a path that would take me to the ancient meadow where generations of my clan had been interred since times untold.

The place where Gran was buried was easily identified by the patch of scorched earth. At the center were a mound of newly excavated soil and a pile of rocks, one for every year she had lived. This coming winter would have been her seventieth winter, but as I counted the stones, I saw that she had been given seventy, even though she had died a few moons short of that mark.

I knelt by the huge cairn, touching the neatly arranged rocks and remembering the wonderful woman they honored. As my fingers ran over the stones, more tears stung my eyes. I had always known that Gran was very aged. In fact, she was far older than anyone else I had ever known, and it was inevitable that at some point I would face this day. However, I still found myself to be unprepared to accept that she was really gone.

I then heard approaching footsteps as they crunched through the many fallen leaves that littered the ground. Raena woofed softly and stood to face the newcomer, wagging her tail in recognition. It was Puh. He carried a spear, and the sight of that weapon reminded me that I should not have gone this far from home without bringing one of my own. Puh knelt at my side, also placing his hands on Gran's stones.

"I thought I might find you here," Puh said quietly.

I merely nodded. I could think of no words to say.

"I come here almost every day to sit by your mother, your brother Dak, and the babies your mother and I lost," Puh told me. "My parents, my older brother . . . so many kin are here. Now Gran is with her beloved Gareth. She waited a long time to join him."

"Did you know him?" I asked, curious about the great-grandfather I had never met, but had heard so much about.

"No," Puh said, shaking his head. "He passed not long after I was born."

"Oh." I was struck by the heartache that Gran had suffered those many years, pining for the man she had loved. I stood to collect my water bag and return to my waiting family.

Puh rose to his feet as well. Although I knew he must have been wrestling with his own grief, Puh reached out and put a consoling hand on my shoulder.

"Tris," Puh said, "she had a good long life. She loved you. Remember that."

I nodded again.

"Yes, Puh," I replied.

Then Raena and I walked away.

No one disturbed my household for those days I spent in seclusion with my family. The children did not seem to mind that we had a few days to ourselves. Perhaps they were just glad to be home after staying with their relatives for a while. Morning Star was horrified at my generally battered condition, and absolutely appalled to see that part of my left ear had been shorn off. I thought I had emerged from the battle in fairly good shape, considering all the carnage that had taken place that day. All the same, Morning Star applied a salve to the raw edge twice a day and kept watch for signs of infection.

Our days were relatively quiet. We did not venture from home except to refill the water bag at the stream or to relieve ourselves at designated spots, making our contribution to the ongoing effort to create an invisible wall of scent around our conclave to keep predators at bay.

One day we sat outside after the sun's rays had melted away the morning frost, enjoying what was probably one of the last balmy days of the season. Morning Star was taking advantage of the bright sunshine to mend the slashed and stained clothing I had worn on our recent trip. She used strands of her own long hair and a bone needle to sew the neat stitches. Meanwhile, I was occupied with showing Fox how to knap a simple cutting edge. Fox watched with interest, Kaw perched on his shoulder, as he often was. Kaw sometimes took wing to fly a short distance to collect a gift for Fox, but he always came back, depositing some little item into Fox's waiting hand.

This day, however, Kaw flew off and remained gone for quite some time. Fox fretted over his missing crow. He was so used to Kaw's being with him that he sometimes reached up to stroke the bird that always sat on his shoulder or lounged in his sling, but when his hand found only empty air, a look of profound sorrow crossed his face.

Nightfall came and still no sign of Kaw. I had become quite fond of the bird myself, and I was sad to think that Kaw might not come back. Fox waited by the doorway, hoping against hope that Kaw would return.

"It is getting cold and dark, Fox," Morning Sat said to him gently. "We must close up the entryway."

"But Muh-Muh," Fox protested, "Kaw has not come home yet."

"I know," Morning Star said. "But Kaw is a smart bird, and he knows where we are. He will come back when he is ready. Do not forget; he is a bird, and he must live a bird's life." Morning Star took him by the hand and drew him to her. For the past year or so Fox had been determined to be a big boy who was too old for cuddling, but this time he did not pull away.

* * *

I knew I could not hide away with my family for much longer. I was sure that the other men were eager to start the fall hunts. The rutting season would be well underway by this time. And, no doubt the Wolfmen were becoming bored with our daily routines; especially considering how particularly sad and humdrum our lives were just now as everyone mourned Gran.

When I walked down the hill to the main compound, I found life going on much as usual, except for the presence of the Wolfmen and the one person whose absence was so painfully obvious.

The Wolfmen, industrious by nature, were erecting a structure for their accommodation, with the eager assistance of Black Wolf's sons Swift River and Hawk. The shelter was partially carved into the hillside just past Puh and Ria's home. The upper part was created from various tree branches topped with layers of dead leaves, more branches, and more dead leaves, and now they were covering it with moss. I hoped it would stand up against the winter winds and bear the weight of snow. Additionally, it appeared to be rather small for twelve men, but like many Old Ones, the Wolfmen were a compact, sturdy people, so perhaps they had room enough.

Black Wolf's mate, Little Fawn, exited her home as I examined the Wolfmen's new dwelling. I had been greeted with a few sedate nods and wishes for a pleasant day, but most seemed unwilling to intrude on my apparent desire for solitude. However, Little Fawn, with her youngest daughter, Dewdrop, in tow, smiled as she saw me. Little Fawn approached and enveloped me in a warm hug.

"I am so sorry, Tris," Little Fawn said. "Everyone loved Gran, but I know you must be taking her passing very hard. There is little I can say that will make things easier, but I did want you to know that I was thinking of you."

"Many thanks, Little Fawn," I told her, somewhat surprised that she was in such good spirits considering all that had occurred lately, and the fact that Black Wolf had not returned home with us.

"You men will probably be leaving soon for the hunts, will you not?" Little Fawn asked.

"Yes, I think so," I replied. "We have had some time to rest from our journey, and the season is upon us. I came down to see if any plans had been made."

"Nothing definite that I know of," Little Fawn said with a shrug. "But I would guess they were waiting for you to be ready. There is no hurry yet." Little Fawn paused. "Is Morning Star prepared to entertain a visitor at this time? I have not wanted to impose myself on your household while you were grieving, but if you think it would be all right, Dewdrop and I will stop by."

"I am sure they would enjoy your visit," I said, smiling. "Fox is particularly in need of a diversion. He misses Gran, of course, but his crow flew away a few days ago and he is very sad."

"Kaw is gone?" Little Fawn responded. "That is sad. We had all come to like him."

"Us, too," I admitted. "But it was bound to happen. I am surprised that Kaw stayed as long as he did. If he had not been so scrawny and nursing an injured wing, I believe he would have left far sooner."

"I will go up and see him now," Little Fawn said, taking Dewdrop by the hand. "Come, my dear Dewdrop; let us go see some of your playmates."

Dewdrop smiled at the mention of spending time with my children, who – since Morning Star was her eldest sister – were actually her nephew and nieces, though she and Fox were only a few years apart in age.

As Little Fawn and Dewdrop departed, Puh and Bror approached.

"Pleasant day to you both," I greeted them.

"Pleasant day to you as well," Puh returned.

"And you also," Bror followed.

"I came down to see if you have decided on a day to begin the fall hunts," I told them.

"We can leave any time," Puh answered. "The Wolfmen are eager to go, but they would like to finish work on their shelter first."

"They should be done in a day or so," Bror said. "We have spoken of going to the North Country before we start the hunt so that we may let Inlee and Trae know they no longer need concern themselves about the raiders."

"That would make sense," I agreed. "Have things been quiet these past days?"

"Amazingly so. Hawk and Swift River are thrilled to have their old idols back, and they haunt the Wolfmen's every step," Bror said with a laugh. "I was afraid that Ru would be upset to have Karno here again; after all, she was so furious with him, and she had claimed that she hoped she would never see him again. But she has taken it in stride, almost as though Karno had never meant anything to her at all. And I must say, I am glad for that.”

“As am I,” Puh said. “I still worry since I now have another daughter approaching the age to be paired. I will feel more at ease when we have taken the Wolfmen away from here, at least for a time. I cannot begrudge them our hospitality after all they have done for us, but I would hate to have Karno try to attach himself to Twie the way he did Ru.”

“Perhaps tomorrow we could leave for the North Country,” I suggested. I really did not want to leave my family again so soon, but as a father of three daughters I could understand Puh’s angst.

“The sooner we go, the sooner we will set Inlee’s and Trae’s minds at ease,” Puh said thoughtfully. “Let us discuss it at our evening meal.”

* * *

The nightly sup was the first of which our compound seemed to have resumed a sense of normalcy since Gran’s death. I still felt an underlying sadness, but I was at last ready to rejoin my family and friends.

The presence of the Wolfmen meant that we were now a much larger group of people. The clearing that housed the main fire pit where we often gathered for our end-of-the-day meal was more crowded than usual. Black Wolf’s boys sat amongst the Wolfmen. The boys had somewhat clumsily hand-drawn images on their skin to replicate the Wolfmen's numerous animal-themed tattoos, and they had managed to fashion impromptu necklaces and wristbands like those worn by their heroes. I suspected that the Wolfmen may have even helped them with these things. At least they had not yet cut their hair in imitation of the Wolfmen's close-cropped hairstyles.

The talk eventually drifted around to hunting, and it was agreed that we would embark on the fall hunt at sunrise, the day after the next. I was relieved to know I would have one more day with Morning Star and the children before I was forced to leave them again. For Fox's sake, I wished Kaw would come home. I would feel much better about leaving if I knew that Kaw had returned by then.

When the food had been consumed, one of the Wolfmen, Bewok, approached us.

"We have been speaking amongst ourselves," Bewok told us, "and we were wondering if it would be all right if we played our music for you. We have not yet played for you since our return and we would like to play a song in honor of the . . ." he appeared to be searching for a word; most of the Wolfmen were fairly fluent in our language but occasionally a word or phrase would stump them; ". . . in honor of the revered grandmother who now resides with the Ancient Ones."

Puh and I traded glances. In my grief, I did not trust myself to speak without weeping. Puh did not speak, either; he just nodded. Bewok smiled and nodded as well, before returning to his comrades.

The Wolfmen had collected a variety of common rocks and chunks of wood, on which at Karno's signal they began to play a slow rhythmic beat. Often Karno led the singing, which was more like a harmonized chanting, but this time, Bewok alone sang in a clear, well-modulated voice. There were no words to the song, like Black Wolf's *Mighty Hunter* tunes, just wonderful soaring notes. We had never heard anything like it. I found myself wishing that Gran were here. She would have so enjoyed this. Perhaps, somehow, she was listening even now.

* * *

The following day was a designated apple-picking day. The apple season was almost over, so we did our best to harvest as many of the hard round fruits as we could. Apples were a valuable crop; if they were kept in a cool place, they usually remained fit for consumption throughout the winter, and often into the spring as well.

It was a pleasantly warm day. As we picked the apples, I noticed that Fox's eyes frequently scanned the skies. There was no sign of Kaw.

Kaw still had not returned home by the time I left early the next morning. The children were still sound asleep as Morning Star helped me prepare for this final lengthy journey of the year. I hated to leave, but it was good to know that it was unlikely that I would be called upon to go on another long trip until the spring hunts came about.

Just before donning my heavy outer layers, I looked in on our children for one last peek before I was to depart, and then kneeled to hug Raena. The dog whined a little; I am sure she knew from past experience that I was about to leave the family for an extended period – which was something she disliked as well. Raena was happiest when all her family was present.

"Good girl," I whispered to Raena, "I know you will watch over everyone while I am away. Such a good girl."

Her tail wagged at my words, and she licked my face. Morning Star stood beside the two of us as I knelt on the floor by the dog, and she pushed my hair back from my wounded ear to check it one more time.

"Stay there a moment, Tris," Morning Star said.

My mate retrieved a shell bowl containing a salve, and using her finger, she painted the ointment onto the raw edge of my ear.

"All set now," Morning Star announced.

I then rose to my feet.

"Many thanks," I said. "I must go. I am sure the others are all ready and waiting for me. The sun must be cresting the horizon by now."

Morning Star just nodded mutely, looking unhappy. I drew her close.

"This will be the last trek until after winter," I said, trying to comfort her.

Morning Star nodded again.

"I am thankful for that," she said, holding me tighter.

I kissed her, hoping that simple act would convey all that she meant to me; the one woman I had ever loved, the mother of my children, the keeper of my home; my reason for living.

"I love you, my sweet," I murmured to Morning Star.

"As I love you," she replied.

I tore myself away from her and pulled a heavy elk skin tunic over my head. Then I slipped my arms through the straps of my pack and grasped my spear. Morning Star was holding my rolled-up wisent cloak, ready to place it over my left shoulder. Last, she bent to tie the rawhide thongs that held the two ends of the cloak together at my waist on the opposite side, so it would not slide off. Almost immediately I began to sweat under all the heavy clothing and gear. After a final kiss for my mate and a pat to Raena's head, I was out the door.

As I had predicted, the other men were already lingering around the central outdoor fire pit in the middle of the main compound, patiently awaiting my arrival. Several dogs milled around the assemblage, tails wagging in hopes that they would be included in our outing. This time, however, they were to be left behind. They were great assets in harassing prey such as boars or bears, but during the fall rut, they served mostly to scatter the deer before we could get anywhere near them.

The men merely smiled in greeting at my tardy appearance, and we promptly set off down the trail that would eventually lead us north. We were a sizable group, since most of the men on the compound were taking part in this hunt. Of the grown men, only my brother Ty and Fish Hawk stayed home. Even with this large party, it seemed odd not to be accompanied by Black Wolf. I had become so accustomed to his gigantic presence, his lung-bursting songs, and frequent chatter that this seemed a quiet trek indeed.

After a time, Karno fell into step beside me. We had not had much chance to converse since the Wolfmen's serendipitous entrance onto the scene of our fracas with the Outsiders. Karno looked up at me thoughtfully.

"Tris, Karno glad we find you, find friend," Karno said.

"I am glad as well," I replied. "We might not be here if not for your help."

Karno smiled at this.

"Karno glad for that too," he said. "You – your family – are Karno's family now."

"You honor us," I told him. "But will you try to get back to your own lands someday?"

Karno shrugged, suddenly glum.

"Karno think there nothing to go home to," he began. "You cannot imagine, Tris. All land choked with ash. Death everywhere. Not go back. Just death there."

"I am sorry for that," I said, sympathizing with his plight. In truth, he was correct. I could not imagine what it was like to look upon a sea of ash smothering the land, and believing it meant that anything beyond, including all those who dwelt in my homeland, were dead. It was too horrible to contemplate.

"Karno sorry too," he went on. "As Karno said before, want to see father, to show him that Karno not silly bad boy anymore. At first, Karno want to show he not care and stay gone very long time. Now Karno lost home forever." Karno paused before continuing, "But if Karno home, Karno dead too."

"Maybe we were meant to be sent away so that our people will survive through us," Bewok pointed out, having overheard our conversation.

"Yes," Mino chimed in. "We can start a new clan . . . assuming we can find mates."

"Karno think on that," Karno said. "Think last village might make good clan, but they did not want new Great Man. Too bad. Good women there. Karno pick several."

I knew that Karno's father had been the Great Man, as they called their Head Elder, and Karno had expected to fill his father's role after his demise. It seemed that Karno still clung to the thought. Karno had shown no inclination to put himself in place as Great Man at our encampment, but I thought that was only because he knew that while he and his men were welcome guests, any such attempt would not be tolerated.

Karno and Mino continued to chat about new directions they might try in search of clans suffering a lack of leadership and an overabundance of available woman.

"Yes," Karno said with a laugh, "Karno want to find many mates and have many children; many children like Tris!"

"I would be happy just to find one mate at this point," Bewok piped up with a grin. "You can go ahead and be a Great Man with eight mates – I do not need so many."

"*Eight*?" Karno repeated, "How many eight?"

Bewok held up eight fingers, which was difficult to do while carrying a spear, without poking your neighbor.

"Yes, that right number," Karno said with a nod.

Puh listened to this exchange without comment. Harkening back to those years ago when Karno had courted my sister Ru, Puh had been extremely displeased when Karno had said it was his intention to bestow upon Ru the great honor of being the very first of his eight mates. Fortunately for Karno, Ru had not been present when he had divulged this bit of information or he might have found himself regretting it. Ru had become a gentle and devoted mother and mate, but at that time her fiery temper may well have gotten the best of her. However, she had already told Karno that she could not accept him. Nonetheless, when Karno imparted this news, it had come as a shock to the rest of us, and Puh had been particularly unhappy at his proclamation. Somehow it came as no surprise to know that his ambitions had not changed.

What with the ongoing conversations with the Wolfmen, this trek seemed to pass quickly. Except for one day of light rain, the weather was agreeable. Nights were predictably cold, but we built trailside shelters each evening that we could also inhabit on our way back. The chill evenings were brightened by a warm fire and the Wolfmen's music. It was as pleasant an outing as I had ever known.

This being the middle of the rutting season, we saw plentiful signs of deer activity. Some trees sported scrapes or, as in the case of saplings, looked as though they had been thrashed by a buck's antlers. On two occasions we saw the deer themselves as bucks pursued does, crashing headlong through the brush, completely unperturbed by our presence. We watched with avid interest; after all, we would be hunting these animals following our visit with Inlee and Trae.

* * *

We arrived at our destination just before dark after four days of trekking. Puh whistled to alert the households that we had arrived. Inlee came out into the cool early-evening air to greet us.

"Tris! Tor! Bror!" Inlee exclaimed. "This is a surprise! And you have brought others with you . . . I do not believe I know them." Inlee peered at the Wolfmen. "I am Inlee," he said to them. "Welcome!"

"We bear good news," Puh told Inlee. "These men helped us put an end to the Outsiders."

Inlee smiled broadly at this.

"That is good news! Come inside," Inlee said, motioning for us to follow him. "It will be a bit crowded, but no matter. Trae and his family are here with Soosha and me just now. Trae's knee is slowly improving.   We are still living off the deer and elk you helped us bring in, but we were just discussing the upcoming reindeer migration, in hopes of taking advantage of the great influx of animals."

As we ducked through the entrance to Inlee and Soosha's large earth-bermed home, the enticing aromas of cooking foods met my nose, and my stomach began to growl almost immediately. We removed our packs and cloaks and set aside our spears near the entryway, creating a pile of belongings in the neat home.

The warmth of the room had us rapidly shedding our bulky tunics. The Wolfmen's heavily tattooed bodies and short hair drew amazed stares from our hosts. They had never seen anything like it before, but they quickly recovered themselves as introductions were made.

"Tor says they have come to tell us good news!" Inlee announced to the gathering. "He said that the raiders are no more, in part thanks to the Wolfmen who have also come to see us."

Trae stood up, eyes wide, and obviously still favoring his bad knee.

"They are gone, or they are dead?" Trae asked anxiously.

"Dead," Puh replied.

Inlee and Trae and their families were jubilant to hear this.

"I never thought I would be celebrating the death of another man," Trae said. "But this is different. Those men have wreaked so much havoc and death on so many innocent people. I am glad they are no more."

"I fear we do not have enough water in our bag to slake the thirst of everyone present," Inlee told us. "I hope you have brought at least a little water with you?"

Food was now being distributed to all in the room, some cooked or roasted, and some dried stores.

"We have water in our bags," I answered. "But do you have enough to feed us? We also carry our own dried stores."

Inlee laughed at my words.

"It is true we were not expecting to feed so many men tonight," Inlee said. "But we will gladly share what we have. We will just make the fresh food stretch a little further with the addition of dried and smoked foods."

Puh then went to his pack and returned with two sacks, placing them in Soosha's hands.

"Soosha, this is for you," Puh said. "We recently picked a great many apples, and also harvested and roasted a variety of nuts."

Soosha seemed delighted. She hugged Puh as she accepted the gift.

"Many thanks, Tor, many thanks!" she said. "We will enjoy these! If you do not mind, I will share them will all present."

Puh simply smiled and nodded at her in reply.

"Tor, have you given more thought to relocating to this area?" Inlee asked.

"Yes," Puh responded. "We thought we might choose a place somewhere near here."

"Why not choose this place?" Inlee asked.

"*This place*?" Puh repeated. "Do you mean here? *Right here*?"

"Yes," Inlee said, nodding. "You would not need worry about encroaching on our resources; most of our children have moved away and we are growing old." Inlee paused. "Look at me; I am not only a father, but a grandfather. And the eldest of my grandchildren are now almost old enough to become parents themselves. How many more winters do I have left? This is good land. There is plenty of food, water, and wood, and every spring and fall there is no need to travel great distances to hunt; the reindeer migration brings the hunt to us."

When Puh did not answer right away, Inlee continued.

"And besides, I like the idea of your coming here," Inlee added.

Puh smiled.

"Many thanks, Inlee." Puh said. "I will bring it up with everyone after Black Wolf returns home. He is staying at the Gathering Hall just now to help prepare for the upcoming Gathering."

"I see," Inlee said. He seemed thoughtful. "I wondered why Black Wolf did not accompany you. I have seldom seen you without him since you two were boys."

The talk turned to reminiscences about days long gone by when they all were much younger, when my mother, Inlee and Trae's youngest sister, was still alive. It had surprised me to hear Inlee speak as though he would not be with us much longer. It was true he had lived many years – he must have been nearing fifty winters in age – but he was still a strong, vigorous man who yet had a few children young enough to still be living at home. In some ways he seemed more youthful than his younger brother Trae, who was slightly stooped and limping with his injury.

As the fire burned low and eyelids began to droop, we were invited to make ourselves comfortable on the matting in the large room where we had eaten our nightly sup. Trae escorted his family to their dwelling next door, and we found places to curl up on the floor, using our cloaks as bedding.

 **Chapter Twelve** 

The next day, we were packing in preparation to make our departure when Trae made an unexpected arrival. He limped into our midst, seeking Inlee.

"A mammoth!" Trae cried out. "There is a woolly mammoth not far from the lake! I saw it only in the distance, but I am sure it is a mammoth!"

Inlee seemed momentarily awestruck.

"A mammoth? A young male, perhaps?" Inlee mused. "Most of the mammoths prefer to stay closer to the Lake Region, but maybe this one was driven from his herd as he became too old to stay with his mother and has not yet established himself among the bachelor bulls. In any case, it would seem that he has found our little lake."

"I was thinking that we might go after him," Trae said excitedly. "As we did those many years ago – when we had over thirty people living here in our clan. Do you remember that bull? It was so long ago, and I was so young, that I may not recollect correctly, but I believe it was an old bull. I just remember that his tusks were enormous."

"I do remember," Inlee said with a nod. "I was a mere twenty-one winters old. I was so proud to be included in the hunt."

"Tor, what do you think?" Trae asked. "Would you, Tris, Bror, and the Wolfmen like to see if we can bring down this mammoth?"

Puh did not answer for a moment. Our last mammoth hunt had not gone well, and he had witnessed the death of his oldest brother during a similar long-ago outing. But this animal also represented a tremendous amount of meat and numerous additional resources. If successful, we would all benefit immensely.

"Let us look at it," Puh suggested. "And devise a plan, if possible."

We left our packs behind, carrying only spears, knives, half-filled water bags and a small amount of dried foods. Puh, Bror, and I also left our cloaks behind, but the Wolfmen donned theirs, as was their habit whenever they went anywhere. The heads of the deceased wolves were situated atop their own, and wolf forearms were tied loosely around their necks to keep the cloaks in place and prevent their necklaces from rattling.

We followed Inlee and Trae through the forest, hoping to approach the mammoth from behind, assuming it had not traveled too far from its last known position. As we walked, I made note of the wind direction. We would be neither up- nor downwind from our quarry; with luck we would be able to conceal our scent from the mammoth. The skies were somewhat overcast, and the sun shone weakly overhead, scarcely strong enough to cast a shadow. A hawk called out from somewhere close by, and a variety of birds twittered from the tree limbs and brush. The more background noise, the better to disguise our footsteps in the dry litter beneath our feet.

At last, the hulking outline of a mammoth appeared on a broad expanse of grassland that bordered one edge of the lake. I would have called it a pond. It seemed a bit boggy at this end, and it was filled with reeds, rushes, and lily pads. He was indeed a young bull, but he had already broken one of his tusks. We watched the beast as he ambled about, grazing as best he could, plowing the ground with his single tusk. He seemed to be digging up roots, which would provide more nutrients than autumn's yellowed grasses.

Suddenly, Puh nudged me.

"Look at the tusks," Puh whispered. "At the one that has broken off."

I looked more closely. I had at first wondered if this was the same young bull we had pursued some time ago, but when I saw he had snapped off a tusk, I had discounted the thought immediately. But upon closer inspection, I could see that a bit of rope was still attached to the broken tusk. It must have been the rope we had used to suspend the lion skin from the trees in which the beast had become entangled.

"Do you suppose he was so panicked by the lion skin, the hyenas, and us, that he cracked a tusk when he tried to rid himself of lion skin and rope?" I asked.

"I would guess so," Puh replied. "He must have lost it sometime later, since we did not find the tusk with the pieces of lion skin. Perhaps fighting with another bull."

"Maybe he lost the cracked tusk while plowing up roots as he is now," Bror suggested.

"Yes, that is possible," Puh agreed. After a pause he went on, "I am sure that we are indelibly imprinted on his memory. He will know us."

"You know this mammoth?" Inlee asked incredulously.

"Tor, Great Man," Karno said. Although I had once told Karno that we had no Great Man, he seemed to persist in thinking that my father was the head of our combined families at our compound. Karno went on, "Tor know all."

"We have hunted this bull before," Puh said to Inlee. "If he sees or catches scent of Tris, Bror, and me, he will bolt."

"What do you suggest?" Inlee inquired. "He seems placid enough right now."

Puh pondered this. Our only successful mammoth hunt had occurred when we had set a trap on a frozen pond by melting an opening in the ice and then allowed falling snow to cover up the skim of ice that formed over the hole. When Ria's arrows spurred the mammoth down a trail and onto the pond, it had fallen partially through the ice and we had then carried on with our attack.

There was no chance of this same plan's being put into effect here. We could hope that the mammoth might become mired in the boggy end of the pond – or lake, as Inlee had called it – but unlike the forest-lined creek where we had last met the mammoth, the open grassland offered escape in any number of directions. Puh looked toward the Wolfmen. Karno smiled.

"We go to mammoth bull!" Karno said. "We poke him on all sides while you *sneak-sneak-sneak* behind and stab him good!"

"That is probably our best option," Puh concurred. "But it will be exceedingly dangerous. Engaging a bull mammoth head-on has cost many men their lives."

Karno waved Puh's concerns aside.

"Not worry," Karno said. "We do this."

Without further debate, Karno motioned to his men to follow him, and they left us without another word. While the Wolfmen got ahead of the mammoth, the rest of us continued to creep closer to where the mammoth grazed. We stopped perhaps ten paces from the bull, where we could remain hidden from sight by the dense brush at the edge of the forest. From there, there was nothing we could do but wait for the Wolfmen to make their move.

We did not have to stand idle for long. Within moments we heard their yips and howls as they ran at the surprised and bewildered mammoth from all sides.   The mammoth wheeled to meet them, trumpeting and rumbling, charging first in one direction, and then another.

We quickly broke from cover and ran toward the rear of the behemoth, striking the backs of his legs and as close to his anus as possible to inflict the deepest injuries we could. The bull now spun to face us, but the Wolfmen raced to block him, while we again ran to his back end and repeated the process of lancing him hard and often, twisting our weapons as they drove in, to widen the wound. The mammoth was now frantic; he scarcely knew which way to turn, so he tried to face all directions at once. We had to run and leap to avoid his formidable tusk and powerful trunk, and also his heavy feet. Blood now streamed freely from his injuries. I felt sure that he could not survive the wounds we had inflicted. However, the question was how long it would take for him to bleed out sufficiently that he would no longer be quite so lethal.

Puh managed to dart in to make a deep horizontal slash across the back of one of the mammoth's hind legs, and an instant later the leg gave out, causing the bull to come down hard on his tail. The mammoth was bellowing with rage and fear, his breath coming in ragged puffs that blew up bits of dust and detritus from the ground around him. He briefly tried to drag himself forward, but then his great head came down on his forelegs. He continued to vocalize, but the sounds were now weaker. His breathing became more rapid. We now stood by, panting, watching his last moments, awed that we had at last managed to bring down this huge beast.

Anguished cries sounded from the far side of the mammoth's huge hulking body.

"Is someone hurt?" Inlee asked us.

We ran around the enormous animal to investigate.

The Wolfmen were at the front of the bull, but they were not looking at him as he passed, or reveling at their kill. They were grouped together, keening piteously. Being tall enough to see over the Wolfmen's heads, I could see that Mino was lying on the ground, cradled in Karno's arms as Karno wept profusely. Mino was oddly positioned, as though he were a discarded toy carelessly thrown down. His eyes were open, but his gaze was vacant.

Just then the mammoth gave a long groaning sigh. He had passed.

* * *

Unfortunately, there was no time for grief. We had to harvest all we could from this animal, and we had to bury poor Mino. Inlee and Trae returned to their homes to bring back sleds and butchering tools. We lighted fires all around the mammoth to discourage predators from trying to take our kill as their own. It seemed cruel to remind the Wolfmen that we had much work to do, so we let them grieve while we gathered armloads of deadwood from the forest to feed the fires. We knew that the Wolfmen would rouse themselves soon enough.

As Puh and I walked past with a final load of wood, I saw Inlee crouch by Karno, who still held his friend. Karno was well bloodied and staring blankly into space, his wolfskin cloak now askew and begrimed face striped with the tracks from his tears.

"Karno," Inlee said gently, placing a hand on Karno's shoulder. "If you would like to leave your friend with us, we will bury him where our family members are interred. We would be honored to have such a brave man rest with our loved ones."

Karno looked up at Inlee with red and swollen eyes.

"Karno could not save him," Karno said as fresh tears flowed down his cheeks. "Could not save him," he repeated.

"My family is preparing a place for your friend," Inlee continued. "It will take a while to get into the permafrost, but it will be made ready if that is what you wish."

Karno nodded and seemed to draw upon some inner strength.

"Yes. Karno thank you," Karno said quietly.

Karno then called to his men and conversed with them in their native language. In his own tongue, he spoke fluently and confidently. The men squared their shoulders and began work on the mammoth, although still suffering through waves of grief. Those of us who knew Mino grieved with them. I also felt much sorrow at his loss, and I wanted to weep along with them, but just now there was too much to do. It would take days to process this animal, and the sun had already reached its zenith. We would need to strip everything off the carcass as quickly as possible and then do all was necessary to preserve it all until it could be consumed or used.

By the time evening fell, many hands had harvested everything usable from the bones. The skeleton itself still contained much marrow, but that could wait for now. We returned to Inlee and Trae's homestead and worked through much of the night, roasting some of the meat and organs for consumption as we worked, and drying and smoking the meat that did not go into a cold-storage cache. At one point I sank down by the entryway to Inlee and Soosha's home, and the next thing I knew the sun was rising. I must have nodded off for a short time. I was incredibly thirsty. I gulped down the last bit of water in my water bag and rose to my feet. I was sore all over. I could see that some of the group was still at work, while others had fallen asleep.

We broke our fast with copious amounts of fresh roasted mammoth meat. When the meal was through, we rested briefly as we prepared for the next round of work.

Trae had left us for a little while, but he now rejoined us. Looking at him limping painfully and covered with dried blood and filth from head to toe, as we all were, I was amazed that he was still on his feet. I wondered if he had slept at all last night. Trae sat next to Karno.

"Karno, would you and your men like to see the place we have prepared for your friend?" Trae asked. "It is just over there." Trae pointed to a location behind the two dwellings.

Karno nodded.

"Yes. Would like see," he said. "Bring Mino there so he take the journey to meet Ancient Ones."

Mino had been cleansed and he was placed on a litter, his wolf cloak carefully arranged around his person, his spear at his side and pack at his feet. I thought of the good-natured young man I had known and of the terrible end he had met. This was life; but it seemed so harsh just now.

The burial grounds looked much the same as the one we had at home. It was a field dotted with stone cairns, some small, some large. A pile of stones waited by the trench in the earth. We gazed into the trench to see the charred remains of the fire that had thawed the soil past the permafrost so the hole could be deepened enough for a burial.

"We did not know Mino's age and thus how many stones we should gather to mark his grave," Inlee said apologetically to Bewok, who stood next to him. "I asked Karno, but in his grief, he could not tell me."

Bewok stood silent as he thought on this.

"He cannot count," Bewok finally responded. "But if you have twenty-two stones, you will have enough. Thank you for all you have done."

Mino was tenderly laid in the trench. Karno wanted to include his spear, but it was too long to fit inside the hole, so Karno broke it in half over his knee.

"It fit now. Mino not need spear any more. No more hunts for him," Karno said somberly. "Now he live with Ancient Ones. We sing for him later. Sadness too sharp now." Karno knelt to drop the broken spear in the grave with Mino. "See friend when I too take the journey."

* * *

We continued to work on the mammoth for two more days. The weather grew progressively colder. Not wanting to sully my tunic and leggings, I had been working naked except for my loincloth, as had the others. We were glad for the large fires that blazed at Inlee and Trae's compound, providing both light and heat. Just seeing how my companions were covered with blood and offal and blackened with smoke, I knew I had to be equally befouled. As we finished putting the last of the strips of meat on smoking racks, I turned to Puh.

"I think this is the end," I said.

"I think so, too," Puh agreed. "Black Wolf would be glad not to have to be on his feet all this time, had he come with us."

"I am sure that is true." I smiled at the thought. I was also sure that Black Wolf had stayed quite clean and comfortable throughout his stay with Willow Woman and Oak at the Gathering Hall. Willow Woman doted on him, lavishing him with attention and gifts, and she fretted if he wished to do anything that resembled work. "I guess we will leave for home in the morning?"

"Yes," Puh replied. "It will take us the rest of the day to get clean. I am not looking forward to immersing myself in any of the local water sources at this time, but there is no alternative at this point."

I shivered involuntarily just thinking about it. But there was no avoiding it; I was now so incredibly dirty and rank that I could scarcely stand myself, never mind go home to Morning Star this way; she would be completely appalled at my condition. This might be far worse than coming home to my mate minus a part of an ear.

In addition to bathing, we also needed to construct sleds to transport our portion of the mammoth back to the family compound. Bathing came first, this being the warmest part of day. That would require a running stream to wash away the filth and stench, so we took turns visiting the nearest stream – a few at a time – so that no one was bathing in the runoff from numerous bathers upstream. Next came the sled projects. We left the bones and hide with Inlee's and Trae's families, who generously offered the one tusk to Karno. Karno seemed to be genuinely moved by the gesture.

"Karno thank you," he said, grasping Inlee by the forearm to demonstrate the depth of his feeling. "Karno always remember you kindness."

"And we will always remember you and your fellow Wolfmen," Inlee assured him. "You are welcome here at any and all times."

"Karno thank you," Karno said again, with a nod.

* * *

We started off early the next morning. It would be a long and strenuous haul to bring five sleds across the countryside, burdened as they were with our hard-earned bounty. If we planned to use the same shelters we had erected on the trip up, we would have to push hard to reach them before nightfall. The one benefit of using existing structures is that we could keep moving longer each day, knowing we would not have to stop in time to build a shelter before sunset.

Now that we were accompanied by sleds heavily loaded with meat, it meant that we must have at least two men guarding the sleds all night long. So we slept in shifts, thus allowing each man to sleep most of the night. Every morning we awoke just before sunrise to prepare to hit the trail once more. The days were long, and the nights seemed all too brief.

One night as Puh, Bror, and I sat by the fire, keeping watch on our sleds while the others dozed, we talked quietly amongst ourselves.

"It is good that the cold dry weather continues," Bror said, "It will help to preserve the mammoth's meat."

"Yes," Puh agreed, "If it will hold out through tomorrow, we should arrive at the compound late in the day. I will be grateful to be home again."

We all nodded; this had been a particularly arduous excursion, and the loss of Mino weighed heavily on all of us. Another thought had been on my mind.

"My Dreams have left me," I blurted out.

"What?" Bror asked. "Can Dreams just leave?"

I shrugged.

"I realized just a few days ago that I have not Dreamed since Gran died," I answered. "I am afraid they are gone. I have regular dreams, but not the kind that bring moments of vision to my sleep. Perhaps it was Gran who gave me the gift of Dreaming, and when she died, they died with her."

Puh placed his hand over mine comfortingly.

"Perhaps. Does it upset you to think they are gone?" Puh inquired.

"I do not know whether to be upset or relieved," I admitted. "They almost always showed me something frightening or disturbing. Or they did not seem to make any sense at all. I will not miss that part. I will not miss feeling as though I have to hide them because their flashes of chaotic insight might worry others – most especially Morning Star; she always knows when I have been Dreaming. But then they sometimes showed something helpful – like that first Dream that showed me when you were in trouble, Puh."

Puh and Bror nodded gravely. They knew only too well what had happened. Bror's father had lost his life, and Puh had barely escaped with his own. I shuddered to think what might have happened if Black Wolf had not believed my Dream, and if he had refused to accompany me on a rescue mission. Then, as it had at many times during our lives, Black Wolf's faithful friendship had proved invaluable.

* * *

Just as we had hoped, we reached the family compound late the next day. Our families and the dogs gave us a boisterous and noisy welcome. We abandoned the sleds where they had ground to a stop to step out of the harnesses and hug our loved ones. Their relief was palpable in the knowledge that we had returned home with a vast amount of meat, enough to easily see us through the winter.

Morning Star helped me slip off my pack.

"You look tired, my dear Tris," Morning Star said. "Sit down," she ordered, "I will get food and water for you."

"Many thanks, my sweet," I replied. I found a spot where I could recline against the side of Puh's home and momentarily closed my eyes, only to reopen them again when Pony clambered onto my lap.

"Puh-Puh!" Pony exclaimed. "You are back, Puh-Puh."

I embraced her and kissed her face as she giggled and rubbed the place where my beard tickled her cheek. Raven soon joined us. I looked for Fox amongst the throng of people, hoping to see him and see Kaw perched on his shoulder. But while I did indeed spot Fox, Kaw was not with him. My sister Saree appeared, toting Lily, keeping the baby entertained while Morning Star worked to make our evening meal. The nightly sup was still some time off from being consumed. The fire had to be built up to burn down to coals, food had to be prepared for roasting or cooking; it was a laborious job to keep so many people fed.

Morning Star soon returned with a small tray of roasted nuts, sliced apples, and thin slices of smoked fish.

"Fox is coming with your water," Morning Star told me after handing me the tray, which I juggled as well as I could with the two girls on my lap. "Would you like the girls to leave you alone while you eat?"

"No," I said, shaking my head with a smile. "Let them be for now. As always, I have missed you all so much."

"We have missed you, too." Morning Star bent to kiss my forehead as I began to eat, pushing my hair back from my face. "Your ear looks good," she said, gazing at it critically.

"It has not bothered me lately," I assured her. "It must be healed by now."

"I think so." Morning Star still looked at my ear, studying it from various vantage points. "It is good that it did not become infected. You must have kept clean."

I almost choked on my mouthful of food at the irony of that last remark, but I just smiled and nodded at her.

Except for the sad news about Mino, it was a happy homecoming. We spent the next days and moons settling into a routine of readying for winter. That meant hewing what wood we could find and dragging it home, and then chopping it into manageable sections for splitting. We occasionally added to our larders with some of the plentiful fowl that still winged south, but fall was nearly over now. When the Wolfmen had recovered sufficiently from the trauma of losing Mino, they resumed their nightly songs, and Bewok sang his farewell song for his lifelong friend.

The time of sharing our nightly sup at the central outdoor hearth was nearly over, since the cold weather would soon drive everyone indoors except for necessary outdoor chores and infrequent hunts.

My Dreams, like Kaw, remained absent. I resigned myself to the fact that both were not likely to ever return.

However, one early-winter day as fat, fluffy snowflakes floated earthward, the dogs alerted us to the fact that someone was coming. Many of us were still laboring to cut tree trunks into chunks that would fit into our fireplaces, but we all stopped working and walked to the center of the compound to see who was approaching.

"This may be Black Wolf," Fish Hawk stated.

I thought it probable that this was true. He would not be traveling by himself, of course. He would no doubt be accompanied by some of those from Willow Woman's household.

Suddenly, the dogs' barks changed to frightened yelps, and the dogs growled and snarled, tails between their legs, some urinating with fear. We still had our axes at hand; and while they could be used as weapons, I regretted not having my spear close by. The men who lived near the wood pile ran home for their spears, but the rest of us stood resolute, ready to face whatever might be coming.

The dogs continued to vocalize, hackles up and salivating. This was most peculiar behavior; I did not think I had ever seen them act this way.

Moments later, a group of men emerged from forest, Black Wolf at their lead. I blinked in disbelief as I recognized him. His great height was hard to disguise, but I had to gaze for an instant before I realized it was he. He stood, grinning broadly, hands on his hips, clad from head to toe in a hooded winter coat and winter leggings all made from hyena fur. The striking russet fur dotted with black was indeed distinctive, and no doubt was the cause of the pandemonium amongst the dogs, who continued to be utterly confused by what they saw and smelled.

Black Wolf was accompanied by Slow Bear and a few other men from Willow Woman's lodge, who were brought to the central fire pit where they could rest from their journey and warm themselves. After a quick greeting, I trotted up the hill to retrieve Morning Star and the children from our home. They would no doubt be glad to know that Black Wolf had returned.

Morning Star and the children quickly dressed in layers of outdoor clothing. Then we strolled down the hill, the children running and slipping and sliding ahead of us in the snow as Raena loped along with them, barking merrily.

Raena's demeanor changed as soon as we neared the compound. She stood at the head of the path, legs stiff, hackles up, and growling. I tried to soothe her.

"Do not worry, Raena," I said, stroking her head. "You know Black Wolf. It is just the fur that worries you."

I then glanced at Morning Star, who had frozen in her tracks and was standing beside me, mouth agape. She appeared to be struck speechless, as were many of the congregation.

"Da," she said finally, "*what* are you wearing?"

"Well, what kind of a welcome is that?" Black Wolf said indignantly. "I am away for several moons, and yet when I return home my family stares at me as though I have crawled out of the south end of a north-facing woolly mammoth!"

Karno approached Black Wolf, looking him up and down.

"Karno think that fine suit of cloth," Karno gushed. "No one have cloth like that!"

"Thank you," Black Wolf said to Karno. "At least *someone* appreciates my attire."

Fox sniffed at his grandfather.

"Grandpa," Fox began, "it does not stink!"

Hyenas had become so well known for their foul odor that even a child knew to remark on the smell – or lack thereof.

Black Wolf picked up Fox and gave him an affectionate squeeze.

"That is right, my little Fox – although you are growing fast and not so little anymore," Black Wolf said. "Great pains were taken to make sure all the bad smell was removed from the fur before it was stitched together."

Morning Star seemed to recover her aplomb, and she too approached to more closely examine her father's outfit.

"Well, Da," she said with a bit of a giggle. "It is very unique. This is by far the most . . . spectacular suit of clothing I have ever seen."

* * *

That evening we had a celebratory feast; it seemed appropriate in light of the events of the past few moons. We had defeated the Outsiders, and we had acquired enough food to feed us until spring. There had been losses as well, but it seemed as though there was always some bad with the good.

We spoke of Inlee's offer to have us take up residence at his homestead, and we agreed unanimously that this would be a wise choice. At long last, the question of where we would relocate had been settled.

* * *

Late that night, as I lay still pleasantly entangled with Morning Star, I was thoroughly contented. Not just sated from making love to my mate, but at ease – as though a great burden had been lifted from me. I kissed Morning Star's forehead and felt her embrace tighten around me. I pressed against her as well, reveling in the soft warmth of her flesh. In a few moments, I felt Morning Star relax and her breathing slow. I felt ready to succumb to weariness as well.

* * *

Fox is sitting on a fallen tree trunk, his red-gold hair catching the sunlight. New leaves flutter on a gentle breeze, and a profusion of flowers bloom. Earthy scents of the warming landscape and fresh greenery permeate the air.   Then, Fox's head swivels as he stares with delighted fascination. All at once, he is surrounded by many crows as they alight all around him, their raucous calls sounding like laughter.

 **Author's Notes** 

As always, I include the obligatory disclaimer that all characters depicted in this novel are completely fictional. Any resemblance to persons either living or dead is coincidental.

* * *

As in the previous installment of this adventure (*The Blood-Red Skies*), *The Outsiders* storyline is affected by a real historical event. Approximately 40,000 years ago, the Campanian Ignimbrite super eruption occurred in what is now Italy. This was one of the most cataclysmic events known to have taken place in Europe during the last 200,000 years. It was thought to have lasted several days and caused great destruction. Immense amounts of sulfur-dioxide were spewed into the stratosphere and it is believed to have created an ash plume that may have been more than 40 miles high. Life might have been completely wiped out in a 60+ mile radius of the eruption and ash deposits are found more than 1500 miles away from point of origin.

There has been much discussion on how human life was affected and how long it may have taken for both the climate and the natural world to recover. It has been speculated that the eruption might have contributed to the downfall of the Neanderthal. However, it was unlikely that the Neanderthal (and other humans) in Western Europe, where these novels take place, would have been significantly affected. Due to the ash content in the atmosphere, skies would have been stained in particularly dramatic colors at sunrise and sunset. Additionally, the temperatures would have dropped by a few degrees for a period of years, but they would not have suffered the dire fates of those who lived in close proximity or those who lived downwind to the Campanian Ignimbrite eruption.

However, when the men from The People of the Wolves clan were crossing Eurasia on an attempted return to their families, they likely would have found a veritable moonscape in their path. Access to clean water, game, and edible plant life would have been severely hampered. They might have been exposed to breathing hazards from the airborne dust and ash as well, as it was kicked up by the group while they made their journey homeward.

They may have trudged across the ash-choked lands for a few days in hopes of discovering an unspoiled countryside on the other side, but when they found nothing but worsening conditions, no doubt they would be forced to turn around. It would have been crushing to give up all hope of seeing home again, but ultimately, survival would have necessitated their decision to abandon the trip. Their sole consolation was the knowledge that they had forged a strong friendships and alliances with Tris and those in his clan, and they could anticipate a warm welcome upon their return.

* * *

Strength of relationships is a common thread throughout these novels. At a time in history when such bonds were paramount to survival, it was an inescapable fact of life. Indeed, on a daily basis, your very existence might depend on the actions of your family and friends.

Even though modern people may not be tested as severely as were our ancestors, I am a believer in maintaining strong connections. I feel that – ideally – relationships should last a lifetime. This isn't always possible, however, I remain grateful to those who have given me with the most important thing they can offer; a bit of themselves. Whether friend or family, there is no higher complement, or greater gift.

It is for this reason that I dedicate this book to my life-long best friend. We first met in elementary school and we have traveled parallel journeys through life as we grew up, shared adventures, raised our families, reveled in joyous occasions, and supported one another through tragedies. The courses we have traveled would have been far duller and much more difficult without this treasured friendship. (And yes, we sometimes still act like a couple of goofy teenagers when we get together, even though we're both grandparents, now.)

* * *

The saga continues in 2022 with *The Dreamer VII ~ The Challenge Circle.* The first volume of Dreamer Books companion children's series, *KAW,* is currently expected to be released by the end of 2021.

Thank you for your continued readership!

With warmest regards; E. A. Meigs

Index of European Ice Age Animals

Antelope (Saiga Antelope) These small antelope (24 to 36 inches tall at the shoulder weighing approximately 80 to 140 pounds) ranged over a good part of the northern hemisphere. They are exceptional in appearance due to their unusual muzzles, which feature a long, flexible snout that looks much like a truncated elephant's nose.

Aurochs (Extinct) Predecessor of domesticated cattle. Size varied between 61 to 71 inches at the shoulder, with weights of 1500 to 3300 pounds. Their horns could reach up to 31 inches in length. Sometimes aurochs is spelled "auroch", but from my readings, I am lead to believe that but the "s" is often included even when the animal is referred to in singular form because it is an alternative form of spelling "ox" and isn't intended to indicate plurality.

Boar Wild boars are the plows of the animal world. They are built for digging. Their heads and massive

shoulders make up a good part of their bodies and their large, sharp tusks, which continue to grow throughout the life of the animal, are very effective at turning over soil. The largest adult male boars can reach weights of nearly 800 pounds and attain a shoulder height of 49 inches. Sows (females) are much smaller and they lack the mane and thick shoulder/back "shield" of the boars. Their tusks are also of a more modest size. The coloring of their coats varies from anything between white and black, but most tend to run towards darker shades.

Brown Bear

(Eurasian Brown Bear) Although this bear is called a "brown bear" its color can range from black to a tawny light brown. Males average 550 to 650 pounds but very large specimens can exceed

1000 pounds. Females weigh 330 to 550 pounds. During pre-history, the brown bear did consume some plant matter, but it was generally carnivorous.

Cave Bear (Extinct) This was a very large, stout bear. The average male weighed in at 880 to 1100 pounds.

Females averaged a little over half that (495 to 550 pounds). Despite their size, bone analysis and other indicators suggest that cave bears were primarily herbivores.

Cave Lion (Extinct) (European Cave Lion) These efficient feline predators were some of the largest known cats in animal history. Based on skeletal

remains, it is speculated that the males may have reached 11 ½ feet in length from nose to tip of the tail, and weighed over 880 pounds.

Chamois A medium-sized goat/antelope. They are 28-31 inches tall at the shoulder and range in weight from 55-132 pounds. Besides being a fine source of meat, their hides were used to make garments.

Crow (Carrion Crow) A large black bird, approximately 18 to 21 inches in length with a large, heavy beak that is well adapted to catching and eating small prey such as mice, frogs, insects, etc., and scavenging off the kills of other animals.

Elk (Eurasian Elk) ("moose" in North America) A medium-sized elk/moose, now extinct in many parts of Europe. They average from just over 600 to just over 1000 pounds, with shoulder heights at 5.6 - 6.9 feet.

Fallow Deer A medium-sized deer, about 30 to 37 inches at shoulder height and weighing 66 pounds (small doe) to 220 pounds (large buck), although unusually large bucks may tip the scales at 330 pounds. Their winter coats are brown, but they are  freckled with white dots on their backs and sides during the summer.

Giant Deer (extinct) (Irish Elk) The giant deer was one of the largest deer ever to walk the earth. Commonly, it has mistakenly been called an Irish elk, although it was neither exclusive to Ireland nor an elk.

This huge deer averaged nearly 7 feet in height at the shoulder and carried antlers with a spread that could span 12 feet. They are estimated to have weighed nearly 1200 to just over 1300 pounds but larger individuals could have reached upwards of 1500 pounds.

Horse   The Eurasian Ice Age horse came in many

different varieties. They were more than likely the size of modern ponies and appeared in all colors, spots and stripes. They may have resembled the Przewalski's   horse that still exist today or the now-extinct Tarpan horse.

Ibex   (Alpine Ibex)   A moderate-sized, dun-colored mountain goat. The bucks' horns sometimes reach 39 inches in length. The does' horns may grow to a length of nearly 14 inches. Similarly, bucks achieve a much larger body size (35 to 40 inches at the withers and weighing from 150 to over 250 pounds) than the does (29 to 33 inches at the withers and 37 to just over 70 pounds).

Lynx (Eurasian Lynx) The biggest of all species of lynx. Approximately 24 to 30 inches at the shoulder, and including its short tail, it may be 31 to 51 inches in body length. The largest males weighed nearly 100 pounds, but the typical lynx will run between 18 (very small female)

and 66 pounds (good-sized male).

Marten (European Pine Marten) A small, weasel-like animal with dark brown fur, often with blond markings or a blond bib on its chest.

At a little less than 3 ½ pounds and about 21 inches in length, the marten was hunted for its beautiful, silky fur.

Mink (European Mink) A small mink,

even the largest is just under 20 inches in length and only about 1¾ pounds. They have been prized for their dense, luxurious winter coats.

Porcupine (Old World Porcupine) This rodent wears an impressive coat of quills, some of which may be up to 14 inches in length (Crested Porcupine). These species of porcupines come in a variety of sizes: the smallest adults run from 11inches to 34 inches long, and may weigh between 3.3 to 60 pounds.

Red Deer (European Red Deer) Another very large

species of deer. The buck weighs in at 350 to 550 pounds (48 inches at the shoulder) and does run 260 to 370 pounds (45 inches at the shoulder). These deer, unsurprisingly, are known for their reddish coats. During autumn, the males often have a short mane on the backs of their necks.

Red Fox The biggest of the fox species, the adult ranges from 14 to 20 inches tall at the shoulder and weigh from 5 to nearly 40 pounds. These animals were often harvested for their fine fur.

Reindeer (Also known as caribou) This important game animal consists of several different subspecies and varied in size from 120 to 550 pounds. Color varied as well, but all subspecies shared many of the same basic characteristics, such as a fairly

impressive set of antlers (in most reindeer, both the bucks and the does grow antlers) and a two-layered coat of fur, featuring a woolly undercoat that thickens dramatically each winter and an overcoat of longer, coarse, hollow hairs.

Roe Deer (Western Roe Deer) This small deer averages just over two feet to two feet, 6 inches at the withers, and a mere 33 to 77 pounds. Nonetheless, they were an important source of meat for prehistoric humans.

Sheep The actual breed(s) of ancient sheep that roamed Ice-Age Europe are unknown, but it is recognized that sheep were hunted and eaten by early man. It is possible that the Mouflon (shown in image) is the modern day link to prehistoric sheep. The Mouflon have a shoulder height of less than 3 feet and weigh from 75 to 110 pounds.

Snow Leopard This beautiful cat is well adapted to life in a cold, mountainous habitat. It has a stout build and long, dense fur that varies in color from white to pale gray, with dark gray to black spotted markings. It is about 24 inches at the shoulder with a weight of 60 to 120  pounds, although larger males have been noted at 165 pounds. Their fur was considered to be very desirable and they have long been hunted for their pelts.

Vulture (Eurasian Griffin Vulture) This large scavenging bird may have a wingspan of over 9 feet and weigh as much as 33 pounds, although most individuals range from 14 to 25 pounds. It is known that early men consumed the meat of  vultures.

Wisent (European Bison) An impressive animal, the

wisent is the heaviest land animal that still resides in modern day Europe. Fully grown specimens range from 5 to 6 ½ feet at the shoulder and weigh 660 (small female) to more than 2000 pounds (large male). The wisent was an important source of food and hides for prehistoric humans.

Wolf (Eurasian Wolf) These are the largest of the

European or Asian wolves. Their sizes vary greatly from 70 to 212 pounds. Although their coats could be black, white, or even reddish, by far the most common color was a grey/buff and white combination of medium length, dense fur.

Wood Grouse (Western Capercaillie) This Eurasian
bird is the largest of the
grouse species, weighing
as much as 15 pounds.
The cocks have an
average weight of 9
pounds and a wingspan
of 36 to 48 inches. The
hen is considerably
more modest in size,
with   a   weight   of

approximately 4 pounds and a wingspan of 28 inches.

Woolly Mammoth (Extinct) This large mammal lived
in Eurasia and North
America, and was
similar in size to
today's African
Elephants, but with
considerably longer
tusks, a shorter tail,
and   much   smaller

ears. The males of this huge species could attain
heights of up to 11 feet at the withers and weigh over
12,000 pounds. Females were somewhat smaller,
although still impressive in size at up to 9½ feet at the
shoulder and weights up to nearly 9000 pounds. Their
hairy hides came in a wide range of colors that could be

anything from blond to quite dark. They were protected from the extreme Ice Age weather conditions by a double fur coat that consisted of a short, dense, woolly undercoat and strands of long outer guard hairs.

Woolly Rhinoceros (Extinct) Looking much like a modern rhinoceros in a heavy fur coat, the woolly rhinoceros sported two horns on its long snout and carried its thick body on short, stout legs.

This animal averaged about 4000 to 6000 pounds, with a shoulder height of about 6½ feet. The larger front horn that grew from the woolly rhinoceros' nose could reach lengths of 24 inches.

About the Author
E.A. Meigs

I was raised on Cape Cod (Brewster, Massachusetts, USA) at a time when the Cape was still a rural area made up of woodlands, marshes, beaches, streams, and ponds. There, my life was divided between the land and sea. My father was a commercial fisherman, backyard boat builder, and an outdoorsman; so I had an early introduction to boats, working in the commercial fishing industry and spending lots of time in the local fields and forests. When I wasn't on a boat or roaming around the great outdoors, chances are I was reading or writing. I have been a compulsive writer literally since I could first put words on paper, producing my first full length novel at ten years old. Even at that age, my goal in life was to someday find a way to combine my love of nature, the outdoors, and writing.

After raising a family and embarking on a long and varied career that included many years working on and around boats and in the commercial fishing industry; a stint with Florida Fish & Wildlife in a small field office; and other jobs that actually allowed me to use my writing skills, I awoke one day with *The Dreamer* in my head. I began writing the novel with the intention of producing just one book, but as the story progressed it became apparent that the plot would require much more than one volume to tell the tale.

I have two wonderful adult daughters and nine delightful grandchildren. I am an avid camper and I strive to get out hiking as often as possible, daily, when my schedule allows.

www.ingramcontent.com/pod-product-compliance
Lightning Source LLC
Chambersburg PA
CBHW072054190726
48294CB00005B/1505